THIRD RAIL

THIRD RAIL

AN EDDY HARKNESS NOVEL

Rory Flynn

Houghton Mifflin Harcourt

BOSTON   NEW YORK

2014

For information about permission to reproduce selections from this book,
write Permissions, Houghton Mifflin Harcourt Company,
215 Park Avenue South, New York, NY 10003.

www.hmhco.com

Library of Congress Cataloging-in-Publication Data
Flynn, Rory, date.
Third rail : an Eddy Harkness novel / by Rory Flynn.
pages cm
ISBN 978-0-544-22627-2
1. Police — Fiction. 2. Designer drugs — Fiction. 3. Drug traffic — Fiction.
4. Boston (Mass.) — Fiction. I. Title.
PS3556.I816T45 2014
813'.54 — dc23
2013021744

Book design by Chrissy Kurpeski
Typeset in Warnock Pro

Printed in the United States of America
DOC 10 9 8 7 6 5 4 3 2 1

For Ann, Amelia, and Claire

The forbidden holds a secret attraction.

— TACITUS

On the Pike

WHEN THE FIRST HEADLIGHTS burn in the distance, Harkness shoves the wire cutters in his back pocket, climbs through the fresh hole in the chain-link fence, and scrambles down the gravel embankment. He pulls on a Red Sox jacket to hide his uniform and finds his place in the center of the road like a pitcher taking the mound—focused and ready for tonight's game. His departmental counselor would see this late-night return to the scene of the incident as proof of risk-seeking tendencies. His brother George would just shake his head and tell him to get over it and move on. Thalia would tell him to have another drink. But they aren't here. Only Officer Edward Harkness, formerly of the Boston Police Department, stands on the Turnpike, ready to see if a stranger in a car will kill him.

The first contender appears, a white BMW that takes the curve at Kenmore Square and races toward Harkness. The roar grows louder and echoes from the cement walls of the Pike. At twenty yards, the headlights set his Red Sox disguise aglow.

Harkness runs west toward the car. *No dodging. Stay on the line.* These are the rules of engagement tonight.

The BMW hurtles closer and the driver hits the horn. Breath steaming in the cool night air, Harkness runs down the yellow line. The horn screams and the car swerves so close that Harkness could reach out and touch the doors as it flies past, its slipstream spinning Harkness to the ground. The driver lays on the horn, the note bending lower as the car speeds away.

"One down," Harkness whispers. He struggles to his feet, palms scraping in the grit, and turns to watch the red taillights smearing toward South Station.

When Pauley Fitzgerald stood here exactly a year ago, the highway was crowded with Sox fans driving home. In the blurry security video, he leaps across the lanes, pivots sideways, ricochets from one lane to the next, and somersaults over moving cars. More than three million people had watched *Turnpike Toreador* the last time Harkness checked YouTube, staring in sick fascination as Pauley Fitz dropped, danced, and died. After it was all over, the Staties couldn't even find his teeth.

Harkness runs down the empty highway, the white eyes of new demons racing toward him.

1

AN HOUR AND THREE DRINKS into his latest visit to Mr. Mach's Zero Room, Harkness still can't escape the roaring Turnpike. It's asking a lot of a four-dollar whiskey special. He stares across the bar and wonders how he ended up here with the drunken secretaries, hipsters slumming it, and Joseph "Joey Ink" Incagnoli, an ancient North End felon drinking Cynar and soda and reading the *Herald* in a corner booth. It's not a hard question. Almost everyone in Boston knows the answer.

Thalia nudges his shoulder as she walks past. "Too much thinking, champ."

He looks up. "Can't help it."

"Turnpike Toreador?"

He nods.

Thalia shuts her eyes. "Forget. Him."

"First anniversary."

"Of what?"

"You know."

"Accidents happen every day. Let it go, Eddy. Really."

The restaurant flickers, orange as a broiler. The drinkers at the bar, the couples eating bowls of *phô* at the half-empty tables beyond the murky fish tank that divides the bar from the restaurant—they're all staring.

Harkness blinks. "What're they looking at?"

"Our customers don't tend to like cops, Eddy."

"I'm off duty."

"I still don't think it was such a good idea to wear your uniform," Thalia says.

"Didn't have time to change after work." His dark green Nagog Police uniform makes Harkness look more like a forest ranger than a cop.

"What time'd your shift end?"

"Nine," he says.

"Where've you been?"

"Playing in traffic."

She shakes her head. "Not supposed to do that. Didn't your mother tell you?"

"Can't help it." The room spins a little and Harkness shuts his eyes for a moment to slow it. "It's just too much fun."

"Count your blessings, Eddy. Be glad it wasn't you who ended up dead."

"Maybe it was."

"Shut the fuck up." Thalia leans closer. "That's bullshit and you know it. You know, you really should drink more. Works for me when there's something I need to chase out of my head."

"Like what?"

"Like my week in lockup before Mach's lawyer bailed me out."

"Told you before . . . ," Harkness says, "I was just doing my job."

"And now I'm doing mine." Thalia fills his glass with whiskey and moves on.

• • •

After the beat cops cuffed Thalia and the other bartenders, they dragged them out of the Zero Room and into a van bound for Central Processing. Half were illegals; most of the rest had priors and outstanding warrants or drugs in their underwear or stuck in the toes of their Chuck Taylors. Only Thalia was clean. They locked eyes for a moment when Harkness walked in, wondering what a red-haired art girl in black jeans and a vintage Sonic Youth T-shirt was doing tending bar in a dump like the Zero Room. But he wasn't at Mr. Mach's to make new friends.

The Boston cops from District A-1 had raided the place and called in Narco-Intel when they couldn't find what they were after.

Harkness walked through the bar, getting a read on it. He started at the cash register. Mach seemed organized, the kind of guy who kept his valuables together — keys and cell phone, wallet and Ray-Bans, drugs and money. Harkness trailed his fingers along the red leather barstools and set them spinning.

The stool closest to the register was scuffed with tiny white scratches, almost invisible in the dark bar. Harkness jumped up on it, boots scraping the leather, and pushed up a stained ceiling tile.

A BPD lifer named O'Rourke pointed his flashlight up into the ceiling to reveal wires and a metal duct.

"Thanks for finding the ventilation system," Sergeant O'Rourke said. "Was getting kind of toasty in here."

Harkness held up his right hand to quiet the smart-ass, then let it move toward the duct like a dowsing rod, his fingers running along the cool aluminum until they found the smudged edge. He peeled back a piece of silver tape, then ripped the metal duct open — a little at first, then more, until the flashlight revealed dozens of foil-wrapped bricks.

O'Rourke's eyes popped open. "Holy crap."

At a sidewalk shooting in Dorchester or a drug dealer's triple-decker in Mission Hill, Harkness could find the drugs, guns, money, shell casings, and tossed cell phones. It wasn't supernatural. Harkness didn't need any help from the spirit world.

From where he sits, a few barstools to the right, Harkness can still see the stained tile that once hid ten kilos of cocaine. But there's nothing to find up there now. After two years in Walpole, his sentence reduced by ratting out his supplier, Mr. Mach's done with drugs, Thalia says.

He's moved on to something worse.

• • •

"Hey!" Thalia's waving her hand in front of his face. "You okay?"

"Peachy." Harkness stands but the room starts to twist, and he sinks back down on his barstool.

"Everything okay?" Mr. Mach appears behind the bar beaming like a good citizen of Chinatown, the kind who funds scholarships and builds parks.

"Sure." Thalia gives a frozen smile.

"Like her?" Mr. Mach asks Harkness, as if Thalia's invisible. "Think she might make a good girlfriend?"

"I do," he says.

"My best waitress ever. So sorry to see her go." Mach smiles, teeth yellow as old dominos. With his shiny black hair combed back and his crisp blue suit, he looks handsome and presidential. Harkness can picture his face on a cheap coin.

"No way." Thalia throws a bar rag on the floor with a wet slap loud enough to stir even the deepest drinkers.

"Had enough. No more cop friends here." Mach points at Harkness. "Especially this one. Very bad luck."

"He was just leaving," Thalia says.

"You leave, too." Mach points at the door. "Get out. Now."

Thalia stares at her boss for a moment. She's a tough girl from Worcester, her sharp edges even sharper after years working in one of Chinatown's last dive bars. But there's no negotiating with Mr. Mach.

Thalia grabs her leather jacket and cigarettes. She raises the hinged wooden section of the bar, walks through, and lets it slam down behind her with a loud crack. Everyone in the Zero Room turns to watch another late-night drama unfold under the neon.

"Come on, Eddy," she says. "Let's get out of this shithole."

As they walk across a galaxy of cigarette burns and carpet stains, Harkness waves at the roomful of night creatures like a celebutard taking a star turn. Because that's what he's become.

Harkness turns at the door. "Hey, Mach. Can I see your *special menu?*" He points to the end of the bar, where creeps in suits leaf through thick black binders.

Mach shows his bad teeth and stabs the air with his finger. "Special menu is for people who don't have girlfriends." Then he points at Thalia. "You get sick of her, bring her back. Then you see special menu."

"Thanks for getting me fired," Thalia says when they're on the street.

"Sorry." Harkness pulls his Sox jacket over his uniform and looks up at the spinning stars. "He'll rehire you. Likes you."

Thalia shakes her head. "The guy's a psycho. I'm sick of his shit."

4

They walk down Beach Street past closed restaurants, windows jammed with faded lunch menus and deflated Peking ducks hanging from greasy hooks.

"What the hell was his problem tonight?"

"No idea," Thalia says.

"Why'd he fire you?"

"Because he thinks I'm your girlfriend now, remember?"

"Maybe you are."

"For five hundred bucks, you could spend the night with your very own underage Thai girl," Thalia says. "Don't forget—virgins cost extra."

"I don't have that kind of money anymore."

Thalia kicks Harkness.

"I mean, no thanks." Harkness imagines the warren of rooms facing the street—stained futons, sweet stink of rancid sesame oil, padlocks on the doors, the giant red *0* of the Zero Room's sputtering neon sign glowing through a grid of chicken wire. "Soon as I'm back in Boston," he says, "I'll make sure Mach gets brought down again. For good, this time."

"You sure about that?"

"Absolutely. Second time's the charm."

"That's great." Thalia puts out her hand. "But tonight I'm driving, champ. You're kind of drunk."

Harkness drops the keys in her palm. "Don't smash it up, girl-friend."

2

T HEY DITCH THE PATROL car and walk toward Thalia's neighborhood, clinging to each other like survivors after a shipwreck — half kissing, half walking, finally giving in to the slow desire that's been building during months of late-night phone calls and texts and the occasional night of drinking at Mr. Mach's.

They stop at a Franklin's, a brass-rail-and-plastic-fern bar on Mass Ave, and drink whiskey until they turn the lights up bug-kill bright to chase everyone home. Then Thalia remembers there's a loft party down the street and they're walking again. The nice part of the neighborhood thins out and they pass into the Lower South End, walking by places Harkness remembers from when this used to be his beat — a meth lab in an SRO hotel in Albrecht Square, a coffee shop that dealt Mexican shitweed.

Whatever the street-corner thugs think of a cop and a girl in a white leather jacket wandering through their turf long past midnight, they keep it to themselves. Harkness and Thalia are protected by the impermeable aura of new love — and the heavy Glock hanging from his belt.

The loft party is on the top floor of a crumbling brick warehouse, entered via a lurching freight elevator perfect for more grappling in the dark. Upstairs, the unfinished drywall hallways are scrawled with drawings and messages lit by a string of bare bulbs. To Harkness, it looks more like a construction site than a place to live. Thalia introduces him to some of her friends — a guy who runs a gallery on Thayer Street, a couple of photographers, and her rabbity friend Marnie, who works at the Zero Room and moonlights as a webcam girl and a *sex worker,* as she calls it.

Marnie's hard to miss with her rainbow hair and pierced eyebrows. Tonight's a halfhearted costume party, though everyone seems to be dressed like some subspecies of hipster.

"Great costume," Marnie says. "You really look like a cop, you know that?"

Harkness is tall and thin and stands up straight. He keeps his black hair cut short on the sides. When he's not drinking, his brown eyes spark with intelligence and enthusiasm. When he's drinking, they go dark and dead. Strangers pay attention to him because his voice is strong and he looks right at them, a lost art. *A natural,* they'd thought at the Police Academy.

"Yeah, Eddy's going for *Bad Lieutenant."* Thalia presses her hand on his chest just below his badge.

Harkness summons up Harvey Keitel lurching through nasty New York City, snorting coke by the bucketful and obsessing about a nun. "I don't think he wore a uniform," he says. "And I'm not a lieutenant."

Thalia leans close. "It's a party, Eddy. Don't be so fucking *literal."*

She steps away and Marnie whispers something in her ear.

"Be back in a few," Thalia says. "Stay where I can find you." She walks across the room with Marnie, and Harkness stands alone in the crowded, dim loft, which thrums with bass and feedback. He drifts toward the band, too arty and slow for him, but better than silence.

The twitchy lead singer looks like a fledgling Nick Cave, pressing his eyes closed and muttering deep lyrics into the microphone. Up front, zombies, goddesses, and nurses dance, faces lit blue by their iPhones when they pause to take pictures of each other.

Harkness hits that magic point when drinking resets his mind. Disobedience is cleansing — one of the many truths they don't teach at the Academy. Tomorrow he'll be whiskey scoured and ready to try again.

He finds the bar, a worktable lined with stalagmites of crusted oil paint and a couple of handles of Yakov. Harkness skips the fake Russian vodka. But there's a trashcan full of ice and beer next to the table. He takes a couple of bottles and twists the tops off, drains one and starts the second.

Little Dorothy dances by, weaving around the dancers' legs, white plastic mask over her face. Harkness pushes through the crowd. She surfaces again for a moment, her blue dress fluttering behind her as she darts around the loft.

Little Dorothy shows up after Harkness hears about any dead girl. Doesn't matter how they die — washed up on a Hyannis beach, rotting in the locked trunk of a car on the Southeast Expressway, or mauled by a pit bull in Franklin Park. They're all Little Dorothy to him.

After a few minutes, when he still hasn't found her, Harkness gives up and decides Little Dorothy was just someone's kid in a costume.

"Hey. Brought you a beer." It's the rabbit-girl with the circus hair.

"Thanks, Marnie." Harkness takes the beer. Why not? Thalia's friends are his friends now.

"Thalia just told me you're that Harvard Cop!"

He shakes his head and drinks.

"Dude. That was like the fucking worst thing *ever?* That happens, then the Sox haven't won ever since?"

That happens — his notorious incident reduced to two words.

"You go to jail?"

"No," Harkness says. "They don't send cops to jail for doing their job."

"Good, 'cause that whole thing was fucked up? I mean way fucked up. What kind of douche would do that shit? Drop a friend off a bridge . . . down onto the Pike?"

It's a question Harkness asks himself every day. And its darker twin — *Why couldn't he stop them?*

"Beantown is a mean town," Marnie recites. "That's what I always say. Looks all nice and historical on the surface. But underneath it's fucking rotten. Boston's built on these piers from the 1700s, you know? When they rot, the whole city is going down. Gonna be total fucking chaos."

With her curling voice and fake tough talk, Marnie makes Harkness feel old at twenty-nine. "I'll remember that," he says. "You seen Thalia?"

"Saw her in the kitchen." Marnie points. "Over there."

"Thanks." He makes his way through the crowd. Like Marnie, half of them think Harkness is wearing a costume. The others sidle away, sure he's here to shut down the party. He walks across the loft floor trying to keep it together, one foot in front of the next. *No staggering. No falling.* That's the order of the day.

His cell phone rings and Harkness clicks it open.

"Thalia, where are you?"

"Don't you know?"

"Who's this?"

"Pauley Fitz," a man's voice says. "*Turnpike Toreador.* Happy anniversary, Harkness."

Thalia's passed out, face down on a paint-stained wooden table crowded with empties, surrounded by a clutch of art guys in thin leather jackets smoking cigarettes. They turn toward Harkness, decide he's not a real cop, and keep talking. The tallest of them, wearing old-style black jeans and a tight white pocket T-shirt, is telling a joke. Harkness hangs back.

"So there's this clown and this little girl. And they're walking into a forest." Art guy bends his shining bald forehead toward the listeners. "The girl says, 'I'm scared, these woods are creepy.'" He pauses. "Then the clown stops, turns to the girl, and says, 'How do you think I feel? I'm gonna have to walk back home alone.'"

They laugh, paper-white faces twisted, crooked teeth flashing. They've never seen a dead girl. Or pieces of one.

"C'mon, Thalia." Harkness shakes her shoulder and her eyes open. "Gotta head out. Now."

Thalia reaches back for her coat. No confusion, no fighting it. Harkness takes her arm and leads her out of the kitchen. The art guys watch them like crows.

"Never seen anyone that drunk," someone whispers in their wake.

"Thalia? Thalia Havoc?" another says. "That girl's legendary."

Harkness shoulders the heavy door to one side and they fall into Thalia's loft, locked in a kiss so hard that Harkness feels her teeth.

She's peeling off his uniform before the door slams closed. She helps him unbuckle the belt and the leather and metal viscera of his job clunks to the floor.

Thalia strides across the dark wood floor. There's a studio with an easel and canvases on one side and a cluster of mismatched furniture and a futon on the other. Ten minutes ago she was passed out at a kitchen table. Now she's wide-awake, buoyed by a brutal second wind, stalking across the splintered loft floor to light candles on the windowsill. The candlelight and a night of drinking transform her from waitress-artist into something much more primitive. As Harkness watches, his head turns heavy. The room narrows and tilts like a funhouse, dropping him to his knees.

"Whoa." He shakes his head to clear it, but it doesn't help.

"Too much whiskey?"

"Maybe." He takes a deep breath and stands, shakily, sure that more than whiskey is messing with him.

"This should perk you right up." Thalia pulls off her tall boots and jeans and kicks them across the dim loft. Glass shatters. She rips off her blouse and buttons click across the floor.

Thalia lowers her thong and flings it across the room with a deft kick. She kneels on the battered red couch, her breasts pressed against the velvet curve of the couch. "M'ere, Eddy."

Harkness sways toward the couch. He reaches out to trace the skein of freckles across her shoulder blades, then runs his finger down her spine. Deep at its base, hidden where no one except her lovers would see it, waits a tiny tattoo of a red hummingbird with a crude black X slashed through it.

She pulls back. "Don't touch that."

"What is it?"

"Bad luck. Ancient history."

Harkness tries to remember where he's seen that red bird before.

"Hurry," she whispers.

Harkness moves his fingers lower to part her from behind. Thalia's breathing turns faster. He inches inside.

Thalia gives a low growl. *"Yes."*

Harkness closes his eyes and the room spins. He opens them to see Thalia's pale back moving in the murky light. "You're so beautiful."

"Don't talk shit." She shakes her head and presses her eyes closed. "No more talking. Need to concentrate . . ."

Harkness reaches out and cups a swaying breast to still it.

Thalia grits her teeth and bucks hard against him. "More. Now, Eddy."

Harkness wraps his arms around her and pulls her to him, then harder. He's about to come inside her but wants her satisfied shout to be the last sound he hears before he passes out. To distract and delay, he goes through a litany of Back Bay cross streets — Arlington, Berkeley, Clarendon, Dartmouth . . .

When Harkness gets to Gloucester Street, his strangled call echoes through the dark loft as Thalia turns her head and screams into the red velvet.

3

H ARKNESS WAKES WITH his arms wrapped around Thalia from behind — one hand on her hipbone, the other tucked under her breasts. Sprawled on the futon, where they finally collapsed, their bodies dovetail, legs tangle, and skin adheres. The planty scent of sex wafts from the wrinkled sheets. Thin October light slants off the splintered floorboards to limn the dusty footprints and the smudged giveaway pint glasses on the windowsill. Morning is about flaws.

He picks up his phone and squints at the screen — a few minutes after six. He uncurls from Thalia. He can't shower, might wake her. He's not even sure where the shower is. He gathers his uniform from the floor. It's wrinkled but should pass. Then he looks for the thick black leather belt that holds his gun and radio. He remembers dropping it on the floor when they came in from the loft party. He nudges the clothes on the floor with his foot.

Thalia stirs and sits up. "Eddy? Come back to bed."

"Can't. Got an early shift." His brain hurts when he talks.

"Call in sick."

"Doesn't work that way."

Thalia reaches out and touches his leg. "Call in well, then. Tell the other cops you can't get out of my bed before noon."

"I wish."

"It's rude to fuck and run. Especially the first night you stay over."

"Got to be at work by seven."

"Minding the meters." Thalia lowers her head back down on the pillow, her hair a red-tinged tangle. "Least you still have a job."

"Thalia, I lost my gun."

"It's probably with your jacket." Thalia points toward the couch.

Harkness lifts his coat and finds the belt coiled underneath but no gun. He pats his coat pockets. They're empty. "It's not here."

"Well, you were pretty out of it last night."

"What?"

"Talking shit. Crashing like a dead man, then waking up all wired and weird. You walked to the donkey place to get me smokes, 'member?"

Harkness doesn't remember. "What donkey place?"

"That gas station on Southampton Street, the one with the donkey on the sign. *Gas that's got kick.* Must've dropped it on the way back or something. Just walk toward the corner."

"No. No. No." Harkness lifts up clothes, newspapers, dishes — and throws them to the floor.

Thalia pulls the creased sheet up to cover her breasts. "Don't get all freaked out."

"This is serious, Thalia."

"Then go find it. Didn't you tell me you were really good at finding things?"

Harkness retraces the straight route to the gas station with a kicking donkey on its sign, scanning the sidewalk and finding only cigarette butts, burger wrappers, beer bottles, receipts, losing scratch cards, crushed vodka nips, and a couple of mismatched gloves. He walks past tow lots with prowling Dobermans, a food bank with a line stretching around the block, and the low, hulking South Bay House of Correction, where Narco-Intel sent dozens of dealers. Harkness wonders if any of them are watching out the tiny square windows as he dives down over and over, hands on cold cobblestones, to look beneath cars.

The Southeast Expressway roars with morning traffic and his head throbs like a slowcore band warming up. He's had rough nights out before, but nothing like this — a lost night giving way to a cold reckoning.

He walks into a cluttered convenience store attached to the gas station, the air thick with the smell of dawn smokers and burnt coffee.

"You!" The man behind the counter waves him forward. "What the fuck're you doing back here?"

"What're you talking about?"

"No, really. Get the fuck out of here."

Harkness shakes his head.

"You really don't know, do you?" The manager's goatee rises and falls.

"No." Harkness almost remembers being here.

"Okay, then. Got something to show you."

"Gotta go to work."

"You, *amigo,* owe me a minute or two." He leads Harkness into the office, and a sullen clerk shuffles from the lottery machine to the counter to take his place.

"Let's roll the tape, okay?" The manager reaches over and presses the buttons beneath a closed-circuit TV. The clerk flails his arms and customers flee backwards through the front door. When the time code hits 2 A.M. Harkness sees a cop barging from cooler to counter.

The manager hits a button and the action slows to show the cop lurching through the store, pawing through bags of chips and knocking candy on the floor. Harkness is reassured and sickened to spot his Glock 17 dangling in his right hand.

"Mind telling me what the fuck you were thinking?"

"Long night." No amount of whiskey and beer could turn him into the monster he sees on the screen.

"Even longer for my shit-shift guy. He called and woke me up, asking if he should call the cops or not. I said *no,* 'cuz the cops were already here."

"Thanks for that." Harkness looks away and his eyes fall on the smudgy photo of the store manager's smiling wife and chubby kids thumbtacked over the monitor. Looks like Dad's been bringing snacks home . . .

"Hey!"

"What?" *Focus, Eddy.*

14

"I was saying that we're glad to see a cop around here. Almost never happens. Even if you were drunk and scaring my customers."

"Look, I'm really sorry," Harkness says. And he is. Sorry he's hit a new low. Sorry to see his gun on the screen but gone from its holster now.

The manager gives Harkness a cold stare for a moment, then rolls his eyes. "No real harm done," he says. "Just don't do it again."

"I won't," Harkness says.

"If you show up here again all wrecked, I'll go viral with the tape, *amigo*. You'll be all over the Internet."

Too late for that, Harkness thinks. "Got it." He rushes toward the door.

"Hey!"

Harkness stops.

"Be careful out there." The manager laughs until he starts to wheeze.

Harkness figures he probably wandered on the way back, so he takes the side streets to Thalia's loft. He's still cringing, replaying the video in his mind, watching the out-of-control zombie cop whirling around the store. Harkness knows rock bottom when he sees it.

Painful as it was to watch, the tape proves that Harkness didn't lose his gun at the Zero Room or the art party. It has to be between the gas station and Thalia's. Or someone else found it already, a possibility that Harkness can't even think about.

Harkness checks his watch. He has to be at the station in half an hour, about as long as it'll take to drive west to Nagog at eighty miles an hour.

Walking down Atkinson Street, trying to scan every inch of the shattered sidewalk and keep the panic down, he almost runs into a kid in a puffy orange parka that encases him like a rind.

"What you looking for, Jim-Jim?"

"My gun," he says.

"Your gun? I can get you a gun."

The guy's all Fubu and Kangol, white unlaced Pumas, emergency-

15

colored parka, and gold-mirror shades. Looks like a street player circa years ago. He's probably on his way to Boston Latin.

"What kind of gun?"

"Nine millimeter. Flexi-action automatic. Like a machine gun. Like a fuckin' mortar, man," Fubu says, fake grilles glinting. "I can get you fuckin' *ordnance*. Stuff left over from Afghanistan. Meet and exceed your expectations. Pop a head off in a jiffy."

"I don't want just any gun," Harkness says. "Has to be my gun. Glock 17, custom issue. Got a scrape on the grip. Lost it somewhere around here. If you find it, I'll pay big." Sweat drips down his sides. Harkness peels back his coat and shows his badge and empty holster. "I need the gun that goes with this."

"Shit, man," Fubu says. "Should of told me you was a cop."

"Thought my uniform might have clued you in."

"That uniform looks fake. Where you a cop at, anyhow?"

"Nagog."

Fubu squints. "Fancy town. Out west, right? Picket fences. White folks."

"That's pretty much it. They need cops, too."

"For what?"

Harkness shrugs. "When they lock their keys in the Subaru?"

"Figured you was an actor or something. They always filming some dumb-ass cop movie on account of it still looks like dirty old Boston around here. I keep my eye out for your gun, though. Things you start looking for have a way of showing up, 'ventually."

"If you find it, I'll pay you a thousand, cash." Harkness's misfiring brain spits out the offer before he has time to think about where he's going to get that kind of money.

"How about two?"

"Sure." Harkness bends down and puts his hands on his knees, breathes deep, and wonders how he ended up haggling to buy back his own gun.

Fubu perks up. "I'll do some looking around and get back to you."

"Wait. Name's Eddy. How'll you know where to find me?"

"You're cribbing with that lady with the red hair. One that lives over there, right?" He points toward Thalia's loft.

"How'd you know that?"

Fubu shrugs. "You'll be back, Eddy, my man. 'Cuz she is *so fine*."

He shuts his eyes and downloads his own private porno, starring Thalia.

As Harkness walks to his patrol car, he knows this kid is never going to come up with his gun. It's not lost on the ragged edge of the South End.

It's not lost at all.

4

SIREN SCREAMING, HARKNESS speeds west down Route 2, parting the cars on the crowded highway and racing past them. "Young, Fast, Iranians" blares from the shitty speakers. The dashboard clock moves closer to seven. The road rises slowly and crosses flatland marshes and low hills, maples flaming and fields blanched by an early frost.

Harkness learned to drive here, going to Cambridge for hardcore shows at the Middle East or to hang out next to the Harvard Square T stop. Although he did stupid things when he was younger, Harkness never would have lost a gun.

He turns down the F.U.'s in midscream and dials Narco-Intel, its number as familiar as his own.

"Harky-Hark. Up with the sun, are you?" Patrick's familiar voice cheers him for a moment.

"Driving to work," Harkness says. "I need you to check something for me."

"You ask, we do it. You know how we are here, Harky. Like your loving family of misfit toys."

Harkness smiles.

"What do you need?"

Harkness thinks about telling Patrick about his lost gun but stops himself. "Guy called me late last night pretending to be Pauley Fitz."

"Sick fuck."

"Can you look up a cell phone number and see if it's his?" Harkness checks his phone and reads the number.

"That dude's dead, Harky. Footnote to history. Stain on the Pike."

"The guy who called me wasn't dead."

"Yet."

"Right. So can you check it out?"

"Not a problem, boss." Patrick pauses. "When you coming back?"

"Future cloudy. Check back later," Harkness says.

"Don't go all Magic 8 Ball on me."

"Wisdom comes from unusual sources."

"No doubt about that Harky. No doubt."

Harkness drives past the exits for Concord and spins through a traffic rotary next to a state prison topped with concertina wire shimmering in the morning sun. He found an inmate's stash of PCP in a drainpipe there once, dangling from a thread of bright white dental floss. Like many hides — great concept, lazy execution.

In a few minutes, the white church spires rise above the thick pine forest. Tumbled walls of gray stones border ancient fields dotted with rusting tractors and sagging barns. Harkness is home now, crossing the town line into Nagog, a colonial town ten miles square, home to ten thousand no-nonsense New Englanders. Cities churn, suburbs strive, but small towns stay the same. Harkness knows almost everyone who lives in Nagog. And everyone knows him.

After the incident, the BPD internal review put Harkness on unpaid administrative leave for a year, a polite way to get him out of the way. Taking a patrolman gig in his quiet hometown seemed like a penance at first. But when Boston scorned him, when his name became a punch line in the comedy clubs, when Sox fans held up signs with his face on it in the Fenway Park bleachers, when *Boston Herald* editorials railed against him — Harkness was relieved to be back home, serving out his time in the minor league of law enforcement.

Like any small town, Nagog can be annoying. Young moms in Lululemon yoga pants clog the booths at the Nagog Bakery. Elders in Outbacks drift from lane to lane, lost in memories or transfixed by foliage. Guys smelling like vodka and toothpaste hog the public computers at the library while they check their stock portfolios. Rich kids in expensive leather jackets skulk around the parking lot of the E-Z Mart. But his hometown has an old-fashioned reserve and politeness that Harkness admires, craves even.

Nagog isn't very exciting, but it's predictable. And sometimes that's enough.

. . .

The Nagog Five and Ten isn't open yet but Harkness knocks when he sees Lee walking around inside.

Lee peers through his thick glasses and comes to the door, twisting the deadbolt open. "Eddy."

"Lee."

Short and owlish, wearing an AC/DC T-shirt and baggy jeans, Lee looks pretty much the same as he did every day in high school. "Need something?"

Harkness pauses for a second and thinks about whether he should tell Lee. They've known each other since grade school. And he really doesn't have a choice. "Yeah," Harkness says. "I need a gun."

"Don't they give you one of those when you're a cop? Even here?"

"They do. But it looks like I . . . left mine somewhere." Harkness lifts his leather jacket and points to the empty holster. "Need something to fill in for it."

"A stunt gun."

"Right, a stunt gun."

"You've come to the right place."

They walk inside. The dark store smells like a laboratory storeroom, safe and scientific.

Lee points. "Over in aisle two."

Three aisles stretch from front to back of the store, lined with office supplies, toys, and cheap candy—all organized by Lee and his acolytes of old-school retail. They come to a pegboard of toy guns—silver cap pistols, ray guns, potato guns, and dozens more. Harkness tries to concentrate but his eyes unfocus. Lee's dark store is cluttered and overwhelming. And last night still hovers like an inexplicable storm cloud.

Lee picks up a brown, furry gun with a smiling monkey face at the end of the barrel. "Want a monkey gun? We've sold lots of them." When he squeezes the trigger a scream echoes through the store.

"I think I need something less furry."

"We had to take the real-looking ones off the shelves a couple of years back," Lee says. "People were using them to rob banks and what have you."

Harkness glances at the clock over the door. There's less than five minutes to get to the station or face the wrath of the Sweathog.

"Let me check out back." Lee runs to the storage room and comes back carrying a gray plastic handgun with a brown grip. Harkness unsnaps his holster and Lee drops in the toy gun. "Perfect fit."

"Handle's kind of shiny. People might be able to tell."

Lee holds a finger in the air then rushes across the store. He comes back with a piece of sandpaper from the hardware aisle and dulls the grip with an expert rub.

"Thanks, looks great," Harkness says. "You're a genius."

"And look where it got me?" Lee points around the store. "Selling candy and trash bags."

Harkness reaches for his wallet but Lee waves him away.

"But here . . . you'll need these." Lee dumps a handful of bright plastic disks into his hand. "It shoots them. Let me know if you need more."

Harkness smiles. "I will."

"And Eddy?"

They stop at the front door.

"I think you might need this, too." Lee throws him a roll of mints from the counter. "You smell like a bar."

5

SERGEANT DABILIS'S RED SOX cap is jammed on his head above a shiny forehead so moist it could seal an envelope. The Sweathog's shirt-drenching sweats are legendary. Harkness signs in and maneuvers through the Pit, crowded during the shift change. He edges toward the squad room for a coffee.

"Do you people know what happened last night?" Sergeant Dabilis gives a wan, sick smile.

No one says anything. Harkness freezes.

Sergeant Dabilis shakes his head. "They clinched it — worst season in American League history. Ever." Sergeant Dabilis turns cardiac red at the thought. "You jinxed us," he hisses at Harkness, then points to his hat. "*The Curse Is Worse.* Heard that one?"

Harkness has heard it a lot. It's the rallying cry of every Yankees fan.

"Well, now that the season is over, it's time for the whole Red Sox Nation to take a steaming dump right on your pointy head. Not millions of little dumps. One really big dump."

"Could you shut up?" From her desk, Debbie the dispatcher gives Sergeant Dabilis the finger without looking up. Ramble, Nagog's excuse for a detective, looks up from a personal phone call. Watt, Fredette, Sorger, and the other cops say nothing. Like kids in a dysfunctional family, the Nagog cops have learned to keep their heads low.

Captain William Munro stands in the doorway of his office. "Harkness, can I see you here for a moment?" He disappears inside.

"He's gonna fire you." Sergeant Dabilis's smile brightens. "You are *so* out of here."

Harkness walks to the far corner of the captain's bright office and stands next to the state flag. "Sir." He hopes that the captain can't smell his sweet funk of sweat, alcohol, and Thalia.

"You've been with us for almost a year now," the captain says. "I'm sure you know that."

Harkness says nothing. A friend of the family, Captain Munro has watched out for Harkness since he was a young punk getting into trouble in town. The captain's like a Scottish uncle, full of honest advice and dry wit. But he's all business when they're at work.

"Received a call this morning. From Boston."

The floor shifts. Someone recognized Harkness running down the Turnpike like a crazed marathoner or staggering out of the Zero Room.

"Administrative Affairs is looking for a recommendation to the commissioner."

"About what, sir?"

"About your performance here. And whether you're ready to go back to Boston and rejoin Narco-Intel."

Harkness focuses. "And what's your recommendation, sir?"

"I'm just a town cop, so what I tell them probably doesn't carry much weight. But I have to say that I don't really want to lose you. Good to have a smart local boy on the force. And you're doing a great job. An example to the rest of them."

"Of what?"

"Of dealing with disgrace, gracefully."

Harkness stares at the state flag hanging in the corner and tries to decipher the Latin. *By the sword we seek peace . . .* then something else.

"I didn't mean that the way it sounded, Harkness. Bad things happen to good cops all the time. Even the best cops. And you're handling it instead of whining about it to the press or running away and getting a cushy job in private security. I admire that. I can't speak for Boston. But I think they'd be lucky to get you back."

"Thank you, sir."

"For now, just keep doing your job. Stay out of trouble."

Harkness stares. Last night he reenacted a running of the bulls on the Turnpike with cars, then went drinking at a notorious Chinatown dump that retails Thai sex slaves. He let a former waitress he met on a raid drive his squad car before making drunken, college-style love to her on a scratchy couch. Just a few hours ago, he was reeling around a convenience store like Mel Gibson on a saint's day. Now he's carrying a plastic gun that fires colorful disks.

Staying out of trouble doesn't seem like an option anymore.

Harkness wonders if maybe he wants to get caught. Maybe he just wants the humiliation to end any way it can.

"Harkness?"

Drifting again. "Sir?"

"You can go now."

Sergeant Dabilis struts around the Pit in his new Sox jacket, red and shiny as cheap candy. "Want to know a secret?" he shouts at the row of desks, where the day-shift cops are working the phones and typing reports.

No one says anything. They just roll their eyes.

"That final game of the '04 Series, when Lowe clinched it? I jack off to that game, I really do." He raises his glistening face toward the fluorescent lights.

"Gross." Debbie the dispatcher shakes her head.

"Shut. Up!" Watt shouts from his desk.

Harkness gets his jacket and keys from the corner of the squad room and takes a careful look at the duty calendar. The next inspection is coming up at the end of the month, giving him a couple of weeks to find his gun or a new job.

"Hey, Harkness." Sergeant Dabilis stares at him as if he's sidelining injuries, bad throws, batting slumps, and Buckner's '86 fuckup patched together into human form. "The Sox are going to bounce back. Next year, we're going all the way. And no one's going to mess it up. Not even you, Harkness. It's going to be perfect."

• • •

The best night of Harkness's cop career started on a stakeout on Commercial Street, stars fading over the harbor as the last bars and restaurants on the wharves shut down.

"Must be nice to be popular," said Harkness's partner, DeFrancesco, when the black SUV with tinted windows pulled up behind their unmarked Ford. "Don't your pal ever sleep?"

"Doubtful." Harkness opened the door and stepped outside. "See you in a few minutes."

"More like a few hours," DeFrancesco said. "If I get shot, it's his fault."

The SUV burbled with the low voices of dispatchers. It was empty except for the silent driver and its lone passenger, Boston Police Commissioner James Lattimore.

Harkness took the black-leather jump seat. "Sir."

The commissioner nodded at him, then shouted at the smoked-glass divider. "Keep driving until I tell you to stop."

The SUV curled around the northern edge of the city, waterfront to the left, darkened bank towers to the right. The commissioner perched like a paratrooper on the edge of his seat, glancing out both windows in sequence.

"Never thought I'd say it," he said quietly. "But I'm starting to like this city."

"Can take a while, sir. Sometimes a couple of years. Or decades."

"Brahmins and *boyos*, students and start-ups, numb-nuts and Nobel laureates—all jammed together. Roads used to be cow paths. Everyone used to be Irish and Catholic. Unless they were Italian or Jewish. Short summers, long grudges. You don't have to say hello or pretend to be polite. Sound like Boston to you, Harkness?"

"Kind of, sir."

"Sure, it's reductive. But that's our job, Harkness. Reduce the city to districts. Narrow down suspects to find the bad guy. Lower crime. We're all about reducing everything down to its essence. Like poets."

Harkness lets the debatable comparison slide. "Poets with deadly force."

"That's right, smart guy." The mayor had lured Commissioner Lattimore from his job as first deputy commissioner of the NYPD three years ago, the same month that Harkness became a new officer. When Harkness got promoted to detective before anyone in his class, Commissioner Lattimore took notice. And never quit noticing. He thought of Harkness as another outsider, a confidant he could trust.

The car streaked past South Station, dark except for the clock glowing beneath a lone cement eagle. The commissioner turned to Harkness. "Got to tell you, it hurts to see one of our best cops out on the street doing speed-and-weed ops."

"It's my job, sir."

The commissioner waved at the city streaking by. "The war on drugs is over. And we lost. Ought to be shutting down digital black markets instead of lurking around the North End waiting for . . ."

"A crank dealer from Dorchester who works the restaurants. They call him Eighty-Six because he always sells out."

"Nice," the commissioner said. "But we need to look deeper, lower. Anonymizing networks, bitcoins, untraceable cell phones, drugs we've never heard of until they start killing people — if you can see the crime happening, it probably isn't that important."

Harkness smiled, knew he'd be telling DeFrancesco about this latest gem from their boss.

"We're not just driving around the city shooting the shit tonight, Harkness," he said. "Got something important to run by you. We're starting up an experimental unit, Narco-Intel."

"Sounds interesting, sir." It sounded like another initiative that might not make it beyond PowerPoint at headquarters.

The commissioner read his mind. "This is the real deal, Harkness. Not just another task force. We need a dozen or so young officers like you. Smart, tough, excellent instincts, willing to bend the rules a little. Maybe a lot." The commissioner leaned forward. "So what do you think? Are you up for it?"

Harkness looked him in the eye. "Yes, sir."

"Good." The commissioner smiled for the first time. "Congratulations, Detective *Supervisor* Harkness."

As he reached out to shake the commissioner's hand, Harkness realized that his career as a cop had just taken an unexpected turn.

After circling most of downtown, the SUV hurtled up Storrow Drive, wound past North Station, and slid to a stop behind Harkness's unmarked car. "One last thing, Harkness."

"Yes, sir?" Harkness hoped the commissioner couldn't tell that DeFrancesco was asleep.

"You'll be running the show."

. . .

Harkness pushes the coin transfer unit down Main Street, stopping to send coins gushing down into its metal belly like a slot machine paying off for someone else.

It's enough to make even the straightest arrow go bent.

As he walks from meter to meter, Harkness asks the question he turns over in his mind every day like a riddle — will he ever get back to Narco-Intel? Maybe the wheels are grinding slowly, like the captain claims. Or maybe the commissioner just wants him to stay here in Nagog, out of trouble and off the front page. Forever.

Harkness moves on to the next meter. He doesn't have the patience of Job. Far from it. His days of emptying meters are full of second-guessing and unanswered questions, revisiting the incident, guilt multiplying like compound interest. Now his missing gun joins his ledger of loss. Harkness zips his leather jacket against the cooling fall afternoon, careful to keep it over his holster, freed of its hard, deadly weight, replaced by an absurd toy.

Glock 17. Glock 17. Glock 17. His mind keeps sending out a relentless text message to the world. Harkness revisits every inch of the gritty path from Thalia's loft to the donkey gas station — sidewalk, rusty bridge over the railway tracks, intersection, parking lot, smoky store — and wonders when his gun left its holster.

Three cups of coffee and an hour of cold air have started to clear his head. But the lost time after midnight remains surreal and confused. He thinks he remembers being in the store, or is he just remembering the security tape? Was he just drunk, or drugged? Though last night remains a mystery, the hard fact remains — his gun is gone.

A river of handguns runs through the land — street nines with rusty grips, fancy suburban SIGs in bedroom drawers waiting for home invasions that never happen, semiautomatics in the hands of fanatics and haters. Harkness has to keep his Glock 17 from falling into that steel-cold water.

He slams the heel of his hand into meter no. 347 over and over until its plastic window cracks and the read-out blinks METER OUT OF ORDER. There's a brief moment of triumph when smashing something, anything. Then Harkness feels guilty for making more work for Stu, the town repairman. Harkness knows his meters the way plumbers know wrenches. Doesn't make sense to beat up on the tools of your trade.

He moves on.

A few meters later, there's a jam. He reaches for the pair of needle-nose pliers that live in his jacket pocket with the pepper spray. He's never used the spray; dogs like Harkness as much as people do. But the pliers are out every day, pulling out nails, wire, straws, euros, toothpicks, gum wrappers. In August, some smart kid squirted Super Glue down the coin slots of every meter on Central Street.

There's just not that much to do in Nagog.

He fishes a bent paper clip from the coin slot, clicks the ejector knob, and the meter's fine again — a small problem solved. But the big one remains.

Harkness is already imagining the worst-case scenario — his gun ends up with some gangbanger who uses it to kill a rival. Or worse, a cop. He presses his forehead on the cool metal of a meter. His father, Edward "Red" Harkness, who found himself in trouble and under fire more than once, used to say there are no atheists in foxholes. Harkness begins to pray.

Please do not let my gun kill anyone. Please help me find my gun.

"Excuse me?"

Harkness opens his eyes. An older woman in a tan fleece vest stands on the sidewalk. She's holding out a coin purse.

"Change for the meter?" The woman shakes the purse to show that it's empty. She's about fifty, wearing jeans and sturdy shoes. Driving a sensible green Subaru. She looks like she just came back from a long, meditative walk in the town forest.

She waves a dollar like a limp flag.

"Can't make change." Harkness moves on to the next meter.

"But you have that whole thing full of it." The woman points at the coin transfer unit, big as a kitchen trashcan. "Must be plenty of quarters in there."

Harkness flicks the one-way steel door where the change falls in. "Can't get to the coins."

She squints. "Why not?"

"That's the way it works."

"So am I going to get a ticket?"

"I don't know," Harkness says. "I don't write the tickets. Just empty the meters."

She stares. "Why?"

It's a question Harkness asks himself all day. "Because it's my job."

She tilts her head slightly. "I know you, don't I?"

"Probably, ma'am."

"Eddy? Eddy Harkness?"

"Yes?" He looks at the woman more carefully and recognizes her. "Mrs. P?"

"Thought it was you." She throws her arms around him. "Eddy!"

"Been a long time, Mrs. P." The close, warm smell of the classrooms, Mrs. Pettengill at the chalkboard beneath the cursive alphabet chart, the green-tiled hallways of Nagog Elementary — it all comes back.

"Even in third grade, you wanted to be a cop."

"I remember that."

"But you actually did it!" She backs away and looks at him. "I heard about your mother, Eddy. I'm so sorry. Best principal we ever had." With that, Mrs. Pettengill bursts into tears.

Harkness steps forward to pull his former teacher close — once comforted, he becomes the comforter. "She's doing okay, Mrs. P," Harkness whispers. "My sister's taking great care of her. Mom's happy." Harkness doesn't tell her that his mother doesn't recognize him. That she shits herself.

"What's happened to your family, Eddy — it's Shakespearean." Mrs. Pettengill shivers in his arms.

"And you don't mean the comedies, do you?"

She shakes her head.

6

THALIA'S SITTING AT the kitchen table drinking whiskey with even more enthusiasm than usual. She flicks ashes toward a chipped Cinzano ashtray on the kitchen table, crowded with bottles and glasses, yellowed sections of the *Globe*, and brushes jammed in a jar.

Harkness wonders why she's hitting it so hard tonight. He's the one with the big problem. "I got to find my gun, Thalia."

"We'll keep looking, Eddy. It'll turn up." After Harkness got off work, they walked down every street in Thalia's neighborhood until the light faded. They stumbled along abandoned train tracks and the sludgy banks of the industrial canal that runs behind her building. They dug through corner trash barrels. They smell like sweat and garbage.

Harkness shakes his head. "The captain's going to fire me."

Thalia moves closer. "Look. You're not going to get fired. You'll find your gun. It just may take a while."

"Think so, do you?"

"Absolutely."

Harkness isn't so sure.

"Hey. We could post a *Have You Seen Me?* sign with a picture of your gun. Like they do for missing cats."

"Not funny," he says.

"Just tell them, Eddy. Be honest about it. What can they do?"

"Fire me. Or worse, not fire me and just keep me in Nagog forever."

"It isn't your fault."

"Yes, it is. You don't go out and drink tons of whiskey and beers without thinking that something stupid might happen." He sees himself careening around the convenience store.

"You could just drive up to New Hampshire and buy a new one."

"There's a waiting period. And they report it. Anyway, that won't work. Even if I got another Glock, it wouldn't be the same. Mine's special issue. They check serial numbers. And it's got a scrape on it from the last cop that had it."

Thalia turns quiet.

"I hate to ask, but I have to." Harkness pauses for a moment, then barges ahead. "Did you take my gun, Thalia?"

Thalia startles, and looks him in the eye. "No. No way!"

"Know anything about it? Anything at all?" Harkness watches her fingers, eyelids, tongue — looking for the flickering tells of a liar.

"Nothing, Eddy."

"Did Mach tell you to steal it to mess with me?"

"The guy's a douche, Eddy. I wouldn't do anything for him."

"You worked for him for years."

"It was a job, Eddy. All I ever did was pour drinks for creeps and sleazy politicians. And the occasional handsome cop. Or make that paranoid cop."

"Paranoid, really?"

"Fuck you, Eddy."

"You're not being very reassuring."

"So why did Mach fire me?"

"Because that would be the world's most obvious diversion. I'm a detective, Thalia. I know how people try to get away with shit."

"All I can say is I don't know where your gun is. I got fired. I'll never work for Mach again or even talk to him."

"Sure about that?"

She nods.

For a moment, Eddy thinks about twisting her arm around her back and lifting, a proven move that draws out the truth. But he can't do it to Thalia. When she's not around, he'll search the loft. That, he can do.

"I don't blame you." Thalia fills her glass. "I mean, even Nancy-fucking-Drew would think I took your gun. I was the only other

31

person around. You stayed over for the first time last night. And I'm not exactly squeaky-clean. But I didn't take it, Eddy. Why would I do something like that to you?"

Harkness looks Thalia in the eye and she holds his stare. No blinking, looking away, fidgeting, or moving things around on the table. A couple of years at the helm of Narco-Intel left Harkness with a built-in polygraph. Thalia's passing, for now.

"I don't know, Thalia. Maybe you're still mad about the raid."

"I don't sleep with people I'm mad at," she says. "I've had an embarrassing girly crush on you for a long time, in case you didn't notice." She jabs out her cigarette. "Though you're doing a good job ruining it, Major Buzzkill."

"That's not what I'm trying to do."

"Look. I would never take anything from you, Eddy." Her voice rises and her lips curl. "I want to be with you. I don't steal things from people I . . ."

"Like?"

"People I like. Sure. Look, you have to know some things about me, Eddy. First, I'm loyal to a fault. Look how long I hung around Mr. Mach's place. And he's a total dirtbag. Second thing. I'm not just a bartender. My gallery sells some of my stuff. And there's even a little buzz going about my paintings. Google me. Thalia Havoc."

"That's not your name."

"Sounds better than Thalia Prochazka."

"Didn't know painters used other names."

"Sometimes you have to," she says, "when you have a Czech name no one can spell or pronounce."

Outside, they hear people on the street, walking to bars. Harkness wishes they were with them, that he could just be in love instead of in trouble.

"Your gun's out there somewhere," Thalia says. "You dropped it and someone picked it up. Probably some kid on his way to school. It's going to turn up. They'll brag about it or show it to someone. I already put out the word with the young dudes on the street and the old guys who hang around the convenience store. They're like Wi-Fi around here. If someone says something, they'll hear it."

"Met your friend in the big orange parka."

"The guy who looks like a supersized Kenny from *South Park?*"

Thalia breaks into a broad smile. "That's Woo-Derek. He's so cute. Talks all street. Dresses like a *playa*. His dad's a dentist. And he sings bass in a youth choir."

"Everyone's got a dirty little secret."

"Want to know mine?"

"Thought you already told me all of yours."

"I like you a lot," Thalia says, "and I like being your girlfriend." She drags out the word and rolls it down her tongue like a butterscotch Life Saver. "Sounds so clean and nice."

"Let's hope not," Harkness says.

"Stay here until you find your gun, Eddy. Maybe even after, if you want."

Harkness nods, not convinced she's telling the truth but sure he should stay. *Keep your friends close and your suspects closer.*

"I'll spend the day tomorrow walking around again, looking on the street while you're at work," she says. "After all, I don't have a job anymore. Might as well do something useful."

"Thanks."

"But right now I'm going to take a shower, Eddy. When we were looking in the trashcans, I picked up a McDonald's bag and something supergross dripped on my arm."

Thalia sheds her clothes as she crosses toward the bathroom. A black and white vision of pale skin and dark tights, she fades into the shadows on the far side of the loft. Harkness keeps staring at the point where she disappeared. Within an hour they'll be rolling on her futon. For now, he takes out his cell phone and texts Patrick, asks him to run a full records check on Thalia Prochazka, aka Thalia Havoc, resident of 640 Atkinson Street, Boston.

7

Harkness looks up from emptying meters in front of the Unitarian church to see a car speeding toward the town green, its center spiked with a tall granite obelisk carved with the names of the Union dead. The silver Volvo's hitting sixty, engine racing. It crosses the centerline and swerves into the oncoming lane, heading toward Harkness and the green.

Must be an out-of-control elder or a student driver heading to high school, Harkness guesses. Too early for a drunk. As the car speeds closer, a low huddle of deer starts to cross North Street. Deer have become a nuisance in the last couple of years, devouring gardens and stopping traffic. Oblivious, they step forward on elegant legs, hooves recoiling slightly on the asphalt as they meander across the road like a pack of toddlers.

No. Harkness shakes his head at the deer. The driver must know the *Don't Veer for Deer* drill that the Public Safety Commission has been pushing on local cable and in the *Nagog Journal.* The Volvo races toward the pack. And the driver's not slowing down.

He's speeding up.

The Volvo passes right through the herd, sending a deer flying over the hood and knocking a couple of others to the side with a thud. The car keeps racing toward the center of town.

The smiling driver grips the steering wheel and laughs.

"Stop!" Harkness steps into the street and draws his gun, drops down into a crouch, and aims at the tires. The lightweight gun in his hand puzzles Harkness for a moment. Then he remembers.

Bent forward, face flushed red, eyes wide, the driver lays on the horn. He's had a heart attack. Or he's insane. The Volvo races by Harkness, jumps the curb, and roars across the green to smash into the town monument. The scream of torquing metal and the crunch of safety glass shattering cut through the morning air. The crushed grille of the car bends around the marble base of the monument, smoke gushing from beneath the mangled hood.

Harkness shoves his plastic gun in its holster and runs toward the green. He has to keep people away from the accident; the car could explode. He keeps one hand on his radio, calling in an emergency and requesting an ambulance, following protocol. Can't make any mistakes. When it's all over, he doesn't want anyone to say he couldn't handle the situation.

The monument creaks and shudders in the cool morning air. The sculpture of a Union soldier, standing at attention atop the monument for more than a century, gyrates slowly for a moment, then tumbles. In slow motion, the soldier dives headfirst to land squarely on the Volvo with another smash. The top of the monument shatters, sending rocky debris raining down on the green. Harkness dodges the stones as he runs toward the car.

The driver slumps against his half-shattered window, trapped in his car, arms flailing. Harkness radios in to confirm that the driver is alive and that they'll need the Jaws of Life to get him free. Dispatch tells him the EMTs are on the way.

"Hey!" Harkness steps over a chunk of soldier and knocks out what's left of the driver's window with his elbow.

The driver turns toward Harkness, his face powder-white from airbag dust. Two straight lines of blood stream from his nose. He looks like a dead baker. Cubes of safety glass shine on his navy blazer.

"Try to hold still, sir. Ambulance is coming."

The driver shakes his head, probably the only part of him that can move, except for his arm, which is still jerking around toward what used to be the passenger seat. He's got the metal door of the glove compartment open and he's pawing around, sending papers flying.

"I don't need your registration, sir," Harkness says. "Don't need anything. Just keep still. The EMTs are coming." Sirens howl in the distance. An ambulance, fire engine, and the rest of the Nagog Police Department are on the way.

The driver grunts, finds what he's looking for.

He holds a gun in his right hand, a fancy revolver that he shoves over his ear.

"No!" Harkness leans through the driver's window and gets one hand around his thick wrist, then another. He smells vodka and gasoline. The sirens come closer.

The driver grunts. His teeth are shattered, and who knows what else. But he's holding tight to his gun. Harkness pries his trigger finger out and sticks his own thumb behind the trigger. With one hard pull, he yanks the blood-slick pistol away. He clicks the safety on. For a moment he imagines how easy his life would be if the gun were a matte-black Glock. But it's a shiny Smith & Wesson — wrong gun, different caliber. He slips the gun behind his belt.

The driver slumps forward on the dashboard. Harkness leans into the car again, its floor crowded with Grey Goose bottles dislodged by the impact. Cockroach-colored vials gleam among the bottles. Harkness remembers a burnt-out Cambridge triple-decker, its floor covered with the same vials, melted into amber pools next to three blackened and blistered college kids, conjoined on the floor like cowering citizens of Pompeii after their makeshift drug lab caught fire.

Harkness picks out a full vial and puts it in the pocket of his leather jacket, a Narco-Intel habit — *Be your own chain of custody.* You never know what might be evidence. And you never know when evidence might disappear.

He looks up. EMTs are running across the grass. Slumped against the dash, the driver opens his dark eyes open for a moment to give Harkness a heavy-lidded stare.

"Edward, right?" he says softly. "You Eddy Harkness, Red's boy?"

"Yes."

The driver starts to laugh, slowly at first, then more and more until a stream of bright blood gushes from his mouth.

"Says his name is Robert Hammond, of Oaktree Court. Know him?" Captain Munro holds out the license to Harkness. It shows a smiling, smaller version of the man now being raced to the Nagog Regional Hospital in an ambulance. Behind them, a tow truck struggles to free the Volvo.

Harkness thinks for a moment. "My father knew him. He's some kind of financial advisor."

"Like half the town. Got anything else, Eddy?"

Harkness stares.

The captain puts his hand on Harkness's shoulder. "Look, I know this isn't easy. I wouldn't ask you if it weren't important."

"He was a big wine guy," Harkness remembers. "Had a cellar. Big drinker, big talker. That's what my father used to say."

The captain holds up Hammond's shiny pistol, zipped into an evidence bag. "Any reason he might want to kill himself?"

Harkness shrugs. "Wouldn't know. Never met him. Dad kept his business friends separate."

"From?"

"Our family." His throat tightens.

"Was he involved in anything . . ."

"Illegal? Like my father?"

"That's not what I'm saying, Harkness. *Christ*. I'm just trying to figure out why a middle-aged guy with a clean record would go off the rails like this. Anyone we could talk to?"

Harkness runs through his Nagog connections. "I went to high school with his daughter, Candace," he says. "She's a couple of years younger than me. Completely wild."

"Did you know this wild daughter back in the day?"

Harkness shakes his head. "Not very well. Haven't seen her in years."

"Get reacquainted. Do some legwork."

"Me, sir? I have meters to empty."

"Don't be clever. You think I should send Detective Ramble? He'll just talk the guy to death," the captain says quietly. "Or worse Dabilis? They don't know this town the way you do. Being a local is a big advantage for cases like this. You're not a stranger. You know everyone. And they know you, trust you."

"Yes, sir."

"Start at Nagog Regional, in the ICU," the captain says. "This Hammond fellow is probably going to die there in a couple of hours. EMTs say he doesn't have a chance."

"No disrespect intended, sir," Harkness says. "But why do we care?"

"If it's an accident, the town ends up paying the whole bill for repairing this historic site." The captain points at the smashed monument. "Which will be expensive. But if it's suicide, it's willful destruction of property and Mr. Hammond's insurance has to pay."

The tow truck pulls the Volvo free from the monument and what's left of the Union soldier rolls off its roof.

"Hey, be careful!" the captain shouts at the wrecker, which runs over the soldier's arm.

"Hammond got drunk, smashed his car into a monument at about sixty miles an hour, and put a gun to his head. You need more proof than that, sir?"

"Lawyers and insurance companies run the show now," the captain says. "Got to get something in writing. That's what the town manager wants."

"So you want me to go talk to a dying guy and get him to confess to wrecking the town monument while trying to kill himself? Sir?"

"Yes, ideally as soon as possible. Before he dies."

Harkness says nothing.

"Would you rather be emptying meters?"

Harkness walks back to retrieve the coin transfer unit. A crowd gathers on Main Street, cars pulled off to both sides of the road. As he walks closer, a clutch of concerned women rushes toward him.

"You have to do something," one of them says.

"What's the problem, ma'am?"

"A deer."

Harkness walks closer. After Hammond did his damage, the injured deer limped into the woods to die. But a big buck has managed to drag itself back onto the road. A group of citizens huddles around the buck, as if it's a dolphin beached on the Cape. Dozens of cars are lined up down Main Street. Harkness radios in and requests Animal Control.

The buck's back legs splay at terrible angles behind him. Harkness can't count how many points the buck has; his antlers are broken and scattered in pieces on the road. Glistening pink gel seeps from the nubs.

The buck rises up suddenly, desperate eyes glinting, and tries to walk, front hooves clicking on the road as he pulls his scraped body and useless legs a few inches closer to the edge of the road.

"We have to help him," someone says. The small crowd shares the solemn but confused look of do-gooders not sure how to do good.

"Look, the animal control officer is on his way," Harkness says. The protocol is to wait. But no one should have to watch an animal suffer. Best to clear people away. "Step back. Get back in your cars, please."

The door of a Toyota pickup opens and the driver strides toward Harkness. Leather tool belt, big boots, greasy Carhartt jacket — he looks like a carpenter from the Cape.

"Just shoot that buck," he says, voice loud and flat. "Gonna die in the woods anyway."

"The animal control officer is on his way," Harkness says. "Please step back into your truck, sir."

"It's in pain. Why make it last longer?" The carpenter points at Harkness's plastic gun. "Just shoot it."

If he had a real gun, Harkness would have by now. But firing colorful disks over the dying deer doesn't seem helpful. He scopes the carpenter out. He seems like an ordinary guy, the kind who obeys cops. "We're waiting, understand, sir?"

"Look, dude. I'm a hunter. If I had my gear in the truck I'd just shoot it for you."

The crowd murmurs. They want to be humane, but they're not sure about just shooting the deer, which would involve death. As a rule, the town of Nagog is opposed to death. A few weeks ago someone asked Harkness to rescue a spider trapped inside a parking meter.

The buck rises up on his front legs and gives out a terrified bleat. He collapses on the road with a thud, black tongue lolling, flanks heaving.

"For Christ's sake, shoot him!" The carpenter stomps back to his truck.

"The rest of you, get in your cars, please," Harkness says. They start to shuffle to their Subarus and Hondas. Then the carpenter comes back carrying a sledgehammer.

"You. Stop." Because Harkness looks and sounds like a cop, the carpenter does.

Harkness points at the crowd. "All of you. In your cars, now." They trudge away.

A car drives up behind him and Harkness turns to see the brown sedan with the green TOWN OF NAGOG seal on the side. Hank Steadman, the town's gruff, incompetent animal control officer, walks toward Harkness, holding a tranquilizer gun sloppily at his side.

Behind him, Harkness hears a fleshy smash and then another. When he turns, the carpenter is swinging his hammer at the buck's head like it's a reluctant two-by-four. There's a crack when he hits the buck's skull and the deer shudders once, legs trying to run one last time. Then the buck goes still.

"There's your fucking *animal control.*" He wipes the sledge on the grass and stalks back toward his truck, shaking his head.

Hank ambles closer. "Looks like you got a dead deer here, Eddy."

Harkness nods. The buck's black eyes are open and staring, his crushed skull oozing dark blood.

"Grab a leg and we'll get him off the road."

8

HARKNESS PULLS INTO the empty parking lot of Nagog Regional Hospital. There's a banner announcing a blood drive, an empty guard shack, and a couple of old men in tan raincoats shuffling outside the Pavilion, the town's elder care facility. Harkness calls the familiar number.

"Sir!"

"Patrick, it's me."

"Thanks for that information, sir!"

"Someone's in your office, right?" Harkness isn't supposed to call Narco-Intel.

"That's correct."

"Call back when you can."

Harkness clicks his phone off and sits in the quiet squad car for a moment. Through the rain-speckled windshield, he can see the semicircle drive that leads to the emergency room — a longtime Harkness family haunt. He remembers going there at seven when his brother George pushed him out of a tree. When they were twelve, they walked deep into the Nagog Woods and shot each other at fifty yards to see if the pellets would break skin. They did. At sixteen, he and George both ended up in the ER when they smashed their father's BMW into a cement wall to see if the airbags would inflate. They didn't. In high school, George taught his punk brother how to make a pipe bomb in the basement. They learned to make do without eyebrows.

Their father, Edward "Red" Harkness, took a perverse pride in his rough sons, their fights, and the trips to the emergency room. Red had a few visits of his own, stabbing himself in the thigh while drinking Scotch and opening Wellfleet oysters with a barlow knife, an anxiety attack triggered by a market drop, and a holiday overdose of Demerol that left him sprawled on the living room floor, pale and unresponsive as a birch log.

It's only funny when someone gets hurt. Like many a truth, the Harkness family motto makes more sense in retrospect. Eddy and George, with encouragement from their father, fought until blood flowed from somewhere—nose, mouth, scalp. They carried violence inside them like a banked fire. They still do.

His phone rings.

"Harky?"

"Yeah?"

"Got some news for you."

"Good or bad?"

Patrick says nothing.

"Out with it."

"Well, that check I ran on Thalia Havoc came up completely clean. But when I ran Thalia Prochazka, I found out your girl's been busy."

"Like what?"

"Drug busts. Junk twice. Blow once. All under a gram. Assault with a deadly weapon."

"What kind of weapon?"

"Dinner plate. Threw it at someone at some Chinatown dump. And breaking and entering. Broke into the Public Garden at night and took a Swan Boat for a spin back when she was in art school."

Harkness has to smile at that one.

"Girl's a pistol."

"Roger that," Harkness says. "What about the call from Pauley Fitz?"

"Someone's got his cell phone."

"That's weird. Didn't it get smashed?"

"He dropped it on the bridge. Ended up in Evidence downtown."

"So a cop took it?"

"Maybe, Harky. All I know is Pauley Fitz's phone is missing and no one signed it out."

"Weird." Harkness sits in the quiet car for a moment, staring at the gray cement hospital.

"Looks like someone's got it in for you, Harky. All we got to do is figure out who."

"That's always the hard part," Harkness says.

"I'll help you."

"I know that," Harkness says. "Got to go."

"Meters?"

"No. Heading to the hospital to bother a drunk driver who's about to die."

"You get to have all the fun," Patrick says. "Listen, I got some other bad news."

"How bad?"

"Real bad. Watch-your-back bad. Leave-town-at-high-speed bad."

"What're you talking about?"

"Can't tell you now, Eddy. Didn't exactly find out via normal channels. Come downtown and we'll talk."

The mound is covered by sheets and blankets, woven with tubes and wires, and surrounded by pulsing monitors no one seems to notice. Harkness can't imagine that it's human or alive. From the door of the blazingly bright ICU, he watches the doctors and nurses connecting tubes and setting up equipment. Their hushed, urgent voices make it obvious that Robert Hammond isn't going to be walking out of Nagog Regional any time soon.

"Can I help you?" A young male nurse with his dark hair pulled back in a stubby ponytail turns toward Harkness.

Harkness takes off his hat and gives the nurse his cop look — serious, concerned, and honest. "I'm here to ask Mr. Hammond a few questions."

"I don't think he's got much to say. We're pumping him full of drugs." The nurse squints at Harkness's badge. "Eddy, right? Eddy Harkness. Nagog High?"

"Right."

"It's me, Andy Singh." The nurse points at his narrow chest beneath baby-blue scrubs.

Harkness digs back through his high school memories. "Right. Hi, Andy." While Harkness was at the Academy, on street patrols in Boston, and with Narco-Intel, his high school classmates turned into townies.

They shake hands and the nurse leads Harkness a couple of yards away from Hammond.

"You were on the baseball team," Andy Singh says. "And you were into music, right? I was in a band. The Andy Singh Experience?"

Harkness remembers a band of shoegazers in the sun at Nagog High's spring music fest. "Guitar, right? Still playing?"

Andy shakes his head. "No. Too busy. Besides, I got way into drugs in college. Had to give up on music. Found a program. Stuck with it. Cleaned up."

"Good. Good for you." Harkness gives him the hard look and Andy's eyes drift. When people say they've straightened out, they probably haven't. Odds are Andy has some weed or a pill hoard tucked away in his locker.

"Now I'm working at a hospital. Surrounded by all kinds of drugs. Weird, huh? How things change."

"Weirder if they didn't." Harkness looks back at the mound. "Is this guy going to make it?"

"Probably not," Andy says. "But you never know."

"Injuries?"

"Broken arm, cracked pelvis, punctured lung, lots of internal stuff, toxemia." Andy holds out his hands about a foot apart. "Going to have to take out a big chunk of his liver. Luckily his is the size of *Tay-hass*. Some cranial trauma. Brain's loose."

"Sounds bad."

"Ought to be dead already. Scrawny little dudes speeding on prom night? They die in wrecks like this. Puffy guys, wedged in their Volvos, it's like they're driving around with extra airbags made out of fat."

"He was drunk at the time of the accident, yes?"

Andy leans forward. "Officially, I'm not supposed to say anything." He flips back a few pages on his clipboard. "But, yeah, when he was admitted his blood alcohol was .23, like three times over the limit. That probably helped him, too."

"How's that?"

"He didn't clench up on impact. He was all loosey-goosey."

"So being totally drunk and morbidly obese helped save his life," Harkness says.

"Worked out that way for him, I guess."

"Any indication that he was trying to kill himself?"

Andy tilts his head.

"Just trying to assess his . . . state of mind."

"Let me take a look." Andy glances back toward the doctors, then goes through the chart and reads. "Patient was confused, difficult to control, convinced that he had been in a plane crash."

"That's strange."

"Not as weird as some of the shit we see in here, Eddy. Preppie girls with infected cuts up and down their legs. Lawyers with eggplants stuck in their butts. Bankers overdosed on animal tranquilizers from their daughters' horses. The other day some guy tried to poison his wife with antifreeze in her skinny-girl mojito. This town seems all normal but it's not, Eddy."

. . .

"Who loves him some Bambi?" the Sweathog says, smiling.

Harkness slips by Sergeant Dabilis but the sergeant follows him across the Pit.

"Couldn't even shoot a deer, could you?"

Harkness says nothing, fills the coffeemaker with water. The other cops look up, sensing a new episode of Harvard Cop versus the Sweathog.

"You're not supposed to shoot a deer," Officer Watt says. "I looked it up. Harkness had it right. You wait for Animal Control. Too dangerous to fire off a shot with people around."

Harkness likes Watt, a slow-talking rookie, a little more now.

"Well, I'd have shot the fucker," the Sweathog says. "Public menace. You can use deadly force if it's endangering people."

"The deer was down with two broken legs," Watt says.

"Still ought to have shot the fucker, instead of letting some jack-off citizen do your dirty work with a fucking hammer."

Harkness says nothing.

"If you're not going to use that gun, maybe we should just take it away from you," Sergeant Dabilis says.

Harkness freezes.

"I don't think those parking meters pose much of a threat."

Harkness grabs Sergeant Dabilis by the shoulders, lifts him off his feet, and slams him against a row of filing cabinets — all so fast neither of them has time to think. Harkness holds Dabilis pressed against the wall like an insect specimen, then forces himself to let the Sweathog slide down, his coffee spilling on the floor. Harkness walks away, arms vibrating, mind spinning.

"Hey, I'm reporting that!"

The normal cops tell the Sweathog to cut it out, that he was asking for it. They like Harkness. And cops are superstitious. Someday they might make a tough call and end up on perpetual meter duty.

The captain steps out of his office and frowns. "Get back to work, people. Dabilis, clean up that coffee and get back to your desk. Watt, I want you in your patrol car in ten seconds. Harkness, I need to see you in my office. Now."

The captain leafs through papers on his desk with a brutal efficiency, not even looking up when Harkness walks in. He knows there's only one explanation for the captain's coldness; his gun turned up, its serial number traced. He's played out the inevitable ending, where he sets his badge on the desk as the captain looks away in disappointment.

"The town manager's been on the phone with me about a dozen times already," the captain shouts, finally. When he's pissed, the captain's Scottish accent comes out, his cheeks redden, and he loses some of his cool. "The historical commission's got its collective tit in a wringer. I've been fielding calls all day."

Harkness nods. Small-town politics, he can deal with today.

"Some people want to tear the rest of the monument down because it glorifies war. The rest want to rebuild it immediately because it 'honors the sacrifice of our nation's heroes.' Do you know how much it's going to cost to fix?"

Harkness shrugs.

"Almost a million dollars." The captain shakes his head. He's a Scot by birth and a Yankee for twenty years, giving him a double dose of thrift.

"Ouch."

"No one knows how to do stonework like that anymore. Have to quarry new granite in New Hampshire and make it look old. And bring in a repair team from Italy. That drunk asshole, excuse my language, intoxicated citizen, triggered a colonial clusterfuck. What did you find out at the hospital?"

"Hammond was definitely drunk at the time of the accident, blowing .23."

"Impressive. Sounds like a pro."

"Now he's a mess."

"Did he say anything about his motivation? Trying to kill himself?"

"He was out cold, sir. He's dying. Won't be long."

"Shit."

"I'm heading back to the hospital. Want to see if his daughter shows up."

"Excellent. Get her to sign this." He hands Harkness a piece of paper.

"What is it?"

"Official acceptance of responsibility for the damage. He can sign if he ever wakes up. Or his daughter can, if she's authorized."

Harkness folds the piece of paper and puts it in the inside pocket of his jacket.

"And Harkness?"

He pauses at the door. "Yes, sir?"

"You were right to hold your fire. With the deer, I mean."

"Thank you, sir."

"This is a quiet town. We don't need patrolmen blasting away on our streets."

Harkness keeps the truth to himself. *Couldn't blast away even if I wanted to.*

9

B ACK IN HIGH SCHOOL, you turned me on to all the coolest old bands — Mission of Burma, SS Decontrol, Flipper, Misfits, Avengers. You were like a punk historian. *Straight Ed.* Coolest straight guy at Nagog High." Candace Hammond reaches over to peer down at her baby, nestled in the car seat next to her. "Used to see you running all those wild all-ages shows. Now you're a cop. Amazing."

"Not really," Harkness says.

"I guess being a cop is kind of hardcore, when you think about it." Her silver bracelets jangle and her baby makes a snuffling sound. "I can't believe you're still around here," she says. "Thought you'd go to New York for sure."

Harkness shrugs. Everyone always expects something else.

"Anyway, I'm glad to see you again." She looks around the hospital cafeteria, quiet in a midafternoon lull. "Even if it's when my dad's about to check out." Candace blinks her coffee-colored eyes. "No. Not going to cry. He's not dead." She shakes her head, as if it might wake her from this bad dream set in a hospital basement smelling of French fries and hand sanitizer.

Tendrils of black hair streaked platinum frame Candace's delicate, pale face. She's as street tough as a Nagog girl can be — bright red lipstick, dark mascara, and a tiny silver nose ring. But her frightened eyes, gleaming and red rimmed, tell another story.

"This really isn't the right time," he says. "But I have to ask you a few questions."

She gives him a hard stare. "I can't talk about Dad."

"Look, I know this is hard."

"You have no idea."

Harkness says nothing, the oldest tactic in the world. It takes about ten seconds to work.

"Here's all you need to know about dear old Dad." Candace counts off her father's salient qualities on her ringed fingers. "He's a big shot who is, in fact, up to his eyeballs in debt. He's fat as a whale. He drinks all the time. And he's a major asshole. Kicked me out of the family McMansion five years ago. I'm doing double shifts at the Nagog Bakery just to pay rent."

"I like that place."

"If you want a cup of coffee and an almond croissant, yes. If you want to make a living, no."

"When was the last time you saw your father?"

"A couple of weeks ago, when we took the baby over for a visit."

"We?"

"Me and Declan, May's father."

"How'd your dad seem to be doing?"

"No idea. We were there for about ten minutes. Dad can't stand Dex."

"Why not?"

"Says he's wasting his time doing carpentry when he ought to be doing something smarter — and that pays better, of course. Dad's all about the bottom line."

"You two married?"

Candace looks like she's caught a whiff of death. "No, of course not. We're living out at the Old Nagog Tavern. Dex and his friends are fixing it up so we can sell it."

"A project, then." A vague memory of breaking into the abandoned tavern with friends flickers through Harkness's mind.

"Right. You could call it that. Or a dump."

Harkness tries to get back on track. "So has your father been acting differently?"

"You mean, like, depressed?"

"Yes, like that."

"Sure. Maybe a little worse than usual. He's got business problems. Something about meeting with the regulators. I don't know anything about that kind of stuff."

Harkness does. When the regulators show up, it's never good news. "Does he ever talk about killing himself?"

Candace stares.

"Sorry to be so direct."

"He doesn't talk about it."

"I see."

"He just does it," she says. "Like, every day for the last ten years. Every steak. Every trip to the cheese store. Every bottle of wine. Every case of wine. Sure, he's trying to kill himself." Candace closes her eyes and this time it doesn't stop the tears.

She reaches into her purse for a tissue, and her other hand stays on the thigh of her black jeans. Harkness notices that its fingers are stiff and ringless.

Candace catches him staring, reaches into her sleeve, and tosses something at him. "Catch."

Harkness slides back in his chair as Candace's hand lands in his lap then bounces to the cafeteria floor. He leans down to pick up the smudged pink plastic hand, its fingernails painted black. Sharks drawn in ballpoint circle the wrist and its shiny metal nub.

"It's fake, Eddy," she says. "That hand sucks. I've got a better one at home but I left in a hurry."

"How'd that happen?"

"Paper cut."

Harkness stares at her.

"Really bad one."

"Back in high school you were . . ."

"Whole?" she said. "Bi-handed?"

"Yes."

"Happened later, after you left town. An accident."

Harkness holds the hand out to her by its stiff fingers. It's like shaking hands with a mannequin.

"It's a long story. I'll tell you about it sometime. But not now. Dealing with one accident is enough." Candace tucks the metal nub into the sleeve of her leather jacket and gives it a deft twist. She gives Harkness a frozen smile and a queenly wave with her plastic hand.

"I'm sorry. Really sorry."

Candace shrugs. "I'm used to it. Adaptation — the great and terrible quality of us humans. We get used to just about anything."

"Still, it must be . . ."

"Being a one-handed waitress is better than being dead. I tell myself that pretty much every day. And you know what, Eddy? Most of the time it's true." Candace leans toward her baby to tuck in the edge of a white blanket.

"Look, I know you have to get back to the ICU. But I have to ask about this." Harkness takes an evidence bag from his pocket and drops it on the table between them.

"Where the fuck did you get that shit?" Candace stares at the amber vial like it's about to explode.

"On the floor of your dad's car along with the Grey Goose bottles."

"Shit. Shit. *Shit.*" She slams her fake hand down on the cafeteria table.

"What?"

Candace pauses. "Forget it, Eddy. Just forget it. All I can say is this is news to me. And not good news."

The baby cries and Candace lifts her gently from the carrier, unbuttons her blouse to cup her breast, and deftly maneuvers her dark pink nipple into May's mouth. The feeding calms the baby and seems to do the same for Candace.

Harkness stares, transfixed by the skein of fine blue veins just beneath the pale skin of her full breast. When he looks up their eyes connect.

"You can watch if you want," Candace says softly. "I don't care. Just don't arrest me or anything."

"I won't." Harkness looks across the cafeteria.

After the baby finishes, Candace buttons her blouse and raises May to her shoulder.

"When he crashed into the monument, your father thought he was in a plane wreck," Harkness says. "Is that the other accident you were talking about?"

"Yeah," she says. "Family tragedy. I got over it. But he didn't.

That's the thing. Dad blamed himself because he was the pilot. But it wasn't his fault. He rented a crappy Cessna. Carbon monoxide leaked into the cabin. We all passed out and the plane crashed. I woke up in a snowy cornfield all cut to pieces. My sister didn't . . . she didn't wake up. Her name was May."

In Candace's glimmering dark eyes, Harkness sees the sadness and strength beneath the jokes and shit talk, the leather jacket and pawnshop jewelry.

Candace bends down to whisper in her daughter's tiny ear. "No one's going to ever hurt you, are they, May?"

They swagger down the long green hallway. The taller one leads the way, his long blond hair swinging in stringy clumps. Harkness figures the other two have to be brothers; they're the same kind of ugly — grimy and short, with ironic beards that make them look like they just stepped off of a Civil War battlefield. The three dudes stop to peer in the holding rooms, making each other laugh, not even trying to be quiet. One of the hairy brothers takes an empty IV pole and pulls it behind him like a toy. The taller one yanks the pole away and gives his hairy friend a practiced shove like he's a misbehaving kid he's tired of herding around.

Candace looks up from her iPad, thick with stickers like a skate-board. "Here's Dex," she says with a palpable lack of enthusiasm. "And his fucktard friends."

They walk into the waiting room. Dex's friends see something amusing on the ceiling-mounted TV and stare at it, transfixed by cartoons. Harkness notices that Dex pauses at the door before he walks through, a moment of threshold anxiety — could be a quirk or a sign that he's stranger than he looks.

Dex floats over to Candace and bends down to kiss her on the forehead. He has a soft, almost feminine face but his cheeks are stubbled, and his hair, dyed Cobain yellow, hangs in front of his flecked green eyes, which he keeps locked on the floor, rarely glancing up. He could be an organic farmer or a musician.

"Hey, Baby May," he whispers.

"Dex, she's sleeping." Candace shakes her head.

"Oh."

Candace points at Harkness. "This is Eddy. Used to call him

Straight Ed, remember him? He went to Nagog High. He was into punk rock. And baseball. Now he's into law enforcement."

Dex's blue eyes widen. "Eddy . . . ?"

"Harkness."

"Wow," Dex says. "Harkness." He gives a small laugh. "Got it."

When they shake hands, Harkness sees the frayed cuff of Dex's white shirt. Back in high school, Harkness wore the same uniform every day—an old white button-down over a vintage Black Flag T-shirt, straight-leg black jeans, and Doc Martens.

"Do I know you?" Everyone in Nagog looks familiar to Harkness. He's seen them walking down the street, sitting in town meeting, getting gas at the E-Z Mart, having breakfast at the Colonial Diner.

Dex looks up, then back down. "Probably not. I finished high school kind of early, but . . ." Dex pauses, looking like he's turning something over in his mind and trying to figure out if he should say it.

He points at Harkness's thick belt. "Hey, I used to have one of those."

"A gun?" Candace says. "I don't think so."

"Fires little plastic things," Dex says. "Round. All different colors."

Harkness stops breathing for a moment, takes a step back, and looks away.

Dex smiles. "Cop with a plastic gun. Cool."

"Quit being weird," Candace says. "Or just stop talking, so people can't tell that you're weird."

Dex shrugs. "Whatever. I'm just saying it seems like a good idea to me. Like, here's a new gun control policy—give all the cops plastic guns!"

His friends laugh.

"Were you in Boston on Sunday?" Harkness tries not to shout. "Lower South End?"

"Sure," Dex says. "Go there all the time. There's a couple of pubs there where I can be with me peoples and have us several dozen black 'n' tans to forget the Troubles."

The hairy twins laugh at Dex's quick shift into an old-style Boston-Irish barfly.

"What bars?" Harkness stares at Dex as if he's trying to reduce him to ash.

"I don't know," Dex says. "O'Halloran's? Franklin's? Bunch of others."

Harkness remembers stopping at both bars on the crawl back to Thalia's loft. "So were you in Boston?"

"What, like, in the last couple of days?"

"Yes."

"Maybe," Dex says. "Why do you want to know anyway? I just came to see the Big Man, not get the third degree from some local cop I kinda went to high school with."

"Dad's still in the ICU," Candace says.

"Then why're you waiting around here?"

"Because I have to be here."

Dex shrugs. "Been here all day."

"They need me here to make decisions."

"They could text you if he wakes up or something," Dex says. "Come back to the farm. Everyone's hungry."

Candace looks at Dex like she just noticed something new wrong with him. "I need to be here, okay? Dad's probably dying. I asked you to come and help out. Maybe make me feel better instead of worse. Honestly, I wonder if you guys are even human sometimes."

"That's easy, Dex is an enhanced human," one brother blurts out. "Like all H+ and shit!"

The other chimes in. "Like fucking Ray Kurzweil or . . . or a squirrel with microchips."

May wakes and her cries echo through the waiting room.

"Shut the fuck up, all of you." Candace kneels down next to the car seat.

"Woke the baby, Mouse." Dex stares hard at the mouthy brother.

Mouse looks at the floor, his head twitching.

"Need everyone to start behaving. Especially you."

"Don't be a dick, Dex."

Dex's hand flies toward Mouse and his fingers wrap around his thin neck. His other hand shoots out and he's got the other brother by the neck. Their faces turn red, eyes widen.

Dex looks at Harkness and shakes his head. "Kids these days. No fucking manners at all."

From Dex's deadpan stare, Harkness can't tell if he's being serious or snide. He knows this, though — Dex is strong and strange.

He lets the brothers go and gives them a shove toward the door. "Scram. We're leaving sickbay. Dullsville, USA." Dex waves his hand in front of him as if he can make the hospital go away with an iPhone swipe.

The brothers stagger ahead, coughing.

"Hey, want us to take Baby May back to the farm with us?" Dex asks Candace.

She shakes her head. "Are you crazy?"

Dex shrugs. "Suit yourself, Little Mommy."

Dex pauses at the waiting room doorway, unable to just barge through with the others. He drops into a gunslinger stance, makes a pistol with his fingers, and fires his silent gun at Harkness. He brings the barrel to his lips and blows. Then he quits the Wild West act and walks out the door with a tired smile, like Harkness is a joke that isn't very funny, one that everyone has heard already.

10

YOU REMEMBER HOW you used to tell me that this place smelled bad since it used to be an instant photo place?" Patrick spins around from his bank of computers. "Because the chemicals smelled like pee?"

"Yeah?" Harkness remembers making that story up to calm Patrick down about their smelly office.

"Not true. I looked up the building records. Used to be a disco called Buddy's downstairs, and disco people used to come up here and piss. And do drugs, no doubt. Probably blow and poppers."

"You had me come into Boston so you could tell me this, Patrick?"

"Thought you should know it really is old piss, Harky, not chemicals."

"Almost managed to forget about your smell thing." Despite his weirdness, Patrick is the unit's best forensic data miner, a savant at finding evidence encoded in e-mails, cash transfers, and prescription trends.

"This place was a drug hotspot, which I think is, you know, kinda ironic and all."

"Thanks for that."

Patrick turns back to the screens and gets lost in Dataland. Harkness stares at Patrick's gun belt, hanging on a metal coat rack, sees his gun safely tucked away in its black holster.

"So what you working on?"

"Brazilian thing they're selling in Dorchester," Patrick says. "Some kind of bodega powder made out of *datura* that takes you to your happy place, then puts you in a coma. And we're seeing a lot of this lollipop painkiller thing, fentanyl on a stick. Supposed to be for hospice patients. Except they're superdeadly and packaged like an innocent little lolly. Cool, huh?"

Harkness just shakes his head.

"Remember how simple everything used to be?" Patrick looks off into the distance with a nostalgic smile. "Weed, speed, blow, acid, meth. Maybe some Valium from Mom's purse. Now there're more drugs than cable channels."

"Think of it as job security," Harkness says.

A shiver crosses Patrick's shining face. "You do have a way of steppin' in it."

"In what?"

"In subjects you don't really want to get into." Patrick turns from his computer screen.

"And that subject is . . . ?"

"Our jobs, Harky. Remember a guy named John Fitzgerald?"

Harkness thinks. "City councilor out of Dorchester?"

"And?"

Harkness stares out the window at the gleaming Hancock Tower. "Uncle of Pauley Fitz, Turnpike Toreador," he says finally.

"He's about to make a run for mayor."

"Good luck with that."

"Dude's popular. Good-looking guy. Campaigned in every bar in Dorchester. Got elected to the council by a landslide."

"Sure he did. He's got two-thirds of JFK's name."

"Now he's making his move."

"Corrupt?"

Patrick rolls his eyes. "Only real question around here is how corrupt. He's squeaky-clean on the surface. But I hear he likes to hang with the hard guys. His big plan so far is to build a casino downtown by the harbor. That pretty much tells you what he's all about."

"Why do we care about Councilman John Fitzgerald?"

"Because he wants to kill us, Harky. Squash us dead like bugs." Patrick watches the closed door of his corner office, once Harkness's lair. "I'll be honest, Harky. You shouldn't even come around here."

"Why not?"

"People are pissed. Check this shit out, Eddy." Patrick reaches into his desk drawer and spins a thick report across his desk.

"What's this?"

"Information. Useful kind. Managed to get my hands on Fitzgerald's campaign playbook. As usual, the devil is in the data." Patrick flips the report open to a fine-print section titled "Strategies for a New Boston, First-Term Goals." "Check out number eleven."

Harknesss reads the last line. "We support a return to a patrol-based, neighborhood-focused solution to address our city's drug trade, eliminating expensive, resource-intensive special departments such as Narco-Intel."

"The guy's got it in for us," Patrick says. "Or more accurately — you."

"Sounds like Fitzgerald wants an old-style war on drugs. That'll work out really well."

"You're not getting it, Harky. This isn't about whether Fitzgerald cares about stopping drugs. Or whether he even gives a shit about the city. He just wants to be mayor so he can run the whole show and do whatever he wants. Mayor chooses the city council president. Appoints the school committee and zoning board. Even controls the damn library."

Harkness nods. "Got it."

"Here's what fucks us up — the mayor appoints the police commissioner, Harky. Remember? The guy wants us out. He's got a fuck-Commissioner-Lattimore-that-Harvard-Cop-and-all-his-friends plan. Couple of months ago he was just another city councilor in a cheap blue suit. The kind who tends to get caught with bribe money jammed in his tighty-whities."

"And now?"

"Now he's a legit candidate for mayor. Dude's got a hot-shit campaign director from Los Angeles, Mark Sarris, TV celebrity. Know him?"

"Don't think so."

"Had that show on Fox, *LA Confrontational?* The one where politicians yelled at each other?"

"Missed it."

"You'd recognize him," Patrick says. "Looks like a pissed-off piglet. But Sarris can spin any story and make it sound good. And it's working. Fitzgerald's got big endorsements and piles of money. Running as an independent so he can split the vote. It's going to be really ugly. The guy is angry — even more angry than most Irish dudes. And he wants a fight."

"Then give them one. Get Communications on it. It's just a personal vendetta."

"We're in enough trouble already, Harky," Patrick says. "Downtown's definitely not going to go to the mat for the Internetty drug-fighting data miners. They got their own asses on the line. Fitzgerald wins, everyone's out — from your old pal Commissioner Lattimore on down."

"Look, we had an eighty-five percent conviction rate last year," Harkness says. "We shut down more pill mills and crooked docs than the DA. And uncovered drugs no one even knew about."

"Yeah, but I'm not you, Harky," Patrick says, voice lowering. "Can't run this place the way you did. I'm just a fat hacker who ended up in charge of a really cool unit when you got banished to the boonies. When I come to work I feel like I'm getting into a sports car I don't even know how to start." Patrick runs his fingers through his hair, scratches his scalp, and sniffs his fingertips.

"Not true, Patrick, none of it," Harkness says.

"If Fitzgerald gets elected, he'll bring in some drinking buddy as commissioner. Some guy named Sullivan, Ryan, or Mc-what-the-fuck-ever. Then we're all out of here. Game over."

"Not over yet."

"That's what Sox fans say, Harky. All the way to the last game."

Harkness walks down the dank back stairwell to Boylston Street, crowded with students, gawking tourists, and bums clutching bent cardboard signs detailing their afflictions. Across the street in Copley Square, elegant Trinity Church sits like a jewel box left at the feet of glimmering Hancock Tower. From his office window, Harkness used to watch visitors stream through the church's arched entryways every day. If he believed in God as much as he believed in the order of law, Harkness might join them today, walking inside the church to kneel in front of the gilded sanctuary and pray for his gun back.

Instead, he walks toward the Public Garden to look for a drug dealer.

. . .

The narrow crescent of Bromfield Street winds past a shoe repair place, a nail salon, and the Café Marliave, where Harkness used to go for pasta and the clear view of the street, a favorite for drug deals. The camera stores are gone, pen places, too. A tequila bar has replaced Boston Stamp and Coin, where Harkness used to stand at the counter as his father — collector of stamps, coins, and other people's savings — leafed through the thick binders.

"So you want to buy your girlfriend a ring, that it?"

Harkness turns from the window. "Definitely. She deserves something nice."

"For putting up with you, right?" The jeweler's tall and bald, dressed old-style in pleated gray pants and red suspenders over a baggy white shirt.

Harkness fakes a laugh. "Right."

"Women put up with a lot," he says. "Got to make sure you respect them. That's what jewelry is, you know. Shiny little pieces of respect."

"Never thought about it that way."

A couple finishes looking at wedding bands and heads toward the door. The jeweler follows them. "Thanks for coming by." He shuts the front door behind them and locks it, then opens the back office door. Two sleek Dobermans rush out, barking and baring their white teeth. They back Harkness against the wall and lunge at his ankles. Froth spews from their sloppy mouths.

"Get them away from me, Gus," Harkness shouts. One of the dogs gets too close, and he kicks at it. If he had his gun, Harkness would have shot it.

"What the fuck are you doing here?" the jeweler shouts. "This is where I work, motherfucker."

"Got a question about a drug. Thought you might be the man to ask."

"Not anymore." Gus "the Chemist" Donovan shakes his head and his glass eye swirls in its socket, making him look even crazier. "I

60

sell rings and necklaces. That's it. You and your pals put me out of business."

"Did that all by yourself." Harkness keeps his eyes locked on the snarling dogs, knowing his stare is all that's keeping them at bay.

"How's that, asshole?"

"Shipping by commercial jet after 9/11." TSA uncovered Vicodin mixed in a shipment of semiprecious jewels, putting an abrupt end to Gus's import business. "Heard of drug dogs?"

"I know all about dogs." Gus nods at his Dobermans, the bold dog nipping at Harkness's shoe, the clever one trying to sidle around and sink his teeth into the back of his leg. "One word and they're on your throat, Harkness."

"You're on probation, Gus. Want to go back in?"

"I'll just say it was an accident. They freaked out. Dogs do that, you know."

"Really?" Harkness bends down and stares into the dog's white-blue eyes. Without breaking his gaze, he reaches under a display case and pulls out a filthy stuffed rabbit. He holds it up for a second and throws it at the window.

The bold dog leaps for it and smashes through the glass. The other circles beneath the windowsill, sniffing a spray of blood on the floor, then giving it a tentative lick.

The showroom turns silent for a moment as Gus walks to the window and looks down through the shattered glass.

"Shit. He's dead." Gus keeps staring down at the alley as he screams. "What are you, some kinda ninja? They been looking for that fucking bunny for weeks."

Harkness shrugs.

Gus herds the remaining dog into the back room and gives it a kick before slamming the door. "Useless piece of shit," he whispers. "All that fucking training."

Back in the showroom, Gus looks out the window again for a second, shakes his head, and pulls the window shade over the broken glass. "You're lucky it's not twenty years ago, Harkness. Because I'd be throwing you out the window on top of my dog."

"Need something from you, Gus."

"You got to be kiddin'. You just killed my dog. Go fuck yourself."

Harkness pulls the amber vial from his coat pocket and sets it on the glass counter above the glittering engagement rings. "Any idea what this is?"

"I'd have to say it's probably some kind of drug. Why don't you ask your other asshole cop friends?"

"They're busy," Harkness says. "You're better and faster than a drug lab. Plus, you owe me a favor."

"Really? I'm already down one dog and a window."

"We busted you with two thousand Vicodins, right?"

"So what?"

"DEA wanted to wait for the twenty thousand you had coming into Logan the next week so you'd look like a big fish. We said move fast. If we hadn't, you'd still be in Walpole."

"Okay, okay." Gus holds up his thick-fingered hands. "I'll look at this shit for one minute because you're such a nice fucking cop. But then you're out of here. And don't ever fucking come back."

"Deal," Harkness says.

Gus reaches for the vial and unscrews the top, then breathes deeply like a wine drinker about to sip a fine Burgundy. He lifts a piece of blotting paper from a drawer and puts a drop on it, then smears it across the paper and holds it up at the light. He licks the paper and moves his face around.

"Not liquid Ecstasy, not dissolved heroin or opium, not in-process meth or anything obvious. Where'd you get it?"

"Car wreck."

"What kind of car?"

"Volvo S80, almost new." Harkness summons up the crushed silver car melded with the town monument.

"Where?"

"Nagog."

"Rich people's drug, then?"

"Maybe."

"I'd say it's some kind of speed but it ain't bitter enough," Gus says. "I'm pretty sure it's this new stuff called Third Rail."

"Never heard of it."

"Takes you places. Even if you don't want to go. And once you touch it, it's too late. Get it?"

"So what is it?"

"Synthetic cousin of meth with a splash of dopamine to wake up your brain and an ephedrine chaser to squeeze it like a lemon. Guanfacine to mess with your memory. All mixed with this Chinese herb, *má huáng*, to make things really batshit crazy. Hard to make. Way expensive."

"Designer meth."

"More than that. It's a wild ride, from what I hear. Nothing else like it. Not that I know. Or care."

Gus tosses the vial at Harkness, who catches it in midair. "Now take this shit, get the fuck out of here, and don't ever come back."

.   .   .

Walking back across the Common, Harkness sees Little Dorothy, pale and glowing, near the Frog Pond, where there's a roller rink in summer, ice skating in winter. It's empty between seasons, and a few kids shuffle across the abandoned rink, pretending to skate on the crushed leaves.

Harkness walks toward her but she slips away. He sits down on a bench next to the rink to wait for her return.

Little Dorothy first appeared on a meth bust on Queensbury Street three winters ago. A couple of small-timers from New Hampshire had come to the big city to make a million in meth but got caught. The cop running the bust told Harkness there had to be major crank hidden somewhere. But they'd ripped the place apart and still hadn't found it, so they brought in the smart guys from Narco-Intel.

Harkness was a dowser, minesweeper, Geiger counter, Ouija board. From the moment Harkness walked into the grim apartment, a kitchen wall sent out a signal. There was no way that meth cookers would bother to hang new wallpaper in part of the kitchen.

Lost things don't want to stay lost. Money wants a warm wallet and street drugs crave a narrow pocket. Rings call out for a finger, cell phones want a hand, and bullets need a gun. Harkness didn't do anything special to find the meth hidden in the ragged Fenway apartment. It called out on subtle frequencies and he listened.

Harkness took hold of the edge of the flowered kitchen wallpaper and used a razor blade and a bowl of warm water to peel it back inch by inch as the cops watched, slit eyed with suspicion. He revealed a flush-mounted gray metal door the size of a school locker. When he opened the door the putrid wind knocked them all back. The upper shelf held a plastic-wrapped cake of backyard meth. The lower shelf, once for mops and brooms, held tubing, bags of chemicals, and a yellow bucket with a doll sticking out of it, feet encased in cheap pink plastic skates from the shut-the-kid-up aisle of a convenience store.

Harkness reached for the doll's legs and felt stiff, cold flesh instead of plastic. He shut his eyes for a moment as he lifted, opening them a sliver to see the head emerging from the bucket of bleach. This was no doll. As Harkness held her emaciated legs, the child's bloated face fell back into the gray chemical ooze like scrambled eggs sliding from a tipped plate, leaving only a glistening white oval of bone with darker voids for eyes, nose, and mouth.

The hardest cops in the room fell on their knees to heave or stumbled out on Queensbury Street. Harkness set Little Dorothy back in her bucket, leaving her reassembly to Forensics. He did his part, revealing the hidden, for what it was worth. He could only drift away, tainted by revelation.

Now Harkness walks slowly through the Public Garden, leaving Little Dorothy behind.

11

WHEN THE MAIL TRUCK finally lumbers around the corner, Harkness hits the flashers and siren. He's spent most of the afternoon lurking near the town forest instead of emptying meters along Bridge Street.

The mailman rolls down his window.

"Need to see all the mail for the Old Nagog Tavern, please."

The mailman shakes his head and blinks. "Not called that anymore, officer. It's 375 Forest Road. Private home."

"Then all the mail for 375 Forest Road."

He shakes his head again. "We can't just hand over mail without a warrant."

Harkness takes off his sunglasses and leans inside. "Ira. It's me. Eddy Harkness. Used to live on Nagog Hill."

The mailman tilts his bald head. "Harkness. Your father ordered clothes from Orvis. Subscriptions to all kinds of financial newsletters. Your mom got *Cook's Illustrated* and *Granta.* You got music magazines from England."

"That's us." Or that *was* us, Harkness thinks.

The mailman looks into a bin. "Still can't give it to you. But you can take a look, Eddy. Just don't tell anyone." He hands Harkness a packet.

"Know a Declan Nevis? Goes by Dex?" Harkness flips through the stack of cable bills and postcards for gutter cleaners.

"Nice enough kid," the postman says. "Doing a lot of work on that house."

"Met him once," Harkness says. "Seems okay."

"His mother was a science teacher. But he's definitely not."

Harkness looks up. "Where did she teach?"

"Taught at the high school for years. Name's Allison Nevis."

"Call me if you see anything unusual in his mail." Harkness hands him his Nagog Police card.

"Is he a terrorist or something?"

Harkness shrugs. "Can't say at this point."

. . .

"George, heard of Allison Nevis?" Harkness stands out on the cement slab around the refueling station, where Nagog cops go to call their sports bookies and girlfriends.

"No," his brother says. "Why?"

"I think she may be on the list."

"There're thousands of people on the list, Eddy. Can't remember them all. Why do you care?"

"Her son may be messing with me."

"I'll look her up," George says.

"Thanks."

"Dinner tonight?"

"Can't." Harkness can't imagine doing anything but trying to find his gun.

"Don't you want to introduce your girlfriend to your favorite-slash-only brother?"

"You really want me to answer that?" Harkness waves at the overnight shift, just leaving.

"I'll see you at the bar at Number 9 Park at six. Bring your girlfriend, she can meet Suzanne. We'll have a nice dinner. I'm buying. And I'll behave, promise."

George hangs up before Harkness can say no.

. . .

"We're having dinner with George and his girlfriend," Harkness says.

His mother brightens. "George!" She's bundled up in her green fall coat.

66

"He's doing great, Mom. Working hard, you know. At the car wash."

"Cut it out," Nora says.

When their mother was first diagnosed, they tried to bring her back. They handed her their father's favorite scarf or showed her a painting they'd bought on their honeymoon, hoping that memories would break through her congealing mind. Then they realized none of it mattered — the resonant objects, their careful words, nothing. She just kept drifting further out of reach, caught in a riptide of forgetting.

So now they just walk through Nagog, past pastel fields of loosestrife, its purple stalks beautiful but obvious, like a plant designed by a hairdresser.

"Cold today, isn't it?" Nora still tries to engage, always the good daughter, even better when compared with her feral brothers.

Their mother nods because she senses she probably should. Once she was a sharp-minded elementary school principal who loved Yeats. Now she nods and walks.

"Mom, I have a question," Harkness says, looking her in the eye.
"Yes?"

"Do you remember a teacher named Allison Nevis?"

She just stares until Nora nudges him.

"Don't make her feel bad, Eddy," she says.

When they cross the bridge, wisps of fog are rising off the black river. The slow-spiraling road, once theirs, leads to the old town waterworks. On Nagog Hill the large houses are set back from the street and the gracious lots are dotted with sheltering maples, lawns cleared of leaves by Salvadorans.

Harkness and his sister lag behind their mother when they come to what they always think of as the Lenoxes' house, even though the Lenox family moved away long ago. No one really leaves Nagog.

"Got a problem, Nora," Harkness says.

"Must be a big one or you wouldn't tell me."

"Lost my gun."

"You mean they took it away from you or something?"

"No. Lost it. I got really drunk. It was the anniversary of . . . you know . . . the incident."

Nora stops and pushes on his shoulder to spin him toward her. "Jesus, Eddy. You're supposed to be the responsible one."

"I am, usually."

"Well, this sounds like a major problem."

"It is."

"You have to get it back, and fast."

"No kidding."

"Any idea of who might have it?"

He shakes his head. "Working on it." He waits for a moment, the silence thickening. "I'm chasing down a guy who may know something about it. Or maybe Thalia does."

"That girl's bad news."

"She makes me feel better, Nora. And she's got a good heart."

"Well, that's not always enough, is it? You look like crap. Like you haven't slept in days."

He gives his sister his you-don't-need-to-worry-about-me look.

"Be careful, Eddy. One piece of bad luck has a way of leading to another." No need to explain — she's talking about the Harkness family's fast slide down Nagog Hill.

They look at their mother, trudging ahead.

"I know you've got your problems, Eddy, but you've got to listen to mine for a second."

"Okay, sure."

"I need you to talk to George."

"About?"

"Money."

"I'm sure he'll love that."

"Mom's gotten a lot worse." Nora's eyes tear up and she reaches into the pocket of her suede coat for a tissue. "We have to get her in some kind of . . ." Nora's voice diminishes to a whisper. "Some kind of facility, Eddy. I just can't handle it anymore." Harkness shakes his head and feels tears welling up behind his eyes, pressed tightly closed.

"We're already paying the home care agency a ton of money so I can go to work," Nora says. "And she needs more care than she's getting. The nursing aides just park her in front of the TV. I came home the other day and she was watching some true crime show about a shoot-out in someone's backyard." Nora shivers. "Blood spraying all over. Explosions."

"I'll help any way I can, Nora," Harkness says. "But I don't have any money right now," Harkness says. "And I don't think George does either. He's still trying to pay off Dad's . . ."

"Mistakes."

"Right, those."

"Well, we need to have a family meeting or something, because I can't take it anymore."

"I'm really sorry." Nora, twenty-six, working at a job she hates, comes home from the hospital to deal with the *mombie*, as they used to call her, back when they could joke about it. Half-Mom, half-zombie.

"Well, sorry's not enough," Nora says. "We've got to actually do something. And before the holidays. I can't take another Thanksgiving. And definitely not Christmas."

They catch up with their mother, staring at the houses more intensely. Somewhere deep in her misfiring brain, she has to remember this road that she drove up and down for years, taking them to school, into town, to the train. The order of the houses — a rambling white clapboard that was once the Jamisons', a brick pile that was Mr. Stephen's place — sends a message that she's home.

They stand in front of what looks like a brand-new prep school, an enormous white house with two wings jutting out, more windows than they can count, and a circular gravel drive that looks like a sports car parking lot.

Their mother stares at the McMansion. "Where is . . ."

"Our house? It's in there somewhere," Nora says. "All gobbled up." A hedge fund manager bought their house from the IRS and supersized it.

"Where is . . ."

"Dad? He's gone . . . on a business trip."

Mom turns to Nora and shakes her head. "No, dear, he's dead. He's *dead*."

They stare. Their mother used to surface in rare moments of clarity, but there hasn't been one in months.

"Is he?" Nora asks.

"Yes. He died because he did bad things. Bad things." She's shaking her head now, holding her right hand in front of her and waving the bad things away like flies.

"Some people . . . ," she says. "Some people are too smart for their own damn good."

12

FROM THALIA'S LOFT they walk past condemned brownstones marked with spray-painted red *X*s, an abandoned Syrian restaurant, and a burnt-out Citgo station. When they cross Albany Street and Harrison Avenue, Harkness remembers sweaty all-ages shows in cavernous warehouses before artists and gallery owners replaced squatters and punks, before the vintage flea markets and artisanal food trucks appeared like mushrooms that grew on money.

"They call this neighborhood SoWa now," he says.

"What?"

"South of Washington Street—SoWa. Like SoHo. Supposed to sound all hip and happening."

"Sounds like 'So what?,'" Thalia says. "I like the old names. Kenmore Square. Winter Hill. The Combat Zone."

"You really want to bring back the Combat Zone?"

"Sure," she says. "It didn't try to be something that it wasn't already."

They walk down the stairs into Ruggles station to wait for a downtown trolley. The platform is nearly empty except for a few tired women slumped on the wooden benches, one with her arm wrapped around a bright red upright vacuum cleaner. When the hair on the back of his neck tingles for a moment, Harkness glances over his shoulder just in time to see two guys in thin leather jackets running toward them. They look like hipsters pretending to be thugs. The bigger of the two shoves Harkness to the ground while the other latches on to Thalia's arm.

Harkness jumps up to pull the skinnier one from Thalia, spin him around, and wrap his hands around his neck. When Harkness presses his thumbs into the soft hollow at the base of his neck, his face reddens and his eyes pop open wide like a stress doll's.

"Want to rob us?" Harkness says. "I don't have any money. I'm carrying a CharlieCard and a Visa that's about two hours from maxing out." He tosses the choking guy down at the feet of his friend, who pulls out a serrated survival knife. If Harkness still had his gun, his right hand would be moving toward reassuring, deadly force. But on this clear fall night, he's just another citizen.

The bigger one's eyes rake over them and he seems to be at a loss for what to say next, like he's lost his place in a script. "Uh, give me those boots." He waves his knife at Thalia. "Those fucking boots."

"Really?" Thalia says. "That's what it's come to now, guys stealing boots?"

"Frye boots, aren't they?"

"So what?"

"Expensive. Take 'em off. Now."

"Just take them off, Thalia," Harkness says quietly.

"Are you kidding, Eddy?"

"Take them off."

She pulls off her favorite boots and hands them to Harkness, who holds them up like a prize. "Okay, come get them."

The guy Harkness choked hangs back. But the bigger hipster has been drinking or thinks he might have a chance just because he has a knife. When he steps forward, Harkness swings the boots and hits him in the temple with the heavy heels. The knife clatters down into the gravel next to the tracks. He goes down hard and stays sprawled on the platform. His friend runs across the empty platform and up the stairs to the street.

Harkness hands Thalia a boot. He sits on the edge of the cement platform and starts to slide down to get the other one from where it's fallen between the tracks.

"Don't do that, Eddy."

"There's not a train coming."

"Just don't. It's dangerous."

72

Harkness jumps down into the gravel. "Some guy just tried to knife us. I think I'll be okay."

He steps over one rail and picks up the boot from the beer cans and trash. Harkness stares at the third rail, taller than the other two and strapped down to the ground with thick metal bands spiked into the railroad ties. It's rust-sided and silver-topped like the other rails. But it sends out a powerful signal, as if temptation runs through the steel instead of electricity. Though it would be foolish as well as fatal, Harkness imagines touching the rail just to find out if it's deadly.

"Get back up here," Thalia says.

He climbs back up onto the platform.

Thalia pulls her boots on. "Let's go," she says.

They climb the stairs.

"Hey!"

They turn to see the failed boot thief swaying on the cement platform as a train pulls into the station.

"Where's your gun, Harkness?" He shouts over the train's squealing brakes. "Where's your fucking gun?"

The train doors open and he staggers inside.

· · ·

"So how would this guy know your name?" George leans forward over what's left of his steak. "Or that you lost your gun?"

"I have no idea." Harkness looks at Thalia for any hint that she knows something, but her gaze stays steady.

"Eddy," George says. "I got to tell you, maybe this is a sign."

Harkness shakes his head. "Don't start that up. It's like listening to Dad all over again."

"Maybe he was right, Eddy. Just come work with me. I could use help from a smart guy like you."

"I already have a job and I—"

Thalia cuts in. "So you're like what, a banker?"

"I'm the Harkness family janitor." A couple of years past thirty and looking older, George still carries the culpable sadness of a spoiled boy who just sat on his favorite toy and crushed it.

"Don't play the victim, George," Suzanne says. "Tell her what you mean."

"Okay, I'm an investment advisor," he says. "But mostly what I do is clean up the mess our dad left us."

"What'd he do?" Thalia asks.

"Screwed over his clients," George says. "Unions, corporate retirement funds . . ."

"Anyone he could talk money out of," Harkness says.

"Anyone he ever met," George says. "Say what you will, Dad was a charmer. Told everyone the returns were better than they were, and siphoned off a chunk of their money, figuring they wouldn't ever ask for it."

"What happened?"

"They asked for it." George pours wine in Thalia's glass, then Suzanne's. "Shot himself in the head when the regulators started sniffing around."

"Shit," Thalia says. "Why didn't you tell me about this, Eddy?"

"Guess I didn't feel like talking about it," Harkness says.

"That's too bad, Eddy," Suzanne says. "Talking about tragedy is one way we process it." A life coach, Suzanne exudes a professional-grade concern.

"Well, I'm at the end of the process," George says. "The deal we worked out is that we have to pay the aggrieved parties thirty cents for every dollar they lost. Couple of months and it's over. Done. Ancient history."

"We ought to be paying them everything we owe them," Harkness says.

"Do NOT start with that again." George slams his glass down on the table. "We'd have to liquidate. You might even have to quit playing cop."

Harkness stares at the lights across the Public Garden, wishing he and Thalia were walking back to her loft. "I'm not playing cop, George. I *am* a cop. I like it. And I'm good at it."

"So what?" George empties his glass. "I like drinking. And I'm really good at it. But I don't pretend it's a career."

Suzanne cuts in. "What do you like about your job, Eddy?" While she waits for his answer, Suzanne tilts her head like a talk show host.

"Every now and then I get to stop someone from doing something stupid."

"Eddy's on an investigation," Thalia says.

George perks up. "Investigating what?"

"Guy who plowed into that monument thing in Nagog . . . ," Thalia says.

Harkness nudges her under the table.

"So you're investigating a traffic accident? Congrats, bro."

Harkness feels his face turning hot. "There's more to it than that."

"You know what Dad would tell you, don't you?"

"No, I don't. And you don't either."

"He'd tell you to cut your losses, Eddy. Write it off. Move on."

Harkness stares at his brother for a moment. "I'm coming back to Boston," he says. "I'm not done."

"Maybe you are but you just don't know it. Because the world's telling you something loud and clear."

"Well, I'm not listening."

"Then listen to me. Come work with me. You owe it to the family. After all, we wouldn't be in this mess without you." George turns to Thalia. "Junior G-man here led the cops right to the evidence."

Harkness shakes his head. "You can't really still be mad about that."

"*Grudge* is our middle name, bro."

.   .   .

Eddy was wearing his clunky Sony headphones, so he only heard a soft thud from his father's office. He walked downstairs in a trance to find his father sprawled forward on his desk, face to the wood, arms splayed above, blood filling the oval they made.

His father's eyes were open but unmoving. Harkness waited for him to turn his head and reveal the cruel joke. The blood came from a joke shop. The vintage silver revolver on the rug was a toy. Harkness looked behind the door, expecting to find George trying to keep from laughing.

He slid his earphones down around his neck and put his hand on the cool indigo wool shoulder of his father's summer-weight Brooks Brothers suit. He shook it and saw nothing but the recoil of his own actions. No breath rippled the blood. No murmur broke the silence. His father slumped lower.

No one else was home to make sense of the still life of his father's body and the bloody desk, to close the gaping red pocket above his pale ear. Like a sleepwalker, Harkness called the police and reported what had happened.

He waited for the ambulance, standing next to the desk like a faithful dog, unable to do anything but wait for someone to come help his master.

His father had left one of the lower drawers of his desk open, the one he always locked so carefully. Harkness inched closer and saw the silver latch at the bottom. He pushed away the papers and turned it. Underneath waited a hidden drawer with ledgers, note-pads, and stack after stack of cash.

A few weeks later, when the lawyers and regulators came, Harkness showed them the little silver handle. It opened up a new world, one that led to audits then lawsuits, to making excuses then making amends. It all started with the glowing silver latch that called out for a hand to turn it.

.   .   .

"George, you're getting angry," Suzanne says. "You need to O-E-E."

"What's O-E-E?" Harkness asks.

"Suzanne runs a workshop called Emotional Composting," George says. "That's where we met. Couple of friends suggested that I needed to do a little work to get rid of some, you know, anger issues."

Suzanne leans forward. "George needed to move from self-destructive to self-*con*structive."

Thalia turns to Suzanne. "So what's O-E-E?"

"It stands for *Own It, Eat It, Excrete It*," she says. "It's a proven process for getting rid of anger. First you own the anger, recognizing that it's there and where it comes from. Then you take in the anger, challenge it, and devour it."

"Side order of anger, hold the fries," Thalia mutters.

"You can make fun of O-E-E all you want," George sputters. "But it helped me with my anger. It really fucking helped."

"Apparently," Harkness says.

"In the final phase, you excrete the anger," Suzanne says, "the way the body naturally rids itself of all toxins. The anger you shed can serve as fertile soil for growth and renewal. That's why we call it *emotional composting.*"

"Good name," Harkness says.

George gives him the dismissive stare that no one but a big brother can. "No one asked for your opinion, Eddy."

Thalia and Suzanne drift off — Thalia to the bar, Suzanne to the ladies' room — to escape a dinner that drags on like a drive to the Cape on Memorial Day weekend.

When they're both gone, Harkness leans toward his brother. "Hey, did you check on Allison Nevis?"

"She's definitely on the list — aggrieved party from the Nagog Teachers' Union."

"How much is she in for?"

"Three-quarters of a mil, maybe more. She's retired now. Lives somewhere on the South Shore. Why do you care?"

"Ran into her son the other day. I think he may know something about my gun."

"Probably wants to get back at us," George says. "I get threats all the time — on the phone, e-mails, even old-style anonymous letters. Hey, maybe that's who was fucking with you tonight."

"Maybe." The inept attackers at the station seemed too normal to be Dex's friends.

"Better just keep emptying the parking meters, bro," George says. "They can't fight back. How much is time going for now?"

"In Nagog, fifteen minutes for a quarter," Harkness says.

George reaches into his pocket for his wallet, takes out a dollar bill, and sets it on the white tablecloth, crumb pocked and splotched with sauce. "I'll take an hour."

Harkness picks up the dollar and tucks it in his pocket, then tosses some coins on the table between them. "Here's your thirty cents."

George's face reddens as he picks up his steak knife, deftly palms it point down, and drives it into the table next to Harkness's forearm. A wineglass rolls off the table and shatters on the floor. Waiters scramble. Businessmen turn and stare.

Harkness raises his arm but the blue shirtsleeve stays pinned to the table. "Hey, that's my best shirt."

"Not anymore." George is still laughing when the bartender hustles them out of the restaurant.

The brothers walk down Park Street with their girlfriends hovering close behind them.

Sudden happiness sweeps over Harkness for a moment, brought on by the saxophone echoing in the distance from Park Street station, the click of Thalia's favorite boots on the brick sidewalk, the glowing statehouse dome late at night, even the familiar presence of his annoying brother.

George takes a swing at the side of Harkness's head and misses.

Harkness shoves George away. "Cut it out."

Suzanne flutters toward them to intervene. She trips and falls on the street, legs splayed, purse dumping out into the gutter. Thalia rushes over to help her but Suzanne pushes her away.

"You people are like animals," she shouts.

George lurches toward Harkness again, hunched down like a pinstriped prizefighter. The extra pounds he's carrying tighten his white shirt, collar overrun by his razor-burnt neck. He's drunk but still pretty fast. He tries to punch Harkness in the stomach but Harkness grabs his wrist and spins his arm behind him in a classic come-along. George yelps in pain.

"Stop it!" Suzanne scrambles up from the ground and rushes at them.

Thalia sticks out a long leg and Suzanne's down again, triggering applause and whistles from bums sprawled on the edge of the Common.

Harkness marches George toward his black Audi. "Your girlfriend's right. Get a handle on your temper."

"Can't help it." George's huffing like a marathoner. "You know that."

"You're just giving in to it like a big baby."

George struggles to get free.

Harkness reaches into his brother's suit coat pocket to find his keys. The car beeps and the trunk pops. He moves a tennis racket to one side and pushes his brother inside. George's kicking but Harkness grabs his legs and shoves them in, slamming the trunk.

"Nice move!" George's muffled voice comes from the trunk.

Harkness tosses the keys to Suzanne. "Drive him around a little to quiet him down, then let him out. He'll be fine."

George's thumping around inside the trunk like a pair of high tops in a dryer.

Suzanne stares at them for a moment. Her face is smudged with street grime and there's a crescent of dog shit clinging to the knee of her pants suit. She opens her mouth to deliver a final assessment but just shakes her head and climbs into the Audi.

George shouts inside the trunk. Then Suzanne roars off and runs the red light at the intersection with Boylston Street.

Thalia and Harkness watch in silence until the taillights disappear into traffic.

"Another night of Harkness family togetherness," he says.

"You guys are kinda tough on each other."

"Dad liked us that way."

. . .

Harkness lifts Thalia gently from the futon at the end of each thrust to push even further inside her. The only light in the quiet loft comes from a bodega candle guttering on the kitchen table next to an empty wine bottle.

"Tell me," he says.

Thalia's been drinking wine and whiskey, followed by an hour on the futon, Harkness intent on extracting the truth however he can, even if it's with sexual waterboarding.

"Tell me," he whispers again.

"I . . ."

"Tell me." His request turns to a demand.

"I . . ."

"Tell me, now." The demand becomes more urgent.

Thalia's breathing faster now, barely able to get enough oxygen. "I want you, Eddy."

Harkness presses his eyes closed and lowers himself to cover her flame-lit body.

Harkness wakes and climbs from Thalia's futon. He walks to the loft window and watches for his gun to drift by in the hand of a local. Or maybe a glowing Glock 17 will appear like magic in the gutter, waiting for him to come downstairs and claim it. But tonight all he sees are damaged night creatures crawling from the banks of the oily industrial canal that runs toward Albrecht Square — hairless rats, a red-eyed opossum with a row of shiny pink tumors along its spine, and scrawny black cats with leering mouths spiked with long white teeth. They lurch down the sidewalk, stopping to nose through garbage, sniffing the burgeoning decay, then moving on to search out fresh rot.

13

CANDACE WATCHES OVER MAY, sleeping in her car seat next to their table. "Where's your uniform, Eddy?"

"I'm off duty this morning."

"So you're not always a cop?"

"I'm always a cop. I just don't always wear my uniform."

Candace's bracelets jangle as she reaches for her coffee with her good hand.

"What's it like working here?"

Candace looks around the Nagog Bakery. "It's okay, I guess. If you want to get knocked up. Cindy the Cougar. Princess Sparkle Thong. Nancy Nothing Fancy. Vicky Veneer. They all got pregnant. Something about breathing the yeast or the sugar or whatever. Me? I can't blame the bakery."

"Did Declan work here?"

"Dex? You kidding? He doesn't work for anyone but himself. Never has, never will. But I'm all about the team." She points over at the overstuffed couches in the corner with her plastic hand. "That's the Mom Pit, where all the moms hang out. Then there's the *Escaladies,* skinny chicks who drive those enormous Cadillacs. Or the earth mothers, always breastfeeding and organizing the community. And now I'm part of their team. Go, Team Breeder!"

Harkness says nothing.

"Remember that Replacements song 'Customer'?"

"Sure."

"It's like that around here. Customers always want something they can't get."

"Doesn't everyone?" Harkness thinks of his Glock 17.

"Well, sometimes it's me they want," Candace says. "Once a week or so, some guy comes up and starts talking shit after ordering a latte or something. I'm like their daughter's age. Gross, right? But I came up with a killer line."

"What's that?"

Candace leans over the table and turns her pale face slightly to the side. Anyone in the bakery would think they're about to kiss. "I get close to them, like this. Then I whisper the magic words."

Harkness takes a deep breath. "Which are?"

You're old.

"Nice."

Candace stares at Harkness, her dark brown eyes inscrutable. She looks around the bakery. "Dudes all think they're special."

"Everyone does," Harkness says. "They think they're different but they're not."

"Learn that at Harvard, did you?"

"No. Picked that up later."

Candace narrows her eyes. "We're not having coffee so we could share our world-weary insights, I'm assuming."

"No," Harkness says. "I have some . . . questions."

"Like what?"

"Dex's friends seemed pretty out there at the hospital. They always like that?"

"They're okay. Just too fucking smart and weird. I mean, Dex may be the only guy who dropped out of MIT because it was too easy."

"Really?"

"That and his mother ran out of money. Got screwed on some investment thing."

Harkness looks across the bakery.

"I've always had kind of a soft spot for strays," she says, "but they can seriously mess you up."

Harkness thinks of Thalia.

"Where'd you meet him?"

"You know, in high school. We co-founded the Club with No Members. We had to shut it down when we joined."

82

Harkness stares.

"Seemed funny at the time."

"People say that a lot."

"I mean, Dex isn't a bad guy. Supersmart. Just not particularly warm and fuzzy. We used to have a lot of fun back in the day — road trips to San Francisco, going to concerts, pulling pranks with his MIT chums — like hacking the state website and posting a bunch of threats from North Korea. What could be more fun than triggering an international incident?"

"Not much," Harkness says.

"But now we have a baby, my dad's dying, and he won't help with anything." Candace stares out the bakery window. "None of them help. They're supposed to be fixing up the house but they just spend hours on their laptops, jabbering on Skype. It's getting cold outside and our living room doesn't even have real windows, just plastic staple-gunned over them. There's cables and wires and Xbox shit all over and it smells like *dude*. I'm fucking sick of it." Candace smacks her plastic hand on the table like a gavel.

"Then get out."

"Not that easy," she says.

Harkness remembers how Dex grabbed his friends. "Ever hit you?"

She shakes her head. "Comes close sometimes, but no. He's smart enough to know that would mean *game over.*"

Harkness pauses before he asks the big question, the one about his gun.

"Listen, Eddy," Candace says. "I really don't want to talk about Dex anymore. I've got to get back to the hospital."

Harkness stops, realizes it was wrong to think that Candace might tell him anything about her boyfriend. Even if she had something to complain about, why would she tell a cop? "Look, if you ever need help, just give me a call," he says. "I can be there in minutes. I know every back road in this town, believe me." Harkness writes his cell number on the back of one of his Nagog Police Department cards and pushes it across the table.

Candace gathers her courier bag from the floor and checks on May, still asleep. Then she balls up her napkin and throws it on the table next to their empty coffee cups.

"Someone else can clean up after me for once. I'm sick of being the world's waitress."

They're almost at the front door of the bakery when Candace stops, puts down the car seat, and reaches into her coat pocket. "Almost forgot to give you this." She hands Harkness a folded piece of paper. "That thing you asked me to sign. Saying Dad was trying to kill himself when he ran into the monument. His lawyer told me not to sign it. But fuck him. It's the truth."

Harkness looks at the paper. "You're sure you're okay signing this?"

"Yeah. Dad left me a long good-bye note back in his office."

"Really?" Harkness thought about his father's office. No note, no explanation. None needed.

"Said being dead seemed better than the life he was living. At least that's how he felt that morning, when he decided to go on his dramatic drive into history. All the booze and drugs probably had something to do with it."

Candace bursts into tears and rushes toward Harkness, wrapping her arms around him. He backs away, then wraps his arms around her and feels her shaking. She pushes her tear-covered cheek against his chest and presses her eyes closed.

They stand in the entrance to the bakery, customers walking around them, Candace's baby sleeping in the car seat at their feet.

"It's going to be okay," Harkness says.

"No," Candace whispers. "It's really not going to be okay."

· · ·

As Harkness walks down Main Street, he considers the quirks of every parking meter he passes. Like people, some are easier to deal with than others. Most simply do their job, taking in quarters and tracking time. But there are always freaks and troublemakers, meters that jam for no reason or that flash error messages just to get attention. And there are victims, meters that get smashed and bent and never work quite right again, even when all the pieces are back in place. As he walks by tilted meter no. 453, nudged by a snowplow last winter, Harkness gives it a consoling pat on its metal head.

Ahead waits the toppled monument, poking from the town green like a severed finger. Its shattered top is lodged in the ground, surrounded by sugar-colored pieces of marble. On one side of what's left of the monument stand a couple of Uncle Sams, a pack of patriots in tricornered hats, a curly-haired woman in a red-white-and-blue-spangled one-piece swimsuit, and a couple dozen old men with signs that read REBUILD OUR HERITAGE AND REMEMBER OUR HEROES. On the other side there's a silent group dressed in black T-shirts and yoga pants, holding a drooping banner that says END ALL WARS — TEAR DOWN THE MONUMENT.

Deep ruts from Hammond's last drive mark the grass. No matter which side of the latest controversy wins, the town will grade the ground, sow grass seed, and cover up the damage. Hammond's incident on the green will fade but never quite disappear, like all small-town tragedies.

His shift over, Harkness gets in his squad car to drive back to the station. His phone rings just as he's getting in. Harkness recognizes the number. "Listen, Pauley," he says. "You got to quit calling me at work."

There's a pause. "Check it out, Harkness."

Harkness gets a message with a tiny photo. When he clicks on it, he sees the familiar shape of a dark gun in the foreground, a black-haired man with a bloody hole above his eye slumped in the background.

Harkness shifts in the driver's seat, his hands tightening on the steering wheel. *That can't be real,* he thinks. *That can't be my gun.*

A Tercel a few cars ahead of the squad car races through a crosswalk and almost clips an elder bent over his walker.

Harkness reaches up to turn on the flashers and give a quick yelp from the siren. The Tercel slows. The driver looks in the rearview mirror. Then he speeds up. Harkness hits the siren full force for a second and zooms up about six inches behind the Tercel. The driver swerves left into the parking lot of the Unitarian church.

Harkness calls in the plate number, tells Debbie he's got a possible DUI. He writes the time at the top of his clipboard and gives the guy a couple of minutes to stew, per protocol.

He does his cop walk toward the Tercel, spine straight, just a hint of *sheriff.* At the driver's window, he rolls his hand and the window

85

lowers. Inside sits a bearded man wearing a tan linen suit, a vision from the mid-1800s.

You've got to be kidding, Harkess thinks. "Driver's license, please."

The guy just straightens his straw hat, wide with a broad black band. A sweet alcohol breeze wafts from him. Then he pulls a twenty-first-century wallet from his coat pocket, rips open the Velcro, and hands over a business card:

HENRY DAVID THOREAU, WRITER AND SURVEYOR

Harkness keeps his cop face on. "License, please."

Thoreau holds out a smudged Massachusetts license showing a long-haired guy in a gray hoodie.

"Thomas Lehmann?"

"That's me," he says. "Spelled *T-H-O-M,* by the way."

"You almost hit a pedestrian back there, Mr. Lehmann. Consumed any alcohol today?"

He gives a twitchy snarl. "Look, I've been wearing this suit all day, talking to third graders. I was way thirsty. So what if I had a fucking beer or two after work?"

Harkness nods. This guy may look like Thoreau but he acts like an asshole.

"Stay in the car." Harkness turns to walk back toward the patrol car for the Breathalyzer. The car door creaks open and the gravel crunches.

Harkness turns just in time to catch the first punch on the side of his head. Then he's face down on the ground, ears ringing, stunned. He rolls over. Outlined by the gray sky, Thoreau raises a walking stick over his head like an ax.

Henry David Thoreau is trying to kill me. The thought is so absurd that Harkness almost laughs. But Thoreau's face blazes furious red and his pinched mouth sputters out *"fuck fuck fuck,"* spit spraying. He swings the heavy stick down with both hands.

Harkness rolls to one side and the stick slams in the gravel next to him. If he had his gun, he would draw it now. Instead, Harkness pulls his long leg back and shoves a heavy boot at Thoreau's crotch. The stick goes flying and Thoreau sprawls in the gravel.

"Shit." Thoreau curls up in the gravel, his linen pants bunched and smudged at the knees. He turns to the side to spew beer into the gravel. When he's done, Harkness reaches down and spins him over onto his back. His boot fits snugly under Thoreau's neat, Amishy beard.

Harkness presses down hard. Thoreau's eyes brighten and his legs flail.

"What the hell is going on?"

Thoreau's shaking his head. He's got something to say. Harkness lets up on his throat a little so he can say it.

"Didn't mean to."

"Not good enough." Harkness shakes his head slowly. "You do not hit a police officer. You do not swing a dangerous object at his head. Doesn't matter who you think you are, you have to follow the rules just like everyone else, otherwise they're not rules."

"Fuck you."

"Okay, have it your way, Hank." Harkness reaches down, grabs Thoreau's shoulders, and throws him hard against the Tercel. He hits the door with a loud gasp and slumps down to the ground.

Harkness picks up the walking stick and points it at him. "Tell me what the fuck's wrong with you. Now."

"Do all cops talk like that?"

"I'm not all cops," Harkness says. "I'm the cop you just tried to kill." He reaches back and grabs a thick plastic zip tie from his belt and secures Thoreau's right wrist to the Tercel's door handle. He draws the end extra tight.

"Not like this, really," Thoreau says, gulping for breath. "Can explain."

"Start talking."

"Hand me my hat?"

Harkness looks over at Thoreau's straw hat, upside down on the ground. He thinks of grinding it into the dirt. But the hat's innocent.

Or maybe not. Thoreau keeps giving it shifty glances. Harkness picks up the hat and runs his fingers around the inner band until he finds a lump. He plucks out a small amber vial and holds it up to the sky. "So what's this?"

Thoreau gives a low groan. "Nothing."

"Oh yeah? Looks about half full of something to me. What?"

Thoreau evades. "Got a doctoral thesis due by the end of the year. And I'm teaching three classes at Tufts. Couldn't get it done." He pauses. "Then I started taking this . . . new stuff."

"Let me guess. Third Rail."

Thoreau nods. "It's incredible." He gives Harkness the awestruck look of the drug connoisseur. "Makes Adderall look like Skittles. Sets your mind on fire."

Harkness realizes he's found an early adopter, the kind of drug user who always thinks he's ahead of the curve, not knowing he's just the latest canary in an old mine.

"Couple drops and you're off to the races," Thoreau says.

"Or to the ER."

"Yeah, makes you lose it sometimes. Can't figure it out."

"Even smart drugs make people do stupid things."

Thoreau shakes his head. "This one was really great for a while."

"That's the problem with drugs. They wear off." Harkness holds up the vial. "Buy this in town, did you?"

Thoreau pauses for a moment.

"Tell me. Now. Or I'll smack you back into the Transcendental era."

"Bought it from a twitchy guy, short, really hairy, kind of a dick. Met him at a party."

Harkness nods. Dex's friend Mouse. "Here's the deal," he says. "I'm taking you in. You'll get released when you straighten out. But if you end up doing anything else stupid, I'll find out, believe me, and I'll make sure you go to jail. And not just for a night, Hank."

"Okay, okay, okay." Thoreau perks up. "Hey, this isn't going to be in the blotter, is it?" Everyone in town reads the *Nagog Journal* police blotter, a long list of the week's drunk drivers, pot smokers, shoplifters, and wife beaters. It's like the town stockade.

"I'll make sure you're at the top," Harkness says. "After all, you're famous."

• • •

Captain Munro puts on his reading glasses and unfolds the piece of paper.

"Hammond's daughter actually signed this?"

"She did."

"You sure she's got power of attorney?"

"Yes."

The captain reads for a moment, then snaps off his reading glasses. "This is excellent, Harkness. You've saved the town a pile of money. The town manager will be off my back. The monument crisis can end, thank God."

"There's something else," Harkness says.

"Yes?"

"I . . ." A confession rises up in his thoughts and starts to form into four simple words. *I lost my gun.*

"What is it?"

Harkness stalls, his confession caught like a fish bone. "I think there's something going on in town, something we need to look into. About drugs."

The captain tilts his head slightly. "What kind of drugs?"

"Third Rail. It's some kind of smart drug, just starting to get popular. Our monument smasher had some in his car. And so did the guy I brought in for DUI this afternoon."

"That's not good, not at all." The captain sits down. "Where's this going on?"

"Old Nagog Tavern, out on Forest Road."

"What're they doing out there — dealing?"

"Not sure yet. There may be a lab."

The captain leans forward. "I'll get Detective Ramble on the case."

Harkness shakes his head. "No offense, sir. But I'd like your permission to check it out myself."

"So how dangerous is this . . . Rail Yard or whatever it's called?"

"Seems kind of unpredictable," Harkness says. "Makes people lose it. Checked online on some gray market drug sites, did a Narco-Intel database search, been e-mailing someone who's writing a book about smart drugs. Not a lot of intel on Third Rail."

The captain pauses. "You have two weeks to find out more. That's it."

Harkness smiles. "Thank you, sir."

"Report anything you find directly to me. Don't mention this to anyone else. And do not, I repeat, do not, do anything to put anyone in danger. That includes you. We'll pull in the State Police or the DEA if it gets serious."

Harkness nods.

"Got to keep you safe," he says. "You'll be heading back to Boston soon."

Harkness scans Captain Munro's creased face, looking for some sign that he's lying. He sees nothing but the captain's clear blue eyes.

14

THEY'RE DRINKING WHISKEY at McCloskey's, crowded with neon-tanned men with XXL Patriots jerseys draped over beer bellies, whiskey-botched women in velour sweatpants. The dim light does everyone small favors.

"You know that politician guy, Fitzgerald?" Thalia says. "The one you were talking about?" She's shouting over the Sox game on the flat-screen behind the bar.

"Yeah?"

"I think he used to come by Mach's. Looked like him anyway."

"For drugs?"

"No."

"Girls?"

Thalia shakes her head. "Liked to hang with the big boys after hours." Thalia stirs her drink with a tiny straw made for sipping, which she's not.

"What big boys?"

Thalia shrugs. "The usual crooks. Old-style Irish mob guys, mostly."

"Why didn't you tell me this before?"

"Wasn't sure this guy was Fitzgerald. Googled him. Still can't tell. Not exactly an original look around the Zero Room — sausage-colored and vicious."

"Can you find out if it was Fitzgerald?"

"There's a guy I can call. Name's Jeet. Worked the back bar, where all the crazy shit happened. Liked to take pictures. Called them his insurance policy."

"Why the hell would he do that?"

"Everyone at Mach's was working some angle."

Harkness sees a glimmer in Thalia's eyes. "Even you?"

She gives him a steady stare. "I stole a couple big bags of frozen tiger shrimp from the downstairs freezer once."

"Were they good?"

Thalia shrugs. "Not really."

"Anything else you want to tell me about?"

"Cut it out, Eddy. No more interro-fucking-gations. I'm your girl-friend, 'member?" She pulls him toward her. "I'd do anything for you." Whiskey burns on her hot breath and her voice drops. "I'd kill for you, Eddy."

"For now, just call Jeet."

The TV catches her eye and she points. "Game's moving really fast."

"It's the season recap, Thalia."

"Right. Sox lost big. Thanks to you, Eddy." On cue, the camera zeroes in on a pinstriped Yankees fan smiling maniacally and waving a handwritten sign that says THE CURSE IS WORSE!

Harkness feels a little worse, too.

"You know, if Pauley Fitzgerald hadn't been wearing a Sox jersey when they dropped him down onto the Pike —"

"I think I get why you majored in history, Harvard Cop," Thalia says. "You're always . . . living in the past." Thalia waves to the bartender to order another whiskey, then weaves toward the ladies' room.

The past points the way forward. Red Harkness told him this once about market conditions, which he ignored for his uniquely larcenous approach to investing. But using this rare paternal insight, Harkness can predict how this night's going to end. He and Thalia will move on to Franklin's or another dump and drink until two in the morning, then head back to her loft to thrash around on the futon. Harkness will wake up in the middle of the night, sure that something's very wrong, like a bad diagnosis that slipped his mind. Then he'll remember his gun is still missing and he's not any closer to getting it back.

Harkness takes a look around McCloskey's. Along the front bar sit the lost, who made some bad bets or had a run-in with heartbreak or their parole officers. They drink to kill time until the smoke clears from their lives. At the back tables sit the gone, dead-eyed drinkers trapped in amber bar light. They quit waiting for their luck to change a long time ago. They'd be nihilists if they knew what it meant.

Harkness reminds himself not to come around here again. He's not disappointed or lost. He's just stuck in a circle of bad luck. And he's about to break free — he's sure of it.

Everyone is.

His phone rings. He checks it to fend off another Pauley Fitz call. But it's Patrick.

Harkness walks toward the door and stands outside the bar, leaning against a brick wall, still warm from the afternoon sun.

"What do you have?"

"Is that the way you say hello to your friends now?" Patrick's voice sounds far away.

"Sorry. Kind of in a bind, Patrick. Girlfriend's getting strange on me."

"Hate that. Hey, the Dex guy you asked me to check out? There's nothing on him. Clean sheet. No priors. Files his taxes on time. Two years at MIT, then he dropped out, just like you thought. No debt. Paid cash for his house in your lily-white town of Nagog."

Harkness looks back in the bar. Thalia's meandering back from the ladies' room, looking for him. She's morphed into a bleary photo of herself with her eyes scratched out. "Thanks. Got to go. One last request."

"Usually people make those when they're about to die, Eddy."

Harkness doesn't laugh. "I need you to hack Pauley Fitzgerald's cell account and find out who's paying the bill. Or better yet, get a fix on where the phone is."

"No can do, Harky," Patrick says. "You're going to have to do your own dirty work. We're getting the stink eye from the commissioner and his chums. Got a full-time Internal Affairs guy camped out in the next office. Not allowed to do anything freelance."

"Since when did we start doing everything by the book?"

"Since you left, Harky." Patrick clicks his phone off.

. . .

93

The dead girl wears a red and white Nagog High Minutemen uniform. The EMTs found Kelly Pierce face down next to the thin woods that surround the track. The impact sheared back a hand-sized patch of her scalp and bashed in a piece of her skull, seeping yellow cranial fluid. Blood slicks her left side all the way down to her running shoes.

The runner's body is stiff, back arched. She's been lying on the edge of the woods all night.

Her shoes look too big to Harkness, track uniform too tight.

He steps back and the EMT loads the runner's body onto a stretcher and pushes her across the bumpy grass to the parking lot.

"Crazy, huh?" Watt says. "Girl runs off the track and into the woods. Smacks her head the wrong way and breaks her neck."

"That's the story they're telling, is it?"

"That's what Dabilis said."

"Where is he?"

"Dealing with the EMTs and the principal. Taking notes for the report."

"That'll be interesting," Harkness says. "Bet they say it's an accident."

"Plenty of those lately," Watt says.

"They want to keep the stats low. Accidents are okay. Anything worse starts messing with the real estate values," Harkness says.

Watt looks at him like he just said something in French. "That true?"

"Yeah, it is." He hands Watt some evidence bags and a marker. "Hey. Help me out for a minute."

"Dabilis is investigating this one," Watt says. "Told me just to keep people off the field."

"We'll help him out," Harkness says. "C'mon."

They walk side by side for a moment, eyes down and scanning the ground. Harkness reaches down to pluck a scrap of black cloth from the browning grass and seals it in a bag. He writes the date, time, and location on the bag. Then scrawls his name and badge number with a Sharpie.

"Hey, here's another one." Watt leans down to pick up another piece of cloth, then another. He stuffs them in separate bags. "All about the same length."

Harkness looks at the pieces of cloth, some dark, some sun faded, edges unraveling. "Come here for a second." Harkness reaches out to tie one of the pieces of fabric around Watt's forehead. It fits perfectly with a couple of knots in the back. "Can you see anything?"

"No."

Harkness unties the blindfold and they walk on. Harkness imagines the girl surrounded by a crowd of friends or enemies — it isn't clear yet. But the trampled grass says the dead runner wasn't alone.

He imagines her body on the ground in the twilight, blood gushing from her head wound. Anyone with her would want to get rid of any evidence fast. The short grass stretches out like hotel carpet, unable to hide anything. He turns toward the woods, ground thick with leaves and pine needles.

"In here." Harkness leads Watt into the woods. The young pines, the width of a fireplace log, are planted in a careful grid. They choose two rows and start walking.

"What're we looking for, Eddy?"

"Anything that shouldn't be here."

"*We* shouldn't be here."

Harkness stops at the end of a row, takes a pen out of his pocket, and kneels down on the pine needles. The empty amber vial rests on its side. He slides the pen into its mouth.

"What is it?"

"Trouble," Harkness says.

Watt holds out an open evidence bag and Harkness drops it in.

When they walk out of the woods Sergeant Dabilis is waiting. "Did you ladies have a nice walk in the woods?" He gives them a tight smile.

Watt holds out the bags.

"Souvenirs?" Dabilis takes the bags. "My scene. My investigation. Get going."

"Found something you should see." Watt points to the vial.

"Looks like something from the science lab," Dabilis says. "Let me guess. There were probably some beer cans and empty vodka nips in the woods, too, right? Maybe a couple of condoms?"

"Didn't see any, sir," Watt says.

"Like I said before, this is my accident scene. Clear out now. Both of you."

Harkness watches the tiny dots of sweat on the oyster-colored skin below Dabilis's eyes.

"Looks kind of sketchy to me, sir," Watt says.

"Don't try to go all *CSI* on us, Forty Watt," Dabilis says. "It was an accident. The victim was putting in some extra laps last night after the rest of the team left. She ran off the track. Maybe it got too dark. Or she had a seizure. Then she hit her head on a tree. Tragic. Talked to the school nurse. Kelly Pierce was on all kinds of meds."

"I talked to some of the kids," Watt said. "Said she was a nice girl. Really smart. Everyone liked her — they're crying their eyes out in the parking lot. Here's the weirdest thing."

"What's that?" Dabilis says.

"She wasn't on the track team."

15

THE FIRST TWO DOZEN oysters disappear so fast that even their tired waitress seems impressed.

"Another dozen?" Harkness asks.

"Sure." A plaque over the bar at the Union Oyster House tells the tourists that Daniel Webster used to down a few dozen oysters and several flagons of brandy in an afternoon. Jeet seems to be trying to beat him. Or at least run their lunch tab into the triple digits. Harkness is paying.

"Haven't been here in years." Jeet's working on a second bowl of chowder, splashing the lobster bib he's tied over his black T-shirt.

"Used to come here all the time." Harkness likes the tall, wood-walled booths near the bar, public confessionals, perfect for meeting with sources. Back when he ran Narco-Intel, Harkness might be sitting in the same booth with a street dealer ready to roll on his friends or a cokehead accused of setting fires in Back Bay alleys. But Harkness doesn't tell that to the man Thalia called the brother she never had.

Jeet eyes the tray of oysters when it arrives. "Same again when you have a chance," he says to the waitress before even tasting them. She smiles. Waitresses love a hungry customer, even a guy with a retro-punk brush-cut bright blue Mohawk and a T-shirt with I USED TO CARE on the front and BUT NOW I TAKE A PILL FOR THAT on the back.

"Saw you around Mach's sometimes, talking to Thalia," he says. "You're that Harvard Cop guy, right?"

Harkness puts an empty oyster shell upside down on the ice. "Right."

"She's a beaut, Thalia," Jeet says, with a look that's not at all brotherly. "*Sassy lassie with a nice little assy.* That's what we used to call her. Didn't put up with shit from anyone, not even Mach. Got your hands full, don't you?"

"Yes, I do."

"But we're not here to talk about Thalia, are we?"

"No, we're not," Harkness says. "I need your help."

"I guess you're not talking about the oysters. Because I'm doing my part."

"I'm talking about your old boss."

Jeet holds up his hands. "Got nothing to do with Mach anymore. Kinda fascinated by the guy, but he is, at the end of the day, a charming psychopath."

"Thalia says you're a photographer."

He shrugs. "Sure, I take pictures."

"Like what kind?"

"Friend of mine worked at a gallery on Newbury Street back in the day. Showed me Mapplethorpe's *X* portfolio one night. Know what I'm talking about?"

"Bullwhips and butts, not calla lilies and light, right?"

"Oh yeah. Got me interested in the dark stuff. Shit people can't believe is real."

The waitress brings Jeet another beer and for the next ten minutes, he drinks and reels out his take on street photography, from Bellocq to Larry Clark. Harkness thinks Jeet may be high. He's getting kind of wound up about the whole subject.

"What about the Zero Room?"

Jeet looks up at the ceiling. "That place is a scumbag hall of fame. Guys waltz in, politicians you see on the news acting all straight and shit, talking family values blah-blah-blah, and at about three in the morning, they're drunk and snorting cocaine out of some girl's ass crack. Or worse."

"Ordering off of the special menu?"

He nods. "Exactly."

"What were you doing there?"

"I was making piles of money, off the books, of course. And I took pictures with my Minox after hours when everyone was too drunk to notice."

"Drugs and girls?"

"Sure, plenty of that," Jeet says. "But some other things, too, things more in line with what you're looking for."

Something hits his knee.

"Take it, Eddy." Jeet's handing him a cardboard box underneath the table.

Harkness nods, puts the box on the bench next to him. "What's in it?"

"Take a gander." Jeet shakes his head. "My life's work comes down to a stack of pictures of a bunch of politicians and criminals."

"That distinction is debatable around here," Harkness says. "What do you want for the photos, Jeet?"

"Nothing."

"Nothing?"

"Thalia told me what you're looking for. Fitzgerald was a regular back in the day. I hear he's running for mayor, God help us. This guy isn't your normal crooked politician, Eddy. He's ruthless, like some kind of virus. He'll do absolutely anything to be mayor."

"What was he doing at Mach's place?"

Jeet shrugs. "Mach can deliver a lot of votes. And pull a lot of strings. And we're not talking League of Women Voters. Check it out."

Harkness lifts the lid and flips through the photos, recognizing the familiar back room of the Zero Room. Fitzgerald sits with a smiling Mr. Mach and assorted bargirls. Then he comes across a photo so unexpected and strange that he can only stare in awe.

"These are real?"

Jeet nods.

"Is that who I think it is with Fitzgerald?"

"Oh yeah."

"When did you take this?"

"The time stamp's printed right on it. Years ago. Back when he was supposed to be on the run."

Harkness squints at the photo in the dim booth. "Unbelievable."

"Well, you can definitely believe it, because I was there," Jeet says. "I call it *The Last Supper, Boston Mob Edition*."

"Why would Fitzgerald do something so risky?"

"Oldest reason in the world. Money. His fucking brother works in the FBI's Boston office. Fitzgerald passed along news about the feds in exchange for a suitcase full of cash. Probably the money that got his campaign going. Like Kickstarter for crooks."

Harkness closes the lid and holds it down with his thumbs, as if the photos might escape.

Jeet shrugs. "You know how it is. Every thug around here likes to have a politician as their wingman. And the other way around."

"Does Fitzgerald still go to Mach's?"

Jeet shakes his head. "No way. He's all corporate now. Romney-fied. But dirt has a way of getting dirtier."

"Yes, it does."

"And if Fitzgerald gets elected mayor, the whole city's fucked. It'll be a crony fest like Boston's never seen before. And this guy's cronies are even worse than he is. Trust me."

Harkness looks into Jeet's jittery eyes. "Why should I?"

"I'm Thalia's friend." Jeet leans forward. "Look, Eddy. I'm not Mapplethorpe. I'm not even Wee-fucking-gee. I was just a smart-ass bartender sneaking pictures when I should have been stopping all the crap that was going on. And still is. That's why I'm here."

"They're going to know where the photos came from, you know that, don't you? They'll come after you."

"Fuck Mach. Fuck all of them." Jeet takes a black plastic square that looks like a battered travel alarm clock from his pocket and slaps it down on the table. The black square sits on the table between them.

"What's that?"

"My liver beeper from Mass General," Jeet says, finally. "Stage four liver cancer. I'm number one hundred fifty-six on the list of people waiting for a transplant. No way that thing's going to ring in time. There can't be enough motorcycle wrecks."

Harkness stares at the black square. "I'm really sorry. Thalia didn't tell me."

"She doesn't know. No one does, except my mother back in Hingham. And now you."

Harkness remembers what Candace told him in the hospital waiting room, about how her father's guilt grew inside him like cancer.

"Look, you can't feel bad about not stopping Mach. There's nothing else you could have done."

Jeet tosses his napkin on the table and lifts his glass, eyes closed, blue Mohawk spiking toward the ceiling, beer dripping down his chin and lobster bib. He puts the empty glass down on the dark table, carved with decades of initials.

"That sounds good, Eddy. But way too many people think they can get away with shit, know what I mean?"

"Yeah, I do."

"When you got the finish line in sight, excuses don't cut it anymore, Eddy. People who do bad shit have to pay for it. Full price. No matter who they are." Jeet stands up and edges out of the narrow booth. "I should have done something to stop it instead of just drinking and fucking around."

"Hey, Jeet?"

Jeet looks back from the doorway to Union Street.

Harkness taps the top of the box. "You just did."

16

S O I'VE BEEN meaning to ask you," Dr. Lauren North says during a break in her monologue. "Do you like to get high?" Harkness stares across the booth at the bestselling author of *Kill the Pain, Free the Brain: Dispatches from the New Drug Frontier.* She's wearing a black business suit and a cream-colored silk blouse, her long blond hair held by a tasteful silver barrette.

"A joke, Eddy," she says. "We're at the top of the Prudential Tower. Get it?" She points across the bar toward the dark windows. It's almost midnight and the lights of the city waver fifty floors below. The Blue Hills lurk in the distance beneath the blinking red lights of radio towers. Jets descend to Logan like slow comets.

"I get it," he says. "I wonder if we'll ever be able to walk into a restaurant at the top of a tall building and not think about 9/11."

"I wasn't thinking about 9/11," she says. "But now I am. Thanks for that." Dr. North shivers.

"I started college a couple of weeks before," Harkness says. "Watched the Twin Towers burn on the crap TV in my dorm room. Kind of altered my educational path."

"That's when you decided to become a cop?"

"That's when I decided to quit pretending I was anything else."

The waiter brings a second round of drinks, a draft IPA for him and for her a glass of Austrian Zweigelt, which is the next pinot noir, Dr. North assures him. They're the last people in the restaurant except for a couple of tourists. Harkness tracked Dr. North down to find out more about Third Rail. But they've been in the Top of the

Hub more than an hour and all Harkness has heard about is Dr. North and her book.

"You really should read it," she says. "I mean, you can't influence policy or anything. But you're in enforcement, kind of. There's a lot of new stuff out there that you're not going to find on the street."

"Looking forward to it," he says. "Haven't had a lot of time to read lately. Been kind of on a . . . mission."

She leans forward. "I know, I know. That's exactly how I feel when I'm writing a book. Like I can't do anything else. Can't drive my kids to school and talk to their dullard teachers. Don't want to hear from my friends about their little first world problems, their tedious divorces and custody battles, hormone imbalances and cancer treatments. I just want to write the next chapter so I can find out how it ends." She sucks in a quick breath.

Harkness jumps in during the brief lull. "So can I run a couple of questions by you?"

She nods.

"Heard of something called Third Rail?"

"Third Rail." Her gaze drifts up to the ceiling. "In the general category of smart drug, though that underestimates it. Taken in liquid form. Also goes by Thrilla, Mindfuck, and ADA. Which stands for Attention in Disturbing Amounts. And also a reference to the first computer programmer . . ."

"Ada Lovelace," Harkness says.

Dr. North squints at him.

"So what is it?"

"A nootropic cocktail," she says. "Powerful. Really hard to make. Has some ephedrine tacked on for focus and energy, the unstoppable kind. Dopamine to shake up your brain. Plus some Chinese herbs no one's ever heard of to make the trip a little strange."

"*Má huáng?*"

Another stare. "How'd you know that?"

"A pissed-off, one-eyed jeweler told me," Harkness says. "What does it do?"

"Delivers focus, of course, that's the cost of admission for the whole category. Plus you get kick-ass cognition and a sense of euphoria."

"Possible side effects?"

"Triggers bad ideation, so users tend to get in trouble. They give in to urges. They reach for things they know they should leave alone. Especially kids who don't know better and older people with nothing to lose."

Harkness envisions Hammond inside his crushed silver Volvo.

"Problem is it's not illegal, per se. At least not yet. In my book, it's one of the drugs in the category I call *invisible menace*."

"Addictive?"

"Absolutely. And dangerous. Really easy to overdose on Third Rail. And even easier to have some kind of accident. Users tend to be grad students, tech guys, high achievers. People who think they can stay on top of it."

"So it's a smart drug for people who are already smart?"

"You could say that. But Third Rail has a sweet spot. Something nothing else does."

"What do you mean?"

"If opiates are about forgetting, Third Rail is about remembering, sort of." Dr. North nods for a moment, her lips moving silently as she simplifies her thoughts for a street cop. "Here's the way I like to describe it. Everyone carries around a ball of string all tied in knots. Not actually, Eddy. It's a metaphor."

"Got it."

"The knots are all the things that went wrong — bad luck, worse choices. The older you get, the more knots you collect."

No need to ask Dr. North to clarify. Harkness knows about the knots.

"Third Rail rewrites history and unmakes the mistakes," she says. "Tragedies become triumphs. Pain seems like pleasure."

"Sounds good to me."

"Sure it does. But when it wears off, the knots all retie themselves, like in a myth. The Fates. Clotho. Penelope, Odysseus's wife . . . but you don't care about mythology, literature. You want to know what Third Rail does. Just the facts, right?"

"Right."

"Eventually, it induces irreversible anhedonia, the inability to experience anything. Leads to extreme behavior. People start looking for new thrills." Beneath the table, Dr. North's leg edges closer.

She leans forward, eyes widening. "Sex on Third Rail is amazing.

Wrote about it in Chapter 16. Check it out. Let me know what you think."

Harkness moves his leg.

"You're not the only one interested in it," she says. "Lange Pharma, headquarters is in that big building right across the river in Brighton? They're in early-stage clinical trials. They call it Valoria."

"If Third Rail makes people lose it, why would any drug company be interested?"

"Think about it for a minute." Dr. North shakes her head. "You're just a local cop. But think international. Third Rail is about focus and clarity. It triggers audacious behavior and squelches messy emotions. Might be just the thing to rally the troops. Makes the pills they handed out in Vietnam look like . . ."

"Candy," Harkness says.

"Well, that's what they all say. For a while." Dr. North tucks her notebook into her black leather purse.

"One last question," Harkness says. "You ever take it?"

She leans forward. "Are you crazy?"

Harkness says nothing, waits for the truth.

"Yes, of course I tried it," she says. "Write about what you know. That's what they say."

"And?"

"Third Rail is in-*fucking*-credible." Dr. North leans forward, green eyes flashing. "Let me know if you find any. I'll pay whatever they're asking."

· · ·

A last-call beer at one of Harkness's favorite bars, Geidt's, isn't chasing away the headache that Dr. Lauren North gave him along with the inside story on Third Rail. Drug dealers are easier to talk to than drug experts. Less to say, faster at saying it. Even her perfume was annoying, a jasmine scent like hotel hand cream, though Harkness knows it has to be expensive. Dr. North is a connoisseur, with rarified taste in clothes, wine, and drugs.

He takes the amber vial from his jacket pocket and holds it up to the ceiling light. The liquid rolls from side to side, innocent as maple syrup.

He unscrews the top and pauses for a moment, wondering

whether this is a good idea, whether any drug can really rewrite his past. Then he tips the vial over his glass until a thick droplet falls into his beer.

Always good to know what you're up against.

. . .

Harkness stands outside the bar and waits to see what Third Rail has to say. It doesn't take long. The Mass Avenue Bridge pulls him toward Cambridge like a magnet. He walks toward it, sees that the sidewalk is marked off in red-spray-painted increments. Instantly, Harkness remembers that they're *smoots*. In the 1960s, frat brothers measured Oliver Smoot, marking how many of the drunk freshman it took to cross the bridge. It's part of the nerd lore of MIT. But now Harkness knows the name of the fraternity — Lambda Chi Alpha. He knows that a smoot is a unit of measure five feet seven inches long, that the bridge is slightly more than 364 smoots long, and that Smoot ended up working in the field of standards.

All of this information resurfaces when Harkness sees the first red line. Maybe he read an article years ago in the *Globe*. Or the information could be beaming from the bridge to his brain.

Harkness manages to turn back toward Kenmore Square. His teeth are grinding from the initial rush and his fingers are gripping and opening, looking for something to pull apart. He has to hold himself back to keep from running. He drops down and does twenty push-ups on the sidewalk. Then twenty more. When he walks by a BU frat house he wants to go in and talk to everyone.

It's already late and Thalia will wonder where he is, but Harkness can't turn back. He's devouring data like an insatiable human search engine. Semaphore glimmers beam from the last lights glowing in apartment windows. Encoded patterns hide in the slate scales of mansard roofs. Sidewalk cracks reveal hieroglyphs that only he can decipher.

In a few minutes, his mind quits racing and euphoria takes over. Everything Harkness sees around him, the events that led him here tonight — it all makes beautiful sense.

When he sees the Citgo sign over Kenmore Square, Harkness knows where Third Rail is taking him. He can't wait to get there.

Standing at the railing of the Brookline Avenue Bridge, Harkness hears the sound of the crowd come roaring out of his memory like static amplified. Third Rail brings back all the memories in high-def, whether Harkness wants them or not, and casts him in the staring role in *The Incident,* now projecting in the home theater of his mind.

The story begins when a three-run Red Sox homer shoots out of the ballpark into the indigo sky and bounces past the Lansdowne Street bars and nightclubs, just opening their doors. The crowd roars. It's the last game of the playoffs and thirty thousand people gush into Kenmore Square to drink, chant, set fire to cars, harass Yankee fans, and beat up their friends — the kind of low-grade tribal violence that passes for celebration in Boston.

The plot turns darker when Harkness spots the Doyle brothers — pale faced, black haired, and swaying drunk. Billy, the bigger Doyle, clutches the ankles of Pauley Fitzgerald with both hands and holds him, squirming, head down over the railing of the Brookline Avenue Bridge, above the roaring Turnpike. His brother Dickie thinks this is the funniest thing he's ever seen.

Harkness knows this film isn't real, that it's just Third Rail bending his memories, but he can't stop watching.

"You!" His cop voice echoes. "Pull him back up. Now."

Bleary and beer soaked, the Doyle brothers turn and squint. "Just havin' some fun with Pauley," Dickie says.

Harkness gives a quick smile. Best to try to keep drunks on the sunny side. "Doesn't look like he's having much fun," Harkness says. "Pull him up now and you head home with everyone else."

"And what if we don't?" Billy sputters.

"What then, fuckin' cop bastard?" Dickie, the smiler, reaches into the pocket of his running pants and waves a black-handled knife.

At least it looks like a knife to Harkness.

Third Rail summons up the circling crowd. *"Drop him, drop him, drop him,"* they chant.

"Fuck yooooouuuu," Dickie shouts, and the swarming crowd laughs. A long howl comes from over the railing.

"Pull him up, now," Harkness says.

Billy pulls Pauley up until Harkness can see his face again, a rictus of fear, forehead bloody from scraping on the bridge. He flails his arms toward the railing and manages to slap a hand on it.

"Stop." Harkness unsnaps the guard and draws an invisible Glock.

Here, the film slows for the crucial final scene, the one Harkness replays in his mind every day.

There's a clear line of sight to the target. Deadly force allowable — the Doyles are about to cause serious injury. Harkness drops into the stance, legs wide, arms out and bent slightly, and points his gun at Billy.

A car crossing the bridge honks at the sight of a lone gunman pointing his joined hands at nothing, shouting at no one.

"Pull your friend up, right now. Or I shoot."

"Drop him! Drop him! Drop him!" the invisible crowd chants.

Billy shrugs, and pulls Pauley Fitzgerald closer so he can grab the railing. The Doyle brothers slip into the crowd. Harkness runs to the bridge to grab Fitzgerald by his wrists and pull him up, inch by inch, until he slides over the railing. "You're going to be okay," Harkness says to the empty sidewalk.

"Thanks, man," Pauley says. "You . . . you saved my life."

Harkness turns. The toes of his boots slam into the chain-link fence, searching for a foothold. He climbs up to stand on the railing, arms outstretched in the cold night air, staring out at the skyline.

He's supreme, triumphant, a hero.

· · ·

After Thalia talks him down, after he takes a cold shower, after Third Rail starts to let go, the knots come back, one after the next, to retie the tangled black ball that Harkness carries with him. He stretches out on the futon and presses close to Thalia's warm back. She murmurs in her sleep.

Harkness replays the crucial moment on the bridge when he had to answer the important question — was Billy Doyle drunk, stupid, and cruel enough to drop his friend down into the swarming traffic? Billy's pockmarked face gave Harkness the answer — green eyes dead as emeralds, his fleshy mouth twisted like he just drank salt water. No, the threat of getting shot wasn't enough to stop him.

So Harkness fired — scattering the crowd from the bridge.

Billy Doyle gave a merciless smirk as the shot grazed his thigh and dark blood splotched his running pants. If the story had stopped here, Pauley Fitzgerald could have climbed back up on the bridge. But the sick smile stayed locked on Billy Doyle's face as he dragged Pauley further away from the bridge, until his hand slipped from the railing.

Until he didn't have a chance.

Pauley Fitzgerald fell with a scream and the chorus of horns on the Turnpike began playing the opening bars of the *Turnpike Toreador* soundtrack.

During the hearings, Billy Doyle lied, saying he was trying to pull Pauley up when Harkness shot him and made him let go of his best friend. That the knife that his brother Dickie waved around turned out to be a switchblade comb from a downtown joke shop didn't help Harkness's case.

The lawyers claimed that rogue cop Detective Supervisor Edward Harkness turned a teenage prank into a tragedy. And though the BPD Disciplinary Board's investigation was inconclusive, the city of Boston seemed to agree.

Harvard Cop Slays Dorchester Son. The story stayed on the front page of the *Herald* for weeks. When the Sox started their losing streak, the Harvard Cop curse was born. And after all the internal investigations and witness interviews, only one unequivocal fact remained — Pauley Fitzgerald was dead.

When the loft brightens to gray and grainy, Harkness is still struggling to sleep. He has an early shift in Nagog in a few hours and hundreds of meters to empty. But he can't stop thinking about Third Rail's chemical rewrite, where Pauley Fitzgerald lives and Harkness is a hero — a version so much better than what really happened.

As the one golden drop starts to wear off, Harkness realizes its power. Third Rail defeats history, for a while — and sometimes that's enough.

Enough to make him want to take it again.

17

T ERRENCE SEEMS DISTRACTED and lost in thought as he walks down the cement front steps of Nagog High — maybe he has an organic chemistry test coming up. Or maybe the Minutemen were making fun of him in the locker room. It's Friday, game day.

Terrence crosses the empty parking lot and clicks open his Prius with his smart key. Harkness slides into the passenger seat before Terrence can start the car.

Too surprised to talk, Terrence just stares at this apparition in a cop uniform.

"How's that advanced seminar in physics?" Harkness says.

"Good?" Terrence stares through the windshield at the rows of light poles and expensive cars.

"Mr. Lombardi teaches that, right? Big guy, not a lot of hair?"

"Yeah."

"Used to work at Raytheon. Developed the navigation system for drone bombers. Felt so guilty about it that he quit. Gets paid a buck a year to teach high school."

Terrence's face blanches and his chin quivers. "Who are you? How do you know all that?"

"Took his class, way back when," Harkness says. "And I'm a cop, Terrence. I'm supposed to know what's going on." No need to mention that the last vestiges of Third Rail are still amping up his memory.

"Am I in trouble?"

"Maybe."

Terrence's confused look says he's not used to trouble, or getting caught.

"Let's take a little drive," Harkness says.

Harkness and Terrence stand at the far end of the playing fields, where the track meets the woods. The dormant grass, part green, part brown, is cut close for the coming winter. The pine trees at the edge of the woods are aligned in rows as orderly as an Indiana cornfield.

"You know Newton's laws of motion, right?"

"Yes," Terrence says quietly.

"An object in motion tends to stay in motion unless . . . Help me out a little, Terrence," Harkness says.

"Unless an external force is applied to that object," Terrence mutters, studying the knees of his tan cargo pants.

"So let's say that object was, in fact, a person — say, the late Kelly Pierce." Harkness holds up an evidence bag holding a strip of black cloth and an amber vial.

Terrence starts to shake.

"So she would stay in motion unless some external force got in her way," Harkness says. "I suppose a tree might be considered an external force."

Terrence turns away from the woods. "I didn't do anything." Tears run down his face and he smears them away with his soft hand.

"Well, actually, Terrence. You did something. You know that, right?"

"Why are you asking me all this stuff? Aren't I supposed to have a lawyer or something?" Terrence's eyes twitch all around the playing fields, empty at midday, as if he might find a lawyer standing there.

"Calm down, Terrence. Here's the deal. I have one question for you. I'm going to ask you that question. You're going to answer it honestly. Then I'm going to let you get back in your car so you can drive to lunch."

"What if I don't?"

"Well, that's where it gets complicated," Harkness says. "You'll have to come into the station and a detective will interrogate you for a couple of hours. We'll have to call your parents, alert the school—you're applying early to Stanford, I hear—I'm sure they'll be sorry to hear you're involved with drugs and implicated in the death of a classmate."

Terrence's mouth moves but no sound comes out. "It's not my fault," he says finally.

Harkness holds up his hand. "Don't tell it to me. Save it for the jury."

"The jury!"

Harkness lets Terrence Jessup—Nagog High senior and drug aficionado—freak out for a few minutes. Set in motion, Terrence's well-tuned mind runs through all of the possibilities, none of them very good.

"Okay, ready?"

Terrence nods.

"Tell me exactly what happened on the night Kelly Pierce died."

• • •

The smart kids called their game *Fate* because no matter how well you played, it could still kill you. Once a week, they drifted from their quiet ranch houses and saltbox Colonials and gathered behind the hulking brick high school, the cool air thick with their whispers as Terrence popped up a window with a crowbar. By now, even the night janitor was gone, which was good news, because they were clueless at breaking and entering, Terrence claims.

Their nervous laughter echoed through the locker room as they tried on the shiny red Nagog Minutemen track uniforms that never fit—the smart kids were all too scrawny from nerves and Adderall or doughy from spending more time online than in the gym. When they burst through the swinging metal doors of the locker room in formation, girls and boys in alternating rows, and jogged out onto the cool wet grass, someone always sang a line or two of "We Are the Champions."

At the far side of the playing fields, Terrence fished the amber vial from his pocket. He smiled, pale skin glowing in the moonlight. They circled him, faces tilted toward the stars, mouths open like hungry birds. Joe Maguire, National Merit finalist and late-night gamer, edged forward to taste the first golden drop. Then came Jack Palmer and Lindsay Doherty, stars of *It's Academic,* the cable show no one but parents and math teachers watched. A thick drop fell into the eager mouth of Kelly Pierce, the red-haired honors student who talked so fast she seemed to be set at the wrong speed.

"One drop," Terrence said that night, every night they played the game. "This stuff's expensive — and strong."

He didn't need to warn them. They knew not to ask for more.

In a few minutes they were pacing in circles, running fingers through hair, and pressing hands on temples as if that alone might calm their febrile minds. Thrumming from the first rush, they raced around the darkened field, stopping only to blurt out half-formed ideas and sudden declarations. They clutched each other like drowning sailors, slipped fingers down past elastic waistbands. Inhibitions dissolved, nervousness transformed to swagger, tongues flickered, cocks pointed moonward, and white legs scissored on the cold grass.

Dr. North was right about sex on Third Rail.

On game night, everyone was hot, everyone was cool. Everyone knew everything.

When their minds settled, Terrence held out the deck and they each took a card. Kelly Pierce won with the jack of spades.

The others gathered around the chosen and tied her black blindfold tight. They kissed her cheek, whispered in her ear, then turned her toward the woods, narrow pines planted in close rows.

They cheered as Kelly ran across the field toward the edge of the woods, red uniform flashing in the fading light, to smash into the pines or rush in triumph and relief into the dark spaces between them. The chosen could never be sure.

Fate would figure that out for them.

· · ·

Terrence sits in the cold grass, sobbing. Remembering Kelly has opened a well of guilt, and Harkness plumbs its depths to get answers.

"This is the part I don't understand, Terrence. From what I can tell, you and your friends played the game every week or so, isn't that right?"

Terrence nods and a tear drops from the end of his nose.

Harkness leans down to put his hand on Terrence's shoulder.

"Chances are someone must have run into a tree before," he says. "I mean, there's no way every fucked-up kid before Kelly managed to just run into the woods without hitting anything. What happened to Kelly? Why her?"

Terrence shakes his head slowly for a moment. "Everyone else just jogged toward the woods," he says quietly. "If they hit a tree, maybe they ended up with a scrape on their forehead or something. But Kelly, Kelly . . ." He sobs.

"Kelly what?"

"She ran," he says. "She ran as fast as she could. Crazy fast."

"Was she trying to kill herself?"

He shakes his head. "I don't think so. I think she was just really high. She didn't weigh that much, and that Third Rail stuff went to her head."

"Thought she was invincible."

Terrence nods.

"But we both know no one's invincible. Can't beat the laws of physics."

"I know that," Terrence says. "But it's so safe in Nagog, you know. Nothing happens here. It felt good to do something stupid and dangerous."

Harkness remembers dodging cars on the Pike. "I know what you mean, Terrence."

"The game was really fun for a while, then it turned into something terrible."

"That's pretty much how it always goes." Harkness reaches down to help Terrence up from the cold grass.

"Am I going to jail?"

Another cop might pin Kelly Pierce's death on Terrence, turning an accident into second-degree murder. But Harkness just shakes his head. Fate's already tying knots in Terrence's life. "No. But when you get home, I need you to find that amber vial of Third Rail and dump it down the toilet."

Terrence nods and they walk back toward his car.

"How much did you pay for it?"

"Three hundred dollars."

"Short, hairy guy sold it to you, right?"

"At first, yeah. Then a taller guy. Long dyed hair, kind of yellow. Called himself Straight Ed."

Harkness stops cold. "Well, that's an ironic name for a drug dealer."

Terrence opens the door to his mint-colored Prius and climbs inside.

Harkness leans down to pass along one final message to Terrence. "Forget you ever heard it."

• • •

Harkness pulls in front of the Old Nagog Tavern, a tilted white Colonial with peeling paint, gap-toothed clapboards, and plastic stapled over its windows. Gray lumber is piled in the front yard, and behind the house, battered cars point in all directions in a weedy field dotted by black trash bags, fifty-gallon drums, and rusted junk. At the far end of the field there's a big red barn, roofline sagging like a telephone wire.

No warrant. No probable cause. No discussion with the captain. No plan. No gun. Harkness knows he has no justification to show up here on a crisp fall morning except that he's pissed off at Dex for selling drugs in Nagog — and for using his old nickname as some kind of joke, or worse.

The unexpected arrival of a cop in a squad car can have a catalytic effect.

Before he gets to the battered door, a barefoot girl in jeans and a T-shirt walks outside.

"Uh . . . like, what're you doing here?" She squints at Harkness through oversized black-rimmed glasses.

Harkness scrambles for the right lie. Noise complaint. Lost dog. Escapee from the Concord prison.

But she talks first. "Right, *the rent*," she says, drawing air quotes with her fingers. "Usually one of the guys brings it out to the car. Hang on." She pads back into the house, then emerges and hands him a white drawstring bag with the Apple logo.

"Usually it's the first Thursday of the month," she says.

"Well, I'm early, then."

"How come you're not the sweaty guy with the Sox jacket?"

Harkness feels a gear click into place. "You mean Sergeant Da-bilis. See him here a lot?"

She nods. "Him or the old cop, the Irish one."

"I think you mean Scottish."

"Maybe. Polite, tall, with an accent. Usually he just waits in the car."

Another gear clicks.

She pivots and walks back into the house without another word. The rent is delivered, her work done.

Harkness walks back to the squad car and pulls open the draw-string to find dozens of neat stacks of hundreds. He shoves the bag under the seat and drives away.

18

HARKNESS JUMPS UP the hospital steps two at a time to the ICU. Candace is stomping around the waiting room in her engineer boots, ripped jeans, and a Ramones T-shirt. Tears stream down her face.

"You okay?"

"No," Candace says.

The TV blares from the ceiling and the chairs are strewn with sweat-weathered copies of *People*. Nothing good can happen in a bright waiting room at four in the morning. That Candace called him here in the middle of the night, sobbing and hysterical, tells Harkness something important—she doesn't turn to Dex when she's in trouble.

"I need you to get them to let me know what's going on," she says, voice quavering. "That Indian stoner won't tell me."

"I'll talk to him."

"Do more than talk to him."

"You can't beat up nurses."

"I can," Candace says.

"Don't."

When Andy Singh walks in, Candace grabs the front of his blue scrubs. "What's going on with my dad?"

"Ouch. Hey!"

"Tell me!"

"Doctor's coming. Just wait a few minutes."

Candace lets go and paces around the room. She jumps up and turns off the television with a slap.

Harkness walks over and stares into the night nurse's bloodshot eyes. "Andy, what's the news?"

"Eddy, just wait for the doctor," he says.

"Why?"

"Because that's the protocol. I can get fired if I do anything else."

"You smell like weed."

"Shut up, please, Eddy."

Candace spins around. "If you don't tell us what the fuck's going on right now, I'm going to tell the doctors you put your hands all over these." Candace pulls down the neck of her black T-shirt to show her full breasts.

Harkness looks away, after a moment.

"TMI." Andy Singh waves his hand.

"Start talking," Harkness says. "Just tell my friend what's going on. She needs to know, right now."

"Okay, okay." Andy Singh shakes his head, then stops and turns slowly to Candace. "Your father's dead," he says softly, keeping his eyes locked on hers. "I'm really, really sorry. He died about half an hour ago. Went into cardiac arrest and we just couldn't get him going again. Whole unit was working on him. But the accident did too much internal damage."

Andy Singh sits on a plastic chair, lowers his head, and starts to cry. "I hate this fucking job."

Candace tilts her face up to the white tiles of the suspended ceiling, eyes pressed closed. She looks like she's praying for a moment, then slumps to the floor. Harkness catches her and wraps his arms around her shoulders, shaking with sobs. Her wailing brings the other nurses running.

• • •

Watt's pacing around on the slab when Harkness pulls in from emptying meters. He parks and walks over, carrying a bag from the Nagog Bakery.

"Want a scone? Like biting into a cinnamon-flavored rock."

"Sounds great, but no thanks," Watt says.

"What's wrong?"

"You see the final report?"

"Which one?"

"On that girl who died," Watt says. "Kelly Pierce?"

"No."

"They said it was an accident. That she got disoriented and ran into the woods.

"Seems pretty unlikely, doesn't it?"

"I saw her parents crying their eyes out on the news," Watt says. "I got a four-year-old daughter, Eddy. Something crazy like this ever happened to her, I'd find out the truth. Accident? I don't think so."

"You want to know what really happened?"

"Sure. How do you know?"

"Asked around, the way cops are supposed to."

Harkness leads Watt to the edge of the slab, where no one can see them from the station. "Kelly and her friends broke into the locker room and stole some track uniforms. Then they went out to the fields, tied blindfolds on, and took turns running into the woods."

"Who came up with that?"

"It was from some metal band video they saw on YouTube. Most of the kids ended up missing the trees. A couple of guys scraped themselves up. But Kelly ran full tilt and took a direct hit."

"That's crazy. What makes a bunch of smart kids do something that stupid?"

Harkness shrugs. "Easiest reason in the world. They were on drugs."

"What kind of drugs?"

"Third Rail. New stuff that really messes with your mind and won't let go." Every day, Third Rail dares Harkness to take it again.

"The final report doesn't even mention that vial we found in the woods. I checked."

Harkness puts his hand on Watt's shoulder. "Exactly. There's a lot going on behind the scenes, Watt. Not exactly the Nagog Police Department's finest moment."

"Heard the captain yelling at Dabilis in his office this morning, Eddy."

"Really?"

"Maybe he'll get fired."

"Don't get your hopes up. Guys like Dabilis rise to the top."

"Like turds," Watt says.

"Like that."

. . .

From where he stood at the front of the stage, Harkness could see the stranger across the crowded VFW hall, moving against the tide of sweaty bodies. It was the last set of the Saturday afternoon all-ages show in Watertown, a triple bill with Art Carnage, Lawless Order, and Temper Fi. Outside it was a gentle spring day with early flowers in bloom and families riding bikes along the banks of the upper Charles River. Inside the VFW hall about a hundred skinheads in leather shoved and danced, yelled at the band, and had as much fun as teenagers could without drugs or drinks. But the outsider had other plans.

Harkness and Skørge, the other unofficial bouncer, watched the big guy in a spiked leather vest and camouflage pants slamming around in the crowd. He seemed to be zeroing in on the girls and young kids in the crowd, slamming into them extra hard and grabbing at them. Maybe he was a kid with attitude up from New York with one of the bands or some North Cambridge joker, the kind who talked like his mouth was crammed with soft serve. But he wasn't one of their tribe.

"Fucka needs a thumpa," mumbled George Perkins, a quiet electrician in a battered leather jacket who lived in a Worcester apartment lined with sagging record crates. During the shows, he transformed into Skørge.

"I'll get this one," Harkness said, as if he'd just volunteered to take out the trash. As he slipped through the crowd, everyone stepped aside to let Straight Ed do his work. He rented the hall, made sure the bands got paid, sent out the e-mails, put up the posters, and kept the outsiders under control.

The welterweight punk's shaved head was marked with cuts and scars, and his eggy eyes shone from afternoon drinking. He thrashed around to the blistering music, the room so packed that no one could get out of the way. Harkness tapped his shoulder, and when the stranger turned, he clamped his right hand over his eyes. In that moment of confusion, Harkness stepped his right leg behind the stranger and shoved him backwards. Harkness slammed the back of

120

the stranger's head twice — just hard enough to stun — against the linoleum floor. The thumper was no more painful than a hard hit during a football scrimmage. But it sent a message — *Get lost.*

Harkness had a repertoire of proven moves, the kind that might look brutal but that stopped fights cold and reduced the danger and damage. The punishment always had to match the crime, no more, no less. He pulled the subdued stranger through the crowd, his unlaced boots dragging across the dusty floor.

Harkness shoved the stranger through the double doors at the front of the hall, and he rolled down the low, grassy hill toward Mt. Auburn Street. He spun around for a minute on the sidewalk, then stood up, shouted, *"Fuck you,"* and wandered toward the bus stop. Problem solved.

Someone always wanted to take the monthly all-ages show and claim it as his own. All it took was one sneering outsider to taint an afternoon. Harkness walked back inside toward the stage and nodded at Skørge. The show could keep going. Order was restored.

Years later, when he first started out as a cop in Boston, Harkness realized that he wasn't enforcing laws. He was stopping the outsiders who turned up on the streets with bad plans and enough muscle and charisma to make them happen.

Now Harkness is still hunting down outsiders, the ones who sold the drugs that killed Kelly Pierce, Robert Hammond, whoever might be next — and the cops who let it happen.

But first, he has to find his gun.

19

OUT OF UNIFORM, HARKNESS can walk unnoticed around the waiting area of the storefront campaign headquarters on Dorchester Avenue. He leafs through the brochures about creating a new Boston. Posters of John Fitzgerald, smiling mayoral candidate, line every wall. Volunteers hover over their laptops at glass-topped desks.

"Can we help you?" The front desk girl looks young and earnest, with blond hair and a tentative smile.

"Sure." Harkness takes out his cell phone, scrolls to Pauley Fitzgerald's number, and presses REDIAL. Music blares from one of the glassed-in offices along the side. A red-haired man in a white shirt and dark tie emerges from one of the offices. He looks familiar — green eyes set wide, tight skin, neck soft and doughy. Harkness remembers seeing him on television.

Harkness points. "I'm here to see him."

The name tag taped to the office door says, MARK SARRIS, CAMPAIGN DIRECTOR. Harkness backs Sarris into his office with distracting banter. ". . . Just had a couple of quick questions about the campaign, thought I'd stop in . . ."

The door clicks closed behind him.

"What the hell do you want?"

Harkness twists the white plastic rod that closes the blinds. The rest of headquarters fades and disappears.

Sarris gives a fake smile. "My lucky day," he says. "I finally get to meet the legendary Harvard Cop."

"And I get to meet Mark Sarris, talking head. And the guy who's pretending to be Pauley Fitzgerald."

Sarris sits down at his desk. "Very clever. You tracked down a cell phone. You must be a really smart cop."

"How'd you get that phone?"

"Guy gave it to me." Sarris turns toward his computer. "Is this going to take long?" he says. "I'm running a campaign here."

Harkness pulls Sarris out of his chair and shoves him down on the gray carpet.

"Shit!" Sarris's eyes open wide.

Harkness steps in the center of his chest and pulls back on his tie, a noose waiting to happen.

Sarris wheezes like a dog choking on a chicken wing and Harkness lets up a little. "Give it to me."

Sarris reaches in his pocket and pulls out a bright red cell phone.

Harkness takes it. "Now tell me where you got it."

Sarris says nothing for a moment, just rises up on all fours and rubs his throat with his fingertips. "You Boston assholes. You're fucking insane. This shit never happens in LA."

"We're not in LA. And we're not on TV." Harkness grabs Sarris by the shoulders and throws him back in his chair. His face is splotched and his tie stretched New Wave narrow.

"Where'd you get the phone?"

"Your friend in Narco-Intel. Patrick."

"No way."

"Maybe you need better friends."

There's a knock on the door and it inches open.

"Everything okay?" A tall man in a suit peers in, his right eye green circled and swollen shut.

"Fine, Johnny," Sarris says. "This guy's about to leave."

The suit gives Harkness a confused scan with his good eye.

"Ever find those Frye boots?" Harkness says.

"Ever find your gun?"

"I'm about to."

Harkness pulls the door closed and locks it.

Sarris points at Harkness. "What do you want?"

"My gun."

Sarris shakes his head. "I don't have your gun. Get out of here before I call the cops."

"That's rich," Harkness says.

"You're trespassing," Sarris says. "And you're not exactly popular around here. You killed the councilman's favorite nephew. And you fucked up my deputy communication manager."

"Cyclops in a suit?"

"Johnny almost lost that eye thanks to you. He's an actor back in LA."

"You sent actors to beat us up?"

"Figured looking tough was enough."

"Not around here," Harkness says. "The gun, Sarris. Now."

"I don't have your gun."

"Someone here knows where it is."

Sarris shrugs. "That's what campaigns are about. Knowing a lot of things."

Harkness hands Sarris a manila envelope. "Well, here's something you should know about."

Sarris opens the folder. His small mouth puckers as he stares at the first photo.

"Left to right," Harkness says. "Unnamed thug. Very young girl wearing bra and thong. Unnamed thug. Mr. Mach, owner of the notorious Zero Room. Girl. Joe 'Joey Ink' Incagnoli, representing the North End mob. The legendary James 'Whitey' Bulger, making a secret visit to Boston from his Santa Monica love nest. Thomas Gallagher, South Boston associate of Bulger. And your man, City Councilor John Fitzgerald. Thought it might make a nice campaign poster."

Sarris shakes his head. "Totally fake. Nice Photoshop job."

"Got dozens of photos. Different nights, same crew. Your man and a crowd he shouldn't be running with."

Sarris throws the photo on his desk. "Get out of here."

Harkness flips through the photos and finds one of Fitzgerald and Whitey sitting side by side like brothers. "Imagine this on the cover of the *Herald*. Or on Fox News. Maybe *LA Confrontational*?"

"For purposes of discussion, let's assume that it's real," Sarris says. "What do you want, Harkness?"

"You mean if this hypothetical photo stays where it is?"

"Yes."

"My gun. And I want Fitzgerald to leave Narco-Intel alone."

"We get every last fucking photo."

"When I have my gun back, I'll think about it."

Sarris shakes his head. "It's not here."

"Then how did Cyclops know I didn't have my gun? You either have it or you know who does."

Sarris holds up his hands. "The councilman was messing with you. He holds a grudge — not my favorite quality. Wanted to embarrass your pal Lattimore and bring him down. Thought he might put out a *once the commissioner's golden boy, now a townie cop who can't even keep track of his gun* narrative."

"Why didn't he?"

"You really want to know, Harkness?" Sarris tilts his head. "I talked him out of it. Told him it was bad politics to be settling scores in the press. Told him that this race was about getting elected, not getting even. And for once, the councilman listened to me."

"Gee, you're making me almost sorry I kicked your ass."

"Look, no one here took your gun. Fitzgerald just took advantage of it once he knew it was up for grabs. We liked messing with you with the dead guy calling on the phone thing. Thought it was funny at the time. Now it's over."

"Thanks for that clarification," Harkness says. "So where is my gun exactly?"

"One of the guys in that photo has it." He points at the photo of the Zero Room. "You're such a hot-shit detective, you figure out which one. And Harkness?"

"What?"

"I hear he's been using it."

. . .

"I don't know how many times I can tell you this, Eddy," Thalia says. "I didn't take your gun. Listen to me. I. Did. Not. Take. Your. Gun." She's stalking back and forth in front of her building, shaking her head. His squad car is parked halfway up on the sidewalk, engine ticking from speeding to the South End from Dorchester.

"Then how did Mach get it?"

"Maybe that asshole guy at the campaign place was lying, Eddy. Ever think of that?"

"All I know is that Mach has my gun, and you're the only one who could have given it to him. It's that simple."

"I didn't do it, Eddy. I hate Mach."

"Everyone does. But he still manages to get people to do things for him. He controls everyone at the Zero Room like they're his puppet collection. You worked for him for years. Jeet put up with Mach even though he hates him. And you told me he got that waitress friend of yours to walk on him in high heels, you know, the short one with the hair?"

Harkness stops. Then Thalia.

"Marnie," they say at the same time.

·   ·   ·

When they force the door to her loft open, Marnie's sprawled on her back like she just fell out of the sky. Her eyelids sag at half-mast, her moist skin shines, and her carnival hair is splayed out on the cement floor.

"Hey! Marnie!" Harkness leans down to slap her face gently, then harder. Nothing. He checks her pulse and finds it, but barely. Her nostrils bubble with opalescent snot.

"What's wrong with her?"

"Overdose," Harkness says. "Call 911."

Harkness straightens Marnie's bird body on the floor, swipes his finger inside her mouth, and presses his mouth against hers. He blows in one breath, then another. Her slick lips taste metallic and dirty, like licking a subway handrail.

Harkness turns away, counts, and breathes again. Nothing. Ten times or more and she's still staring at the ceiling in frozen astonishment.

Thalia comes back holding a small plastic bag full of powder. "Here's what's wrong with her — Redbird."

"What's that?"

"Shitty heroin." Thalia looks at Marnie. "Eddy, is she dead?"

"Almost." Harkness presses Marnie's chest, gently at first, then harder. Her head and shoulders rise up with each push and almost convince him that she's alive.

Thalia's circling. "Shit, shit."

Harkness turns to blow air into Marnie again, harder this time. Sweat drips down his sides. "Did you call 911?"

"No."

"Why not?"

"Just no," she mutters.

"Call 911! Now!"

"She's going to . . ."

"Now, Thalia. Call now."

Thalia stalks around Marnie, then rushes toward her. "Wake up, you stupid little shit! Wake the fuck up!" Thalia kicks Marnie hard between the legs. Then again. Then over and over, as if trying to kick her across the loft.

Marnie rises up like a sleepwalker and turns to the side to spray the floor with milky clots. She rolls onto her hands and knees and heaves over and over, the murky pool beneath her spreading.

"Feel really weird," Marnie whispers, her mouth connected to the floor with glistening threads. She wipes her mouth on her sleeve.

"Better weird than dead, dumbfuck." Thalia holds up the bag. "How much of this shit did you do?"

Marnie shakes her head. "Just a corner. Something's wrong with it."

Harkness stands. "Get that from Mach?"

"Yeah."

"Trade my gun for it?"

She pauses for a moment. "No."

"Tell us, Marnie." Thalia pulls her foot back, ready to kick Marnie in the crotch again.

"He gave me five hundred bucks to steal your gun," she says. "And that bag of Redbird."

Harkness grabs her by the narrow shoulders. "How'd you get my gun?"

"Got it when you finally passed out, asshole."

"Eddy just saved your fucking life, Marnie," Thalia shouts.

Harkness waves her down. "What're you talking about, Marnie?"

"I put two Valiums and an Ambien in that last beer at the loft party," she says. "Couple of hours later you were still walking around like a zombie, going out for cigarettes and shit. When you finally passed out, I snuck into Thalia's loft and lifted it."

Harkness shakes his head. An answer, finally, at least part of one. "Why?"

Marnie shrugs. "Mach hates you because you busted him and because . . ." She points at Thalia. "Because you're fucking her."

Thalia's eyes narrow.

Harkness knows there's got to be more to it than that. The bust was years ago. And Mach saw him with Thalia for months. "More, Marnie. Or we stick your face back in this and say good night."

Harkness tosses the bag of Redbird on the ground in front of her. She shudders, spews more dirty water on the floor.

"Tell Eddy!" Thalia stabs her finger at Marnie.

"Tell Eddy what?"

"Whatever the fuck you know about Mach."

Marnie stares at the floor. "Mach's working some angle in Nagog. Knew you were a cop there. Figured stealing your gun would put you out of commission."

"Out of commission?"

"You know, like you'd quit."

"Oh really?" Harkness remembers almost quitting dozens of times. He didn't need Mach's help. "What angle?"

"Got a business deal going with some dealer named Dex."

Harkness smiles as another gear clicks into place. Nagog's a small town. But still.

Thalia leaps in, teeth flashing, rabid. "Did I have anything to do with it? Any fucking thing at all? Tell him!"

Marnie shudders for a moment. Then she starts to speak, her voice so squelched that it sounds like it's coming from the bottom of a deep, dark well. "I did it on my own," she says. "Knew where you hid the extra key under that brick out on the sidewalk."

"So you didn't tell me anything about your stupid plan, right, Marnie?"

"No," she shouts. "Knew you'd tell someone with your big mouth. You always pissed me off at the bar, Thalia. You were such a total bitch."

Marnie drops her head, carnival hair hiding her tears.

•   •   •

An empty coffee cup still rests on the kitchen table after they forced Marnie to walk with them to Thalia's loft to get some air and straighten out. They spent an hour in the kitchen, asking Marnie questions, making her cry, scaring the shit out of her, and finally letting her go home to try to sleep.

"She'll be okay," Harkness says.

"Guess that's a good thing." Thalia picks up the bag, no bigger than a dollhouse pillow, the tiny label stuck on the side stamped with a red hummingbird.

"A couple of years ago, bunch of kids in Mattapan died from Burmese Red," Harkness says.

"Redbird is way strong." She tosses the bag down on the table.

"Explain why you have a tattoo of that red hummingbird right above your ass."

Thalia looks out at the yellow streetlights. "Might have noticed that tattoo has a black X through it.

"I get kind of distracted."

"Crossed out my demons." She drinks from a smudged glass of whiskey. "Threw 'em out."

"Sometimes they don't get too far." Harkness stares out the window at leaves skittering across the sidewalk.

"You believe me now, don't you, Eddy?"

Harkness says nothing.

"You have to believe me, Eddy. Marnie was jealous. Mach paid more attention to me, not that I wanted it. The customers liked me better. And I made more tips. But one thing's my fault, and I'm really fucking sorry about it. You never would have run into her if I hadn't dragged you to the stupid loft party."

"Was Mach trying to kill her?"

Thalia shrugs. "Who the hell knows? Probably. She's not exactly a drug amateur. But if you send this bag to the lab, I bet they'll find something extra in it."

"Call Mach tomorrow," Harkness says. "Tell him you made a big mistake and try to get your old job back."

"That'll never work."

"Use your legendary charm." Harkness pulls on his jacket and picks up the bag of dope and a bottle of whiskey.

"What're you doing?"

He grabs Thalia's arm. "We're going out."

Long after midnight, the cool air smells of rot and ocean. They stand on the hard banks of the industrial canal that runs behind Thalia's building, its gray water oily and still, banks lined with weed-woven grocery carts and moonlit shards.

"Got to clean up our act." Harkness drops the whiskey bottle in the canal, where it gives out one small splash, then sinks from view. *If only all temptations disappeared so easily,* Harkness thinks.

"You sure we should just throw shit in the water?"

"People have dropped a lot worse in here." Harkness hands Thalia the bag of dope.

She holds it for a moment, glowing in the moonlight. "Later, Redbird." The bag spirals down into the iridescent canal.

A green-gray creature, eelgrass clinging to its back, swims toward the bag.

"Shit," Thalia says. "What the fuck is that?"

Harkness squints down at the water. "Looks like a *canaligator.*"

"What?"

"Alligators that live in canals. People buy them for pets and dump them when they get too big."

"Thought that was one of those urban legend things."

"Guess not."

They stare at the creature gliding toward the bag of Redbird.

"If you think about something long enough, maybe it shows up," Thalia says.

"I'd like to think so."

20

THE CALL COMES from Debbie the dispatcher. "Near the town mill, Eddy?"

"Two minutes away."

"Report of a suspicious object in the water. Check it out."

Harkness walks toward the mill, once the center of Nagog commerce and gossip, now the town's most popular tourist site. A guy in full Colonial getup — breeches, billowing white linen shirt, a snug brown waistcoat, and tricornered hat — paces in buckled shoes.

Harkness squints. "Hey, don't I know you?"

Thom peers through his wire-rimmed glasses. "Are ye a good citizen of Nagog?"

"Are ye Henry David Thoreau?"

"Not today," Thom whispers. "I'm Amos Garrett, the guy who sold out the Colonials, like Judas. Told the Brits where the rebel guns were hidden down in the mill. Ended up hanging from a tree in the center of Nagog until his face got pecked off by crows."

"Thanks for that," Harkness says. "Isn't there more than one guy around here who likes to get dressed up?"

Thom leans closer. "The National Park Service pays me fifty bucks a pop to do Citizen Garrett tours," he says. "They want to *tell the untold tales of the Revolution.*"

The smell of beer wafts from Thom's little mouth.

"Why'd you call 911?"

Thom clomps forward. "There's something down in the mill. I

don't think it's anything, but this annoying teacher made me call. I'll take you inside." He nudges the heavy door open with his shoulder and cool air billows out. They walk down a hallway to the dank mill chamber.

Thom picks up a lantern from the floor and clicks on a flickering bulb designed to look like candlelight. The wet rock walls of the small room glisten in the dim light, and the hair on the back of Harkness's arms rises. The town mill is just as creepy as it was years ago when he came here on school field trips.

The narrow wooden stairs creak as they walk down them. A school class gathers in stunned silence in the dim room. Their teacher rushes toward them.

"Thank God it's you, Edward."

"What seems to be the problem, Mrs. P?"

Mrs. Pettengill points at the glistening wooden millwheel, the waters of the milldam rushing around its base and flooding across the floor. "We were in the middle of our tour and I saw something strange in the millwheel." The class stands in silence, boldest near the millwheel, timid pressed against the back wall.

"I assured this fine teacher of children that a stick, or perhaps a barrel stave, is miring the millwheel," Thom says in his faux-Colonial accent.

"I'll handle it, Citizen Garrett." Harkness takes his lantern and walks toward the waterway and the still wheel. There's a roll of sod clogging the works.

Mrs. Pettengill stays back. "I don't like the look of it, Edward," she says.

Harkness smells the familiar sweet rot he remembers from alleys, vacant lots, and car trunks.

Thom holds a long finger aloft. "Perchance there are some tree branches lodged in ye olde millwheel."

"I think you need to take the kids outside, Citizen Garrett, okay?" Harkness says. "Now."

Thom leads the class toward the entrance.

"Probably sod or a bag of leaves, Mrs. P," Harkness says to calm her down. "Just stuff a landscaper dumped in the river."

"I don't think so, Eddy."

"I'll check it out. You go on outside." At the millwheel, Harkness reaches out to try to move the clog. In the dim light from the fake lantern, it's green and slick, bobbing awkwardly in the water, half trapped. Harkness pushes it to shift its clammy weight, then pulls his hand away. Water splashes as the millwheel starts to turn.

Harkness holds the light closer. Wrapped with vines and leaves, the bloated body wants to break free of its green uniform. Harkness rolls the body over until the blanched face surfaces through the murky water and the captain's blue eyes stare at him.

. . .

Harkness's cell phone rings in the middle of the night, and he rolls over to keep Thalia from waking up.

"You awake, bro?"

"No." A candle gutters on the kitchen table, where he and Thalia spent most of the night talking.

"Been out partying?"

Harkness pauses, decides to tell his brother to truth. "Look, George. I found Captain Munro floating in the town mill. Dead for a couple of days."

"No way."

Harkness says nothing.

"I remember him from when we were kids," George says. "Really nice guy. Always kept us all out of trouble."

"Right."

"Got Dad off for DUI about ten times. And me for vandalizing the school and a bunch of other stupid stuff I did. He was a real friend of the family."

"I . . ." Harkness wants to say more, about how Captain Munro alone took him in after the incident, about how he checked up on Nora and their mother every week. But he can't.

Thalia sits up on the futon and puts her hand on his arm.

"It's George," he mouths in the gloom.

Thalia gives a vigorous jack-off gesture.

"So what happened?"

"Not sure," Harkness says. "Looks like he drowned. I'm checking it out."

"I'm really sorry, Eddy. I know he wasn't just your boss or commanding officer or whatever they call it."

"Yes." Tears stream down Harkness's face. Thalia's nestled next to him now, running her hand along his back.

"Look, Eddy. I know it's not a good time to talk. But I just wanted to tell you something."

"Then just say it, George."

"The Revolving Gallery?"

"What?"

"The gallery your quote-unquote girlfriend told me about at dinner, you know, when you locked me in the trunk of my own fucking car, remember? Thalia said it was her gallery but it's been out of business for years."

"Thanks, George. I'll correct my art walk map in the morning."

"Might want to ask her about it."

"Why don't you stick with investing and I'll do the investigating."

"All I know is this, bro. People don't tell just one lie."

. . .

Lee unlocks the door and Harkness slips inside the Nagog Five and Ten, radiators ticking against the crisp morning. "Need another gun, Eddy?" Lee whispers, even though there's no one else in the store.

"Baseballs," Harkness says.

"Getting back to your roots, are you?"

"Kind of."

Lee runs down the narrow aisles and comes back with a baseball boxed in thin cardboard. "Like this?"

"Yeah, but a couple dozen," Harkness says. "In a gym bag. Need a bat, too."

"You were a pitcher in high school, right?"

Dozens of Nagog High ballgames replay in his mind in blurry fast-forward until Harkness shuts them off. "For two years."

"Still like it?"

"Baseball? Sure."

"Weird, then."

"What?"

"That you end up getting hated by every Sox fan in the world."

"Thanks for that, Lee."

"Sorry." Lee trots down the aisle again, coming back with a bulging red gym bag and a gleaming aluminum bat.

"How much do I owe you?"

Lee shakes his head. "Just knock one out of the park for me."

"Oh, I will."

. . .

In less than a week, Sergeant Dabilis has already colonized Captain Munro's office. Red leather chairs circle the big new desk and a Red Sox banner hangs next to the Massachusetts flag.

He waves Harkness into one of the new chairs, which creaks when he sits in it. "Listen, Harkness. I know you and the captain were friends."

Harkness nods.

"He was a good man," Dabilis says. "We go way back."

Harkness stares, then traces the outline of the office with his careful gaze, imagines it filling up with black water.

"Turns out he was up to his eyeballs in debt," Sergeant Dabilis blurts out. "That alone might be enough to send him over the edge. But there's this other thing . . . he had some kind of leukemia that was going to kill him in a couple of years. So we're classifying it as suicide."

"And you and Ramble are running the investigation?"

"Investigation . . ." Dabilis rolls his hand in front of him.

" . . . the investigation, *sir?*"

"We think he jumped off the Carson Avenue Bridge. Found his car near there."

Harkness used to jump from that bridge with his friends in the summer. It's only fifteen feet above the water even when the river's low. To drown, the captain would have had to force himself underwater. Harkness sends out a truth-inducing stare but Sergeant Dabilis just looks away.

"I know that you and the captain had some side projects going. Like investigating the town monument accident." Dabilis pauses. "Anything else you were looking into?"

Harkness shakes his head, puts on his most honest face. "No, *sir*," he says.

Sergeant Dabilis circles the room and stops next to Harkness. "From here on in, no side projects. No investigating — except for why a meter doesn't work. I don't want anything funny happening.

135

Just do your shifts and empty the meters until I tell you to stop. Got it?"

"Yes, *sir*."

"Until then, we'll try to get along. Like cops do, Harkness. Right?"

. . .

One of Dex's drug dudebros walks out of the hardware store, lips moving to voice some private complaint, biblical beard waving in the breeze. He's getting a lot of stares on the sidewalk and giving back plenty of sneers. Harkness rolls down the window of the squad car. "Hey, Mouse. It's Mouse, right? Want a ride?"

Mouse looks at Harkness and just shakes his head. "No, thanks."

"Looks like rain," Harkness says. The late-afternoon sky is dotted with dark clouds, air thick with the smell of the ocean.

"No thanks, really."

Harkness trails Mouse along Main Street. "Look, I just finished my shift." He points to his shirt and jeans. "Not even a cop this afternoon. Just a normal civilian. Nothing to be afraid of." Harkness pauses. "Unless you have something to hide."

Mouse stops walking and gives Harkness an annoyed look.

"I'm a friend of Candace's," Harkness says. "She told me you were an interesting guy."

"Sure she did." Mouse laughs.

"The girl has a way with words."

"Mostly *fuck* and *fucktard* and *assberger fucktard*."

Harkness leans over to open the passenger door and gives Mouse his best smile, the one that says *Trust me* in every language.

Mouse rolls his eyes and slides into the seat.

Just like a mouse, Harkness thinks.

"You play baseball?" Harkness asks when they drive by the town park. The playing fields are empty, the pool's drained, and the summer crowds are long gone.

"No."

"Not even catch? You know, when you were a kid?"

"Of course," Mouse says. "Everyone plays catch."

Harkness reaches into the back seat and tosses a new glove to Mouse. "Well, here. Let's break this in a little." He pulls up next to the fields where he spent almost every afternoon as a boy.

"Look, I have to get back to the farm."

"Important things to do, huh?"

Mouse says nothing.

"Maybe Dex doesn't want you staying out without his permission?"

"That's not it."

"So Dex doesn't tell you what to do? Seemed like he was the alpha dog."

"You got that all wrong, dude."

"So just spend a few minutes out on the field with me. A little catch. Some fresh air. No big deal."

After the first dozen pop flies, Mouse almost gets the hang of it. He quits running up to catch the ball only to watch it fall yards behind him. He doesn't try to catch the ball with his glove turned the wrong way.

"Nice," Harkness says. He tosses a ball in the air, and when it drops he sends a line drive heading right at Mouse. The ball knocks the mitt off and sends it rolling across the field.

"Shit." Mouse circles with his hand jammed under his arm.

"That's right, walk it off."

"Why'd you do that?"

"Because if I hit you with this bat, it's assault."

"What?"

"But if you get hit by the ball, well, it looks more like . . . an accident."

Harkness tosses a ball and fires another line drive inches from Mouse's head.

"What do you want, you psycho?" His screamed question echoes across the empty playing fields.

Harkness leans on the bat. "I want to know if your pal Dex had anything to do with the death of a town cop."

"No way."

"Ever meet a Captain Munro? Scottish guy, short gray hair, blue eyes?"

Mouse shakes his head.

"Someone drowned him in the Nagog River. Sound familiar?" Harkness sends another ball just to the other side of Mouse's head.

"Stop it."

"Anything to say?"

"No."

"Because you won't say, or because you don't know?" Harkness fires another line drive right at Mouse, and he drops to the ground, hands over his head.

"I don't know anything about it! I'm only out at the farm a couple times a week."

"Did Dex say anything?"

"Dex doesn't say much." Mouse stands and brushes off his skinny jeans.

"Well, here's something you can tell him," Harkness says. "Tell him to get out of Nagog."

"Why?"

"Because I know what you're doing out there," Harkness says. "And pretty soon everyone will. So get out now." Harkness sends a couple of bounding grounders toward Mouse, who twitches to dodge them.

"I'll tell him. I'll tell him!" Mouse says.

"One other thing," Harkness says.

"What? What!"

"I'd start running if I were you. I'm just getting warmed up."

Mouse's narrow back turns smaller and smaller as he runs across the playing fields, baseballs speeding toward him like white bullets.

21

PATRICK TURNS ON the light and backs against the office door when he sees someone standing at the window.

"Harky, what the hell are you doing here?"

Harkness holds up the red cell phone.

"*Shit,* man. I'm sorry. I thought . . ."

Harkness holds up his hand but Patrick keeps talking.

"They said I'd still have a job even if Fitzgerald gets elected mayor."

"And you believed it?"

"I'm a walking, talking preexisting condition, Harky. Can't get health insurance anywhere else. Probably can't get another job. All I know how to do is track down drugs and money in Dataland."

Harkness tosses him Pauley Fitzgerald's red phone.

Patrick stares at the floor. "I know this looks bad. But if there's a new commissioner coming in —"

"I don't want an explanation or an apology," Harkness says. "I just need your help. And some gear."

·   ·   ·

Mourners in black fill Our Lady of the Fields, the stale air smelling of wood polish, wet wool, and smoking candles. They sit in the back, Thalia in her black dress and Harkness in his dress uniform. He leans his forehead down on the empty pew in front of him. Harkness thinks of his father, and not for the first time today.

Thalia nudges him. "Talking to the Man?"

He opens his eyes. "Maybe."

"Well, forget about it," she whispers. "You have to have his private cell phone number."

"That's how it works, is it?"

"That's how I figure it." She glances around the church as if casing it for enemies.

Candace's sitting on one end of the first pew, Dex on the other, the rest of the family sitting behind them. No mourning dress for Candace. She's wearing a black leather jacket, jeans, and a flannel shirt. She's bent forward and sobbing. The minister strides in from the side, black robe fluttering, and Candace stands with everyone else. Sunlight filters through stained glass to fall on her pale, tear-streaked face.

Over on his end of the pew, Dex sits hunched and smiling, head pivoting as he scans the choir stalls and pulpit with his cold stare. He twirls a finger in his dirty yellow hair.

First blessing over, the minister asks the congregation to please be seated. In front of the family and the somber townspeople rests Robert Hammond's coffin, flame maple with burnished gold handles. Like the foundation of a burnt-out building, it looks smaller than seems possible.

Thalia nudges Harkness again. "Are they really going to let her stay up there all alone for the whole service?"

"Her mother and sister are dead," he says. "Dex isn't exactly empathetic. Her father didn't have many relatives left, from what I can tell." Harkness nods to the rows behind Candace. "And those people don't really know her. They're just here because it's what people do in Nagog — they show up when someone dies."

Thalia's eyes glimmer. Not drinking makes her get teary. "She shouldn't be sitting alone at her father's funeral," she says. "It's completely fucked up." Thalia points. "Is Dex that asshole at the front?"

"Yeah, that's him."

Thalia stands and pushes past Harkness, walking toward the stained-glass Jesus hovering beyond the Communion rail, his hands outstretched. She bends to cross herself, slides into the front pew, and puts her arm around Candace's leather-clad shoulders. They've never met but Candace huddles close to Thalia as if she were her lost sister.

Dex doesn't seem to notice Thalia, just keeps scanning the church like a security camera.

The organ music rises as the minister puts on his glasses and begins to speak. Harkness stands with the congregation. He hears fragments of the eulogy for the late Robert Hammond — *hardworking man, committed to his family, survivor of tragedy* — as he walks quietly down the aisle, gliding past the good citizens of Nagog and pushing through the heavy doors.

. . .

From the edge of the woods, Harkness takes a closer look at the smudged white house. It looks abandoned, windows sheathed in opaque plastic, lumber scattered on the front lawn. Three tilted gables jut from the roof, covered with rippling blue tarps. Misshapen boxes of additions trail behind the house until it connects to a small outbuilding. In the field behind the house, a small crew is building a stage, their hammer strikes echoing. At the far edge of the field behind the house, the barn's sloping roof is a patchwork of missing shingles and thriving moss.

Harkness reaches into the inside pocket of his leather jacket for the metal case. He opens the digital wiretap. Patrick didn't want to let it leave Narco-Intel, reminding Harkness that it costs about ten thousand dollars, which he already knows. And it requires a court order, a technicality that Harkness also knows about, but decided to skip.

He puts on the black headphones and points the device at Dex's house, tracing a path along the eaves, braided with cables, each ripe with data.

The screen starts to glow.

One by one, their screens pop up — e-mail accounts, blogs, and a couple of porn sites. Someone's watching a Hitchcock movie, the one with the swooping biplane. Even with Dex at a funeral, his house has more traffic than an Internet start-up. Music blares and people chatter.

His warning to Mouse didn't make a difference. No one is leaving.

Harkness watches for a few minutes as fast keystrokes send more data beaming out from the tilted house. There's no mention of drugs. Or the captain. They aren't stupid.

Dex's friends keep going back to a password-protected site that shows nothing but a few words.

HEADLESS AT FREEDOM FARM. HALLOWEEN NIGHT.
COME FREE YOUR MIND. A DETAILED AGENDA
WILL BE PROVIDED FREE OF CHARGE.

For a moment, Harkness wonders what kind of party needs an agenda before he remembers the other name for Third Rail.

ADA will be provided free of charge. Clever. And tempting.

A gleaming dot wanders around the screen like a bee. Harkness clicks on it and a registration form pops up — name, e-mail address, favorite number, mother's middle name, secret vice. In exchange, you get the password to a party and free drugs that might kill you.

Harkness closes the silver case and slips back into the thick woods.

A narrow, meandering path cut through the tall grass leads from the house to the red barn. A century ago, children wandered the path at daybreak to milk the cows. But what makes the barn so popular now?

Harkness walks out on the field, cautious to keep the barn between him and the house. The heavy sliding doors are locked, but a small side door opens with a shoulder slam. Inside the cavernous barn, there's a stack of lumber on one side, next to a radial saw circled by a narrow band of sawdust. Harkness walks closer, picks up a pinch of sawdust and smells it, finding it almost scentless, resin dried. Work on the house stopped months ago, when Dex and his friends found something more profitable to do with their time. Next to the back wall wait a couple of fifty-gallon barrels stuffed with trash.

From outside, the barn ends with a row of high windows, but inside it's windowless, the white drywall quilted with nail-gun dents. Even a quick look shows that the barn's shorter on the inside than the outside. He walks to the white wall and feels along it for some kind of door, but finds nothing. The sawdust is tracked with dozens of footprints. Harkness shoves one barrel of trash and it glides across the floor. The other is locked to the floor with an unlikely set of brass nautical latches. He unfastens them and pushes the barrel aside, lifting a heavy wooden hatch to reveal wooden stairs that lead down into darkness.

In the light from his cell phone, Harkness climbs down the stairs, walks a few feet, then climbs another set of stairs up into the cordoned-off end of the barn, where a bright room waits. Beneath blazing overhead lights, an intricate maze of glass tubes rises like coral from steel flasks and plastic drums. The droplets turn from clear to amber as they traverse the intricate apparatus. The room is filled with the low burbling of fermentation and distillation and the hiss of burners.

Harkness has seen dozens of meth labs in backyards and back bedrooms, each jiggered together with duct tape, soda bottles, and science hose. But Dex's lab—and he has to assume this is Dex's work—is immaculate and beautiful, a glass reef of pipettes as brilliantly crafted and delicate as a spider's web glowing in morning sunlight. The windows, painted black, shut out the world to create a private universe.

The lab inspires a reverential awe, as if salvation pours from the condensation tank into a half-full Erlenmeyer flask.

On one side of the lab there's a desk with a laptop, a row of colored notebooks, and schematic diagrams pinned to the wall. On the other side wait racks of hundreds of familiar amber vials, some filled and closed, others awaiting the precious syrup. And neatly marked boxes of chemicals, herbs, and other raw materials line the wall.

Harkness looks at the vials for a moment and reaches out to lift the rack and smash it. Instead, he plucks a couple of full vials from the rack and shoves them in his jacket pocket.

He climbs down the stairs and back up into the barn, where he drags the barrel of trash over the opening and locks it down.

His phone vibrates—a text from Thalia tells him Candace and Dex just left the church. Peering outside, he sees the stage builders walking across the field, hammers still in their hands, on the path toward the barn. In the final seconds before he has to slip out the side door and into the woods, Harkness rummages through the trash barrels, looking for insights no digital device could uncover.

Beneath a layer of newspaper waits a jumble of dozens of empty Chinese takeout containers, still crusted with black bean sauce and maggots of old rice.

Each bears the bright red *0* of the Zero Room.

. . .

Late into the night, Harkness sits at the kitchen table, staring at his laptop and sorting through hundreds of Jeet's photos. He's creating a *Greatest Hits* of boldface names from the permeable worlds of Boston crime and politics. Then one inexplicable photo stops him cold.

"Thalia."

"What?" She's painting her toenails on the edge of the bathtub.

"Come here for a second."

"They're wet."

"Walk on your heels."

When she's standing behind him, he zooms in on one section of a photo on a relatively quiet night in the back room of the Zero Room — a couple of strippers down to their thongs and bras; a serious-looking older man with a short gray beard; Mach and his slit-eyed henchmen; a famous chef with perfect hair and his Japanese girlfriend, ragdoll drunk.

"Who's this?" He points out a solitary figure sitting in a booth across from the gray-bearded man.

"Don't you know?"

"Of course I do. I just want to make sure I'm right. Ever see him at the Zero Room?"

"Nope, never did." Thalia walks back to the corner of the loft. "But everyone goes to the Zero Room eventually. It's like a magnet for lost souls."

22

"B ILL THOUGHT OF YOU as the son he never had, you know," says Katherine Munro, an old-style Scottish *mum* with silver hair and pink-flecked skin. She's friendly on the outside, steely on the inside, like a butcher knife sheathed in a knit tea cozy.

"Yes, I do." Harkness perches on a brittle side chair in the Munros' living room, now crowded with flowers and cards, pies and cakes.

"Thought the world of you. Loved his daughters, of course. But Bill was a man's man, as they tend to say."

"Yes, he was." During the first dark months after the BPD put Harkness on administrative leave, the captain invited him to the Munros' simple house for many quiet dinners. With their daughters in college, they were glad to have Harkness for company. Over boiled beef, roast potatoes, and good whiskey, they talked about Nagog — how the farmers were dying off and the developers swooping in, how they hoped that the town would never really change no matter how much new money arrived.

"You've been talking to Sergeant Dabilis, yes?"

"A nice enough man," she says. "But a bumbler."

"Can't argue with that, Mrs. Munro. He told me I'm not allowed to talk to you. Or even come here this evening."

"Why not? You're a friend of the family. All of Bill's closest friends have come around. It's what you do when someone . . . when someone passes."

"Sergeant Dabilis is running the investigation and I'm supposed to stay completely clear."

Mrs. Munro puts down her teacup to clatter in its saucer. "He's already making a mess of it."

"How?"

"Showed me some . . . papers . . . some old electronic mails supposedly sent to him from William. They were truly disturbing. And they didn't sound at all like Bill. After thirty years of marriage, I know what my husband sounds like."

Harkness knows how simple it would be to backdate fake e-mails and make them look like they came from the captain. Even Sergeant Dabilis could do it. "What were they about?"

"About how he hated his life, and how he was desperately in need of more money."

"Really?"

"Now, that last part might have a grain of truth in it, Edward. Look around here." She waves at the simple room. "It's not like we're living in luxury. But we certainly get by."

Harkness notes the slip. They got by. Now, everything is less certain.

"William was not a man who indulged in appetites and sin," Mrs. Munro says. "Not liquor, fancy food, gambling, other women. Beyond his family, his work was what he loved and held dear. You know that. He was a leader."

"Of course, one of the best," Harkness says.

"Everyone carries something with them as they make their way through the world—something they want but can't have, or a disappointment over something that never came to pass," she says. "But he bore his small burdens well."

"Gracefully, even," Harkness says.

"So I don't believe that he killed himself, not for a moment," she says. "None of us do. He was a good Catholic and a devoted husband and father. Not the kind to just go out some night and throw himself off a bridge."

"Not at all," Harkness says.

"Only selfish men commit something as irresponsible and cruel as suicide," Mrs. Munro says. "He wasn't a selfish man."

An ancient telephone wire, painted into the ceiling molding, winds along the edge of the room. Harkness traces its progress and thinks about the conversations that once coursed through it — the captain calling to say good night to his young daughters, the captain taking important calls from headquarters. Not desperate calls, not late-night rants or early-morning lies.

"I'm sorry." Mrs. Munro reaches over and puts her soft hand over his. "I meant nothing by that last remark, Edward. Your father wasn't selfish, I'm sure."

"Actually, he was," Harkness says. "That and a lot of other things, some good, some bad. Like everyone."

"Yes, like everyone." Mrs. Munro's eyes shine with loss and anger. "The dead can't tell us what they were thinking. That's the terrible part of it, Edward. I have so many questions for Bill and I don't know who to ask."

"I know that feeling."

"I'm sure you do," she says. "Anyone who's lost someone close to them is left with unfinished business."

Harkness shifts the conversation gently. "I was surprised to hear Captain Munro had health problems, ma'am."

"What problems?"

"Didn't he have some kind of leukemia?"

Mrs. Munro shakes her head. "No, Bill was very healthy. Never missed a day at work. Always got a clean bill of health at the doctor's. I would know. I always accompanied him to make sure he actually went to his annual checkup. He hated doctors almost as much as lawyers."

"Sorry, I must have heard wrong," Harkness says.

Mrs. Munro stands and straightens her black dress. She walks into the kitchen and returns carrying a thick white envelope with Harkness's name written on the front in the captain's familiar, precise hand. "I found this in his desk," she says. "I'm assuming it's some kind of police business."

Harkness takes the envelope. "I'm sure it is," he says. "Thank you."

"If you hear anything at the station, anything I should know, I hope you'll pass it along to me," she says. "I don't have electronic mail, but I think you know where you can find me." She smiles. "Somewhere between this house and Saint Michael's Parish."

"I hope you'll let me help out in any way that I can, Mrs. Munro."

Harkness stands. "I loved the captain. I really did. From when I was just a boy."

"Of course, Edward," she says, then stops. "I believe there's one way that you could help honor his memory. One that could ease the burden of his passing."

"What would that be, ma'am?"

Mrs. Munro's hand tightens on his and she pulls him close. He smells whiskey and toothpaste.

"Find whoever drowned my husband, Edward. Hunt him down and make him pay. Without an ounce of mercy."

. . .

The floorboards creak as Harkness paces around the loft.

"Nothing you can do can get Mach to call tonight," Thalia says. "I left a message that said we knew he had your gun and we were ready to deal. But he does whatever he wants, whenever he wants."

Harkness knows that cases aren't always about action, about breaking down doors and barging into apartments. There are lulls and empty stretches waiting for one piece of data to show up and click into place — though this realization doesn't make the waiting any easier.

Thalia goes to the fridge and pours two iced coffees. "Here, drink this. We can get all wired and stay up all night waiting."

A week ago, she would have been handing him a bottle of whiskey. Harkness welcomes this cleaning up of their act. Thalia is less convinced.

"Got any ideas about how to keep busy until the phone rings?"

Thalia reaches to her shoulders to push the straps of her dress to the side. The dress falls to her feet like a stage scrim to reveal her breasts and the auburn delta between her pale, strong legs.

"May not be that original," she says. "But it definitely passes the time."

When Thalia's cell phone finally rings, gray morning light is already filtering through the loft's tall windows. She jumps up from the futon and stalks across the dark loft.

She sits at the kitchen table and shouts in what sounds like

Hmong to Harkness. The only words in English are *motherfucker* and *douchebag*.

Thalia clicks the phone closed.

"You speak Hmong?"

She nods. "Mach taught me a little on slow nights at the bar."

Harkness sits next to her. "What'd he say?"

"Says he'll think about selling your gun back to you."

"Think about it?"

"It's just his way of starting the negotiations."

Negotiating with a grudge-holding sociopath is a challenge, one that Harkness would rather tackle himself. But only Thalia can get through to Mach. She's an insider — though how much of one isn't clear.

"What does he want?"

Thalia shakes her head. "Wouldn't say. Wants us to make an offer."

"Any ideas?"

"Fitzgerald and his chums were willing to pay ten grand for it just to fuck with you," Thalia says. "Now Mach's going to want even more."

Harkness closes his eyes. His Glock is worth about seven hundred dollars without the extortion bonus. "That's crazy."

"Besides a lot of cash, Mach wants Jeet's photos — prints, files, everything."

"Surprise." Somewhere in Dorchester, mayoral candidate John Fitzgerald is sweating Guinness.

"So what do you think he'd take?"

Thalia shakes her head. "I don't know, Eddy. What does it matter? We don't have that kind of cash."

Harkness walks to the refrigerator and pulls open the freezer door. He reaches his hand behind the bag of flour and the ice trays, then tosses the frost-rimed Apple Store bag on the table.

"What the fuck is this?"

"My offshore bank account."

"Really, Eddy."

"You don't want to know," Harkness says. "And I don't want to tell you."

Thalia opens the bag and flips through the stacks of cash. "Jesus, Eddy. That's a lot of cash."

"Depends on how you look at it," he says. "Tourists drop that on a couple of handbags and dinner on Newbury Street."

"We could get the hell out of Boston." Thalia's eyes widen. "Move to New York and start over. Think about it."

"I have, believe me."

"Might be a smart move." Thalia lights a cigarette, her last remaining vice, as far as Harkness can tell. Besides the occasional lie. "Maybe we should short him and keep some of the money."

"We're just going to make him an offer, pay him, and be done with it."

"Mach isn't just going to take your money and hand you your gun. He doesn't work that way. He hates *obvious*. He's always working a second angle. Maybe a third."

"I know that."

"You think you do."

"So?"

"So we were just at one funeral. And the captain's is coming up. I don't want you to end up like him."

"I don't intend to."

"Neither did he."

23

L EE SQUINTS AT the two tapes on the counter in front of him. "Wow, this is like audio archaeology, Eddy. Analog media. These tapes ought to be in a museum." They're sitting in Lee's office in the back of the empty Nagog Five and Ten.

"Look like little cassette tapes to me." The two tapes were the only contents of the white envelope that Mrs. Munro gave Harkness.

"The one on the right is a microcassette." Lee points. "The one on the left is a minicassette."

"What's the difference?"

"I think one format may have been more popular than the other," Lee says. "But I honestly don't know which one. Maybe one was for answering machines back in the day. Not sure. Do you ever think about all the information on cassette tapes that's just going to get lost forever — mix tapes dudes made for their girlfriends, interviews, messages?"

Harkness pauses. "Not really."

"I do." Lee's eyes turn a little misty. "I mean, what if you never heard these tapes? Would it matter?"

"I don't know, Lee. I have no idea what's on them," Harkness says. "That's why I came here."

"Maybe you never will. Let me see what we have for tape players." Lee disappears into the storeroom.

Harkness stares at the tapes.

Lee rushes back with a package so old that the plastic has turned opaque. He tears it open to reveal a gray plastic tape player. "This one's mini. From like 1994 or something, Eddy. I can probably find a micro player on eBay."

"Thanks."

"But for now, let's see if this works." Lee opens up the hidden cavity in the cassette player and presses in two thin batteries.

Eddy hands him the tape.

Lee clicks it in place, pauses for a moment, and presses PLAY.

Harkness startles when he hears Captain Munro's familiar voice, distant and tinny, come through the speaker.

For Edward Harkness upon the occasion of my . . . death.

Captain Munro pauses, stopped cold when he realizes that the words he's saying will outlive him, like an echo. Then he continues.

In 1981 I met Anne Harkness, a school principal, and fell in love with her. She was beautiful, vivacious, intelligent. And we were both married to other people.

Lee clicks the tape player off. "Eddy, Anne Harkness is your mother, right?"

Harkness nods. "Right."

"This sounds pretty personal, Eddy. Maybe you should just take it home and listen to it."

"Why?"

"Just want to make sure I'm, you know, respecting your privacy."

"I don't care, Lee. We've known each other since . . .''

"Third grade, Mrs. Pettengill," he says.

"Right. If I can't trust you, I can't trust anyone." Harkness reaches over to press PLAY. "Anyway, I hate secrets."

In time, our relationship grew closer and closer. We became . . . intimate in 1982, and in 1983, Anne gave birth to my son, though I couldn't claim him as my own. I am recording this tape to register my shame at bringing a child into the world that I could not acknowledge until now, after my death. And to tell you, Edward, as I should have so many years ago, that . . . you are my son. I almost told you hundreds of times. But Anne forbade me to. Red suspected but never knew. And it would have broken Katherine's heart and destroyed my family. So it remained a secret, revealed now by my death. Don't be angry at me. Just know that I loved you as much as I could, given the unusual circumstances of our . . .

Now Harkness shuts off the tape. The captain's words slow time and make the air feel close and under pressure, as if the store has dropped suddenly to the ocean floor.

"Wow, Eddy. Do you think it's true?"

"Makes perfect sense," he says.

It explains why the captain always seemed to be around, keeping an eye on him as a boy, visiting his mother. It explains why his father played Harkness and George against each other like pit bulls. Red must have known, in some way, that his second son was his in name, but not by birth. And it explains why, when no one in hardhearted Boston would show him any kindness, the captain invited him back to Nagog, a homecoming motivated by love, Harkness realizes only now, too late to return it.

"Thanks, Lee. Look . . . I got to get to work." He picks up the tape player and the second tape and barges out of the store, leaving Lee sitting dazed in the back room.

·   ·   ·

Watt shuffles around the slab, hands jammed in the pockets of his leather jacket.

Harkness closes the squad car door and walks toward Watt. "You okay?"

Watt nods. His brow is visibly furrowed, parallel lines marking the pale skin of his forehead beneath his buzzcut. He looks like a glowing human question mark.

"Want to talk about it?"

"About what?"

"Whatever's bugging you."

"The captain," Watt says finally. "I know you were his friend and all, so don't get all freaked out."

"Okay." The captain was much more than a friend, but this news will remain a secret.

"He didn't kill himself, Eddy. I mean, everyone knows that. It's not exactly rocket surgery."

Harkness puts his hand on Watt's elbow and leads him over to the far edge of the slab, out of sight of the station. "Something else you want to get off your chest?"

"Yeah."

Watt huddles close, his breath steaming in the cold morning air. "Sergeant Dabilis and the captain were getting payoffs from someone, maybe at that drug lab you've been checking out. Captain tried to stop it, maybe he started to feel guilty, maybe . . ."

Harkness just stares. "Watt, I got to tell you, I'm surprised."

"Surprised about what's going on or surprised that I know about it?"

"Little of both."

"You're not the only one who pays attention, Eddy," Watt says. "They call me Forty Watt and Blinky and give me a hard time and all. But I've been staying late and digging into Dabilis's files. And I can tell you this — the guy is definitely not on the straight and narrow."

"Why're you doing this, Watt?

"What?"

"Messing with your superior officer. Doing freelance investigating — the kind that can get you fired."

"I like this town a lot."

"So do I, Watt. Maybe too much."

"There's worse things than giving a shit, Eddy."

"That's right." Harkness pauses for a moment. "Watt, given what you already know, I think you need to know about a side project I'm working on out at the Old Nagog Tavern."

"Sure, Eddy. What?"

Harkness leans over and tells him.

24

HARKNESS IS ON FOOT patrol along Main Street when a red Porsche convertible glides by with its top down.

"Hey, hey, hey." A stranger in cargo pants and a white T-shirt grabs Harkness's arm and steps into the street to get a better look. "Know who that was?"

"I don't even know who you are."

"It's me . . . Thom. Henry David Thoreau? Citizen Garrett?"

"Oh yeah," Harkness says. "Sorry, Thom. Didn't recognize you in civilian clothes. So who was that guy in the nice car?"

"Seth Braeburn." Thom whispers the name like an incantation.

"Never heard of him."

Thom pulls off his Ray-Bans. "The Dark Prince of Biotech?"

"Got nothing," Harkness says.

"Started out at Google. Now he's doing biotech venture capital—investing in stuff that's way out on the edge. Enhanced LED lights that beam down antidepressants. 3D printers that make human cells. Can't believe he's here in Nagog."

"Can't believe *you're* here in Nagog," Harkness says. "Didn't I throw you in jail?"

"They let me out when I sobered up."

"Sorry to hear it." Harkness waves Thom back onto the sidewalk. "Aren't you supposed to be wearing a costume?"

"Aren't you supposed to be emptying meters?"

Harkness says nothing. His Taser is in the trunk of the squad car, parked blocks away. Otherwise it might be touching Thom's soft places.

Thom follows Harkness down the street. "Sorry, sorry," he says. "I'm kind of an asshole. Even without Third Rail. Can't help it."

"Maybe you should try a little harder." Thom's the human equivalent of a cover band, familiar and annoying. "So who are you today?"

"I'm not reenacting." Thom raises an eyebrow. "I'm enacting. I'm in the moment, experiencing history in real time."

"That sounds like grad-student talk. Why don't you just call it living?"

"Doesn't sound as impressive."

"So watching a biotech celebrity drive by in a convertible qualifies as experiencing history?"

"Why not? We'd be watching General Gage on a white horse back in 1770. Same diff. History's just whatever people manage to remember." Thom's digging in his backpack. "Here! This should clue you in." He hands Harkness a dog-eared copy of *Wired*. Seth Braeburn stares from the cover, a tangle of fiberoptic cables running from his forehead. The headline screams NEW FRONTIERS OF COGNITIVE PHARMA. Below it, the byline reads *Dr. Lauren North*. Harkness remembers walking through Boston, mind racing on Third Rail. Part of him wants to do it again.

"The guy's a freakin' genius," Thom says.

"No doubt," Harkness says. "Must be in town for the big smarty party."

"Headless at Freedom Farm? Everyone's going to be there."

"Except you, right? Because you're not doing drugs anymore, smart or otherwise, remember?"

Thom looks away. "Right."

School's out early and the streets are packed with young kids diving for candy along the parade route and teenagers wandering around in awkward packs. Salem has its witches. Concord has the Shot Heard 'Round the World. Nagog has Headless Hallows Eve, the town's annual parade, a warm-up act for Halloween, still a couple of days away.

Vintage cars pass — two-tone turquoise Chevys, ancient black

Fords, and Elvis-worthy Cadillacs — each with a gray-haired driver. They're followed by every citizen with a micron of Native American blood, wrapped in furs and beating drums. This crew is all but drowned out by the Nagog Minutemen, who march behind them with fifes and drums, faces drawn and stoic, as if they're facing a line of redcoats. Their costumes are flawless, billowing linen shirts and brown woolen trousers buttoned at the ankles over high leather boots. Not a spot of battlefield dirt on these sanitized soldiers.

The soldiers stop and shift their muskets from one shoulder to the other in unison. They aim at the cloudless sky. Their leader raises his arm and shouts. When he lowers his arm, the muskets crack. Babies cry, kids cover their ears, and Harkness's hand jerks toward the handle of his plastic pistol. He lowers his arm to his side and walks on.

Nine decapitated redcoats march in bloodied outfits, each holding his head in front of him. The younger kids in the crowd start crying when they see the sprouting cords from their severed necks, gleaming glass eyes rolling back in their heads, and blood dripping from leaf-matted hair.

A smoke-sodden, ragged Colonial woodsman steps forward and shouts, revealing blackened teeth, "Have ye heard the Legend of Nine Men's Misery?"

"No!" The crowd shouts, though of course they have. It's been part of Nagog history for hundreds of years.

The woodsman unfolds a piece of parchment to tell the tale they've all been waiting to hear.

"After the Battle of Concord, a group of nine young redcoats found themselves lost in the Nagog Woods, unsure of which direction might lead them to Boston town. There came no word from these soldiers for many weeks. Then nine heads and eighteen hands washed up in the town mill, a bloody gift from the forest. *In the trackless wilderness nine men found their fame, their red coats gone, heads and hands the same.* These are the words of the dark bard Nathaniel Hawthorne."

The woodsman bends down to point at the kids. "No one knows who butchered them. Some say minutemen. Some say Indians. Others say the angry spirits of the forest rose up to join the battle.

Just remember this, young friends, to avoid their misery. *When all seems lost, ye must keep your head about you.*" He gives a maniacal grin and walks on with his headless charges trudging in front of him.

With palpable relief, the crowd turns its attention to a squad of realtors doing synchronized briefcase drills, followed by a tae kwon do class side kicking its way down Main Street.

Dabilis leans against a light pole across the street. He raises his hand to his mouth and Harkness's radio crackles. "Officer Harkness, get moving. Up and down the whole parade route. The meters are waiting."

"I emptied Main Street this morning," he says.

"Empty it again."

Harkness unloads the coin transfer unit from his squad car and pushes it along the crowded street. Sergeant Dabilis just wants to embarrass him in front of the entire town. It's worse than being in the *Nagog Journal* police blotter.

Harkness thinks that this may be the moment when he stops being a cop. He could toss his badge on the ground and walk. But letting Dabilis chase him away would be more than humiliating. Harkness keeps walking down the street, asking kids to move over so he can get to the meters. Meager handfuls of change rattle down the craw of the transfer unit. And all along the parade route, the citizens of Nagog watch his progress, their stares loaded with varying amounts of pity and scorn.

Harkness glimpses Candace between rows of marching bands and gymnasts, stroller brigades and veterans. She smiles, raises one of May's tiny hands, and waves it.

Harkness sidles up to the next meter. Candace looks away.

Further down Main, Harkness sees Dex, Mouse, and their friends sprawled on the sidewalk and staring at the parade, not with openeyed astonishment, just the gleaming eyes of Third Rail. Outliers among the children and families, they look out of place away from their laptops. They laugh as the oldest veterans hobble past. They stare when the town manager's white Cadillac glides by, escorted by six motorcycle cops.

Dex and his friends aren't impressed or amused by anything as hokey as a small-town parade. They're just waiting for their party to start.

The parade ends, the balloon vendors and roasted chestnut carts move on, and the town cleanup crew starts sweeping the streets. His shift almost over, Harkness pushes the coin transfer unit toward his squad car.

"Hey!" Candace pushes May's stroller with the determination of a marathon runner. "Saw you . . ."

"Emptying meters?"

"Yeah," she says. "Doesn't look like much fun."

"Don't knock it till you try it," Harkness says. "Did May like the parade?"

"Every kid likes a parade. Even if it's kind of creepy," Candace says, then closes her eyes and starts to sob.

"Hey, what's wrong?"

"Everything." She holds up her hand and pulls herself together.

"May looks happy. So something's going right."

"Don't make me count my fucking blessings, Eddy," Candace says quietly. "I know I'm lucky. It's just . . ."

"What?"

"Our house has like twenty people crammed in it. A French neuro-scientist who asks annoying questions all night and complains about the food. This skinny Australian photographer who takes hundreds of Polaroids of herself naked in the woods and calls it art. Anyone with a PhD and no fucking clue."

This sounds like good news to Harkness. If these are the kind of people going to Headless at Freedom Farm, it might turn out more like a TED conference than a drug fest.

"I'm a waitress, Eddy. This time to a bunch of smarty-pants. And I got to tell you, the tips suck. Dex is acting like a boy bridezilla right now. He could freak at any minute."

"This party of his, it's tomorrow night?"

Candace nods.

"Be careful," Harkness says. "Halloween always gets weird around here."

"You talking about more than smashed pumpkins?"

"Right," he says. "Never know what people will do given the chance."

Candace moves closer. "These people at the house? They don't have babies. They don't know what life is really like. They're thirty and they're still in school. They listen to electronica shit. Their entire lives are in ironic quotes. They're serious about nothing. And I hate Dex for inviting them all to camp out like his stupid party is the next Woodstock or something."

Harkness just shakes his head. With free Third Rail, the party's not going to be about peace, love, and understanding.

"I'm really worried," she says quietly. "These are smart people, Eddy, but fucked up. They think they know everything, but they don't know anything."

"I'll keep an eye on the party."

"Thank you." Candace leans forward and kisses Harkness on the cheek, then backs away. "Sorry, forgot you were a cop for a minute."

"That's okay, so did I."

"I think you may be the only person I trust in this whole town."

Harkness tries to think of what to say, something reassuring. But finding the right words is a struggle when Candace is around. And by the time they come to him, she's already walking down Elm, pushing May's stroller with her good hand.

25

THE BOATHOUSE IS CLOSED for the season, front gate padlocked, the chain-link fence cold on his fingers as Harkness climbs over it and walks to the stack of canoes and kayaks on the dock. He picks out a kayak and eases the bow slowly into the Nagog River.

Minutes later he's gliding along, the full moon glimmering on the dark water, low wisps of fog lofting from its surface as the night cools. Starting in the west as a wild, narrow creek, the Nagog widens and slows in the inland marshes west of town until its current is almost imperceptible. The same slow current carried the dugout canoes of the Wampanoags and Micmacs, brought the hands and heads of Nine Men's Misery floating into Nagog, and bore the bloated body of Captain Munro to the town mill.

The river takes what it's given.

After a few minutes in the kayak, Harkness sees the back of the familiar white saltbox with its plastic-covered windows gliding into view — once the Old Nagog Tavern, now Freedom Farm.

From this angle, Harkness can see a deck jutting out toward the river. It's crowded with bulging black trash bags, stacks of newspapers, and bicycles tossed in a jumbled heap.

Setting his paddle down carefully, Harkness reaches into the inside pocket of his leather jacket for the metal case. He cracks it open, takes out the digital wiretap, and points it at the cables running along the eaves of the house. In a few moments, dozens of computer screens flicker into view, stacked up like a game of solitaire.

Harkness jumps from screen to screen, looking for any shred of evidence that might link Dex to the death of Captain Munro. In the story that he tells himself, Captain Munro came to the house to tell Dex and his friends to get out. Unable to stop himself, Dex or one of his crew attacked the captain, knocked him out, then threw him off the back porch into the river to float down to the town mill.

But there's a second explanation. Maybe the captain just came to the house to get his "rent," only to be told that another cop had already collected it. The captain accused Dex of lying and threatened him. Amped up on Third Rail, Dex and his friends shoved the captain into the river and held him under the tea-colored water.

In this version, Harkness plays a role in his father's death, a possibility that he can't even consider.

Either way, it seems likely that Dex and his friends killed the captain. With Sergeant Dabilis running the show and Detective Ramble investigating, truth and justice will be hard to find. All Harkness wants now is revenge.

Ten minutes of going from screen to screen tells Harkness that Headless at Freedom Farm is going to be more than a backyard keg party. The comments stream:

> JACCUSE: *Who's comin?*
> DX1: *Everyone.*
> JACCUSE: *Costumes?*
> DX1: *Course.*
> JACCUSE: *Liquid inspiration?*
> DX1: *Buckets of it.*

Harkness reads on, the chatter reminding him of high school guys trying to lure girls to a party in the woods. Mouse turns confident online, more like a handsome frat boy than a pocket-sized drug dealer. Dex claims that Headless at Freedom Farm will be a *night that will change everyone's life forever.*

———

162

Dex's friends spill out of the house. It takes powerful detection software to spot the digital wiretap, but Freedom Farm has it now. They're staring up at the cluster of cable boxes and satellite dishes on the roof. Harkness puts the wiretap down. Before he can put his paddle in the water, he senses someone staring. Dex stands on the deck behind the house, lit by moonlight. He's wearing jeans and a rumpled white shirt. He's too far away to see Harkness in his black sweatshirt, but he can tell someone's out there. Dex starts throwing plastic chairs from the deck out into the river.

Harkness takes a full stroke along one side of the kayak, and then the other. At the sound of churning water, Dex jumps off the deck into the weeds and disappears. Harkness is already slipping down the river, each stroke moving him further from the house. Being spotted doing surveillance is bad enough; that tonight's visit is illegal makes it even worse. Harkness doesn't want to explain what he's doing on the river with an expensive wiretap and no warrant.

Harkness turns to take a last look behind him. Dex is dragging a canoe down to the riverbank like a crazed fisherman. The moonlight flashes from the canoe's aluminum sides as he tosses it into the river and jumps in. Harkness smiles. Despite Dex's chemical enthusiasm, Harkness is already far ahead, and in a sleek kayak instead of a clunky canoe. He digs in to put even more distance between them.

The kayak sails by empty swimming docks and glimmers of headlights from the river road. Ahead, luminous moonlight falls on white church spires and the clock tower of the town mill. Harkness turns when he hears water splashing and heavy breathing. Dex paddles so hard that every stroke raises a whirlpool. He's barely sitting in the stern seat. He curves forward like a pale, skinny claw or an ambitious letter *C* reaching out his paddle on one side, then the other. He's moving down the river at motorboat speed, coming close enough to recognize Harkness.

When all seems lost, ye must keep your head about you.

Harkness veers to the left to take the kayak down the narrow branch of the river that leads into town instead of the wider channel that leads back to the boathouse. He knows this stretch of river from when he and George used to float down the old millrace on hot summer days, gliding through the ancient wooden tunnel that runs under the town to the mill. They pushed their faces up into the rot-scented air at the top of the millrace, shouting the whole way to keep away the fear, then emerged screaming in the sunlight on the other side of town.

A cluster of lights at the edge of town comes closer but Dex is right behind him, breathing as hard and loud as a marathon runner.

High water from fall rain leaves only a sliver of air between the river and the top of the millrace, just enough room so Harkness can slip under. But the water's too high for Dex and his canoe. Harkness takes a final stroke, then leans back as far as he can.

He enters the dark tunnel flat on his back, face up and still, eyes locked open. All Harkness hears is his rasping breathing as he floats under the town in the dark. He reaches up to grab the ceiling and urge the kayak through the black tunnel, but something cold and slimy writhes beneath his fingers. He pulls his hand back and the kayak ricochets off one wall, then another. He can't tell where he is. The kayak should have come out on the other side of Main Street already. But he's still staring at the rotting underside of his hometown.

A spider web brushes his face, and Harkness claws at the stale air above him. He's floated down a hidden channel. Or there's chicken wire blocking the far end of the millrace. He stops himself from rolling the kayak into the cold river and swimming back upstream. He takes a deep breath and waits.

When he opens his eyes, the kayak has emerged from the millrace and floats under the Main Street Bridge, where Dex stands, holding a cinderblock over his head.

Their eyes connect. Dex's gaze narrows. He gives a dismissive shake of his head, like a clever boy losing interest in a simple game. "This is for my mother," he shouts down, then hurls the cinderblock.

Harkness dodges to the right and the cinderblock smashes the kayak, clipping off the last couple of feet of the bow. The kayak lurches and slips underwater with the digital wiretap and his other gear, dumping Harkness into the cold river. He's dragged downstream, swept under, sucking in mouthfuls of sour water.

Opening his eyes in the murky river, current holding him down like a vengeful hand, Harkness knows what the captain felt in his last moments. From underwater, the streetlights look like distant stars and Harkness fights his way toward them, rising and clawing for anything to hold on to. He catches hold of a rusted metal ladder bolted into the waterway's rock walls and pulls himself up, sputtering and coughing.

He climbs up to the street. Dex is gone. Parents walk their children through town, trying out their costumes before Halloween. They don't pay any attention to a sodden cop in SWAT team gear bent over on the sidewalk, spitting out water. They just walk on.

Anything can happen in Nagog on Headless Hallows Eve.

.   .   .

They're counting out twenties on the wide, dusty floorboards of the loft long after midnight. While Harkness was floating on the river, then under it, Thalia was shouting into her cell phone like a telemarketer trying every angle. In the end, Mach took their offer. If they bring him twenty thousand dollars in cash tomorrow at noon, along with all of Jeet's photos, he'll give Harkness his gun back. To Harkness, it sounds like a good deal. They count the money, bundle it up, and put it in Harkness's red gym bag, emptied of baseballs.

"Don't even think of shorting Mach," Thalia says. "He'll chase you down if he finds twenty bucks missing."

"Why would I even think about that?" Harkness says. "You're the one who wanted to keep a little money for ourselves."

"Well, now I don't. He sounded ever scarier than usual."

"Doesn't matter." Harkness snaps a rubber band around a stack of cash and throws it in the bag. "It's simple. He has my gun and we're getting it back."

"So what happens then?"

"What do you mean?"

"You moving back into your old apartment?" Thalia looks up with smeary eyes. The smell of breath mints gives her away—she's been drinking at McCloskey's down in the square.

"No."

"Good. I don't want to think you were just staying here . . . you know, to look for your gun."

"You know me better than that." Harkness wonders why Thalia's drinking again. But he knows the answer. A meeting with Mach is enough to send anyone backsliding.

"Maybe."

165

"Things are going to get a lot better soon, promise."

"I hate promises," she says.

"Let's just get through our field trip to Chinatown tomorrow and take it from there."

Thalia says nothing. When she's painting, Thalia doesn't hear her phone ringing or Harkness talking to her. Now she's working with the same focus and attention. Her red hair dangles in graceful strands as she counts the cash, stacks it, and slips rubber bands from her narrow wrist to hold it together.

What holds them together remains unstated and unexplored tonight. It might be love or desperation. They wouldn't be the first to confuse the two.

He needs Thalia tomorrow in Chinatown. That Mach still has a soft spot for her gives them some protection, but it's not clear how much. For all Harkness knows, his slippery girlfriend's cut a side deal.

"I'm worried you're gonna get killed, Eddy," Thalia blurts out. "I had a completely real dream about it last night. All this blood . . ." She holds up her hand and turns her eyes toward the dusty floorboards.

"That's not going to happen," Harkness says.

Harkness sits at the kitchen table with his laptop in front of him. It's late, the ill-defined hours between night and day when most of the city sleeps. He clicks on the inexplicable photo and studies it like a crime scene, then picks up his cell phone.

"What, Eddy." George's voice is low and tired.

"Thought you might want to head down to Chinatown," Harkness says. "You know, go to some dive bar for some drinks and a bowl of *phô.*"

"Some what?"

"Vietnamese noodles."

"Are you drunk, Eddy?"

"No. Haven't had a drop. I'm back to Straight Ed again."

"Then why are you calling me in the middle of the night to ask me about some kind of noodles I never heard of?"

"Oh, you've heard of them," Eddy says. "I'm looking at a picture of you right now, sitting in a *phô* place with some friends. Zero Room, heard of it? Located at Zero Beach Street in Chinatown. There's a bowl right in front of you. And a bunch of criminals all around you."

The phone goes quiet except for George's slow breathing.

"Shit, Eddy. Where'd you get that?"

"Guy I know."

"Get rid of it, bro. Please."

"Tell me what you were doing there."

"Take a look at that photo. I think you'll see a guy with gray hair and glasses sitting somewhere near me."

"Yeah."

"That's District Court Judge Jack Callahan," George says. "I went to that shitty bar right before our bankruptcy hearing to slip that asshole five thousand bucks cash."

"Why?"

"He told me I had to. Said otherwise he'd hold us to sixty cents on the dollar. Or worse, shut down the company."

"So you were on a family mercy mission?"

"I'm not proud of paying him off, Eddy. Not at all."

"You shouldn't be."

"Everyone does something that they shouldn't," George says. "That night was my mistake. Tell me that you're getting rid of the picture. You're my brother, Eddy."

Harkness stops himself from correcting George. After the captain's confession, they're half-brothers, but that distinction hardly matters now. He deletes the photo. "It's gone, George."

"Thanks."

"But from here on in, you're on the straight and narrow, right?"

"No worries. I'm not following in Dad's footsteps, Eddy."

"Neither am I." Harkness clicks the phone off and stares across the loft at the red gym bag stuffed with cash.

26

THE OLD HANCOCK BUILDING rises off to the left, a stalwart gray office building upstaged by its taller, flashier brother, the mirrored Hancock Tower, more Miami than Boston. Harkness remembers the rhyme about the lights at the top.

"*Steady blue, clear view,*" he says. "*Flashing blue, clouds due. Steady red, rain ahead. Flashing red, snow instead.*"

"What?" Thalia rouses in the passenger seat of the battered tan Chevy Malibu that Harkness requisitioned from Narco-Intel.

"The weather, according to the Old Hancock Building."

"Oh." Thalia stares out at the Boston skyline like she's never noticed it before.

"When the Sox finally won the Series, both lights flashed for the first time. *Flashing blue and red, when the Curse of the Bambino is dead!*"

"Well, that won't be happening any time soon, will it?" Thalia puts her hand on Harkness's shoulder. "I mean, what lights go on when the Sox have the worst season ever?"

"I think all the lights stay off," Harkness says. "All I know is the light is red now, so it's going to rain. The Hancock never lies."

A storm's on its way, the first nor'easter of the fall, the one weathermen love to announce, sending the city running to the supermarkets and liquor stores to hoard.

Harkness pulls the Chevy past the fancy end of Newbury Street, where tourists are buying dresses that cost more than most mortgage payments. Harkness is on his way to buy his own gun back from a human trafficker with stacks of cash he took from a drug dealer. He smiles at the irony, but only for a moment.

They wind through what used to be the Combat Zone, past the site of the Liberty Tree, now a plaque on the side of the Department of Motor Vehicles. They pass crooked streets Harkness walked as a boy, then as a young punk, and finally as a cop. Each corner is laden with memories, but he's not delving into history this morning. He's looking forward.

Thalia's phone rings. "It's Marnie," she says.

"Let your freaky little friend know we're about to get my gun back," Harkness says. "In case she wants to steal it again."

Thalia clicks open her phone. "Call you back later," she says, then closes her phone.

"Arranging for a little Redbird to celebrate if we survive?"

"Don't start."

"Marnie's got problems, Thalia. Big ones. You sure you want her around?"

"What about your fat brother? He's mean and jealous. You sure you want him around?"

"Good point," Harkness says. "But he's my brother. So caring about him isn't optional."

"Everything's optional."

They drive into Chinatown in silence, past community housing, tiny stores, sidewalks crowded with grim-faced women carrying bulging plastic bags, stocking up before the storm.

"Been reading about the mayoral race," Thalia says.

"Didn't know you followed politics."

"Only when it might mean something to us."

"To us?"

"Yeah, like you and me."

Harkness doesn't take the bait. "Look, all we have to think about now is paying Mach, getting my gun, and not getting killed."

Thalia shrugs. "Thought you might want to know that Fitzgerald's way ahead in the polls."

"His campaign manager could get a dead dog elected."

"Now that his friend's on the way up, Mach's going to be even more cocky. We got to be really careful, Eddy."

"We're being careful."

"Not enough." Thalia reaches into her purse and pulls out a silver handgun, chrome peeling from its stubby, scratched barrel. "Thought this might help."

"Where the hell did you get that?" Harkness looks back and forth between the street and Thalia's gun. It looks like a Saturday night special with its barrel cut even shorter with a hacksaw.

"Bought it from Woo-Derek."

"Your man in the orange jacket? Neighborhood choirboy and arms dealer?"

"Yeah, him."

"Why?"

"You're smart and all, Eddy," she says, "but guys like Mach don't just make a deal and shake on it, then do what they said they'd do, like fucking Boy Scouts. They want to nail you for good."

"So what exactly do you think you're going to do with that thing?"

"Shoot anyone who tries to hurt you."

"Thanks, I guess," Harkness says. "Do you even know how to handle a gun?"

"Sure."

"You a good shot?"

Thalia shakes her head. "Terrible."

Harrison Avenue is packed with the lunch crowd. Harkness turns on Beach Street and drives past the medicinal herb stores and bakery windows stacked with mooncakes. The crowds thin the further they go. Harkness pulls over when he sees the unlit neon-red *0* hovering above Mr. Mach's Zero Room at the end of a deserted block. They're conspicuous even in the generic Chevy, his favorite undercover car.

"Okay, now what?"

"We're just supposed to wait," Thalia says. "Won't be long. News travels fast."

"Will Mach show?"

"No way," Thalia says. "He'll just send one of his boys."

Harkness scans the empty street, warehouse buildings lining both sides. A car could be waiting in any alley. There could be a lookout or shooter in any window. No street traffic, not that many people on the sidewalks. One way in, one way out. It's about the worst place to make a drop in the entire city.

About the time they start worrying that Mach's not going to show, a tiny woman in a green jacket taps on the window and holds up a paper bag.

Thalia reaches into the back seat for the money.

Harkness rolls down the window. The woman looks a little too authentic, as if she's an actress playing the role of Old Chinese Woman in a movie. "Got something for me?" he says.

She hands him the paper bag.

He opens it and looks inside.

"Your gun in there?" Thalia says.

"Not exactly." A small turtle claws at the sides of the paper bag. Its jade-green shell is painted with red Chinese characters.

"Is very good luck," the woman says. "Only twenty dollars."

"What is it?" Thalia says.

"A turtle."

"Gross." Thalia shudders.

Harkness hands the bag back. "No, thanks."

"Why not? Too 'spensive? Fifteen dollars, then."

"We're too irresponsible to take care of a pet," Harkness explains.

"Is only a turtle."

"And we may be dead soon," Thalia adds.

The woman shrugs and trudges away. Thalia puts the gym bag on the floor and they wait.

Half an hour later, a boy in a thin white T-shirt and baggy pants walks down the street toward them, smiling. He looks about ten years old, carrying a takeout bag loosely in one hand. When he stops next to the car, Thalia rolls down her window.

"Scram, smiley."

He walks around to the other side of the squad car. "Food for you, mister." He hands Harkness the paper bag.

Harkness sets the bag on the seat next to him and rips it open. Inside is a pint takeout container marked with the familiar red *0*. He opens the top to reveal a blue, sticky mass on top of steaming white rice. He lifts it. There's a swath of coarse blue hair on one side, shiny white scalp on the other. Harkness drops it back in the container, presses the paper lid closed, and shoves the whole mess under the seat before Thalia can see it.

"What the hell is that?"

"A message," Harkness says.

"From who?"

". . . Jeet."

"About what?"

"About how we need to be really careful."

The smiling boy is still at his window. He hands Harkness a fortune cookie in a plastic wrapper. Harkness opens it, cracks the cookie, and reads its message:

COMPLIMENTS OF MR. MACH'S ZERO ROOM!

Harkness crumples the slip of paper and tosses it on the floor.

"What'd it say?"

"That today is our very lucky day." Harkness leans across the seat. "Here, take this. And go home. Now." He hands his plastic gun to the boy, a gift to get him out of here.

The boy takes the toy and smiles. He wanders away, shooting the bright disks up at the gray sky. They catch the wind and soar, then rain down on the sidewalk and roll into the gutter.

A thin man with short black hair walks toward the car. He's wearing a shiny gray suit and mirrored aviator shades.

"I know that guy," Thalia says. "Works for Mach. Nervous fucker. Major douche."

When Harkness rolls down the window, Shinyman jams the nose of his automatic inside and starts shouting. "Give me the fucking money!"

Thalia scrambles for the bag.

"Just hold on," Harkness says.

Shinyman's gun shakes in his hands. "Fuck you! Get out. Give me the money!" Shinyman backs up and waves his gun back and forth.

Harkness takes the gym bag from Thalia, opens the door, and steps out onto the street. Shinyman backs up a few steps and steadies his gleaming gun. Harkness walks toward him, one hand in the air, the other holding the gym bag. Tiny versions of Harkness advance in each lens of Shinyman's glasses.

"It's all in here." Harkness waves the red bag like a bullfighter. "Twenty grand. And all the photos. Prints and files. Just like we said. Give me my gun."

Shinyman backs away a little further, swinging his gun from Harkness to Thalia in the car. He reaches in his jacket pocket and takes out a wadded-up paper bag, then bends down to slide it across the sidewalk toward Harkness.

"Now — the money!" Shinyman's waving his gun around.

Harkness picks up the bag and opens it. "Just shut up for a minute, will you?" A Glock 17 sits heavily at the bottom of the bag, barrel up. Harkness grabs it and sees the familiar scratch on the grip. He checks the serial number. It's his. Harkness sticks it in his waistband and pulls his shirt over the grip. He's been waiting for this moment for weeks but now there's no joy in it.

He tosses the gym bag at Shinyman's feet.

"Here you go, scumbag."

Shinyman rips back the zipper and pushes his hand around in the bundles of twenties.

Thalia flies out of the passenger seat and stands on the sidewalk, legs wide, pointing her crappy gun at him. "You got our money. Now get the fuck out of here!"

Shinyman freezes.

"Thalia, I got my gun back," Harkness shouts. "What're you doing?" But she just starts shouting in Hmong.

Shinyman shouts back.

Thalia shouts again.

Harkness can't understand any of it, but it doesn't sound good.

Then Thalia's blasting away, shots echoing in the narrow street. Shinyman's about ten yards away, eyes pressed closed, hugging himself. Thalia hits a store window behind him and it shatters.

Shinyman looks at Harkness, his eyes wide.

Harkness shrugs. He has no idea what his fierce girlfriend is up to.

Thalia squints, takes aim, fires.

Shinyman reaches up to press his hand where his right earlobe used to be, now a slow faucet of blood dripping on the shoulder of his cheap suit. His eyes widen as Thalia aims again, this time with her gun in both hands.

All they can see is Shinyman's narrow back and the red gym bag flailing as he runs down Beach Street.

"Okay. Show's over." Thalia tosses her gun down a sewer grate. "Let's get out of here."

Thalia keeps looking back long after they leave Chinatown.

"You're lucky that guy didn't shoot back."

Thalia turns toward Harkness. "Mach told him not to shoot me."

"How'd you know that?"

"Marnie told me."

"And me?"

"You, he was okay about shooting." Thalia twists to look out the back window.

"It's over, Thalia," Harkness says. "Calm down."

"It's never going to be over, Eddy," she says. "Mach won't let you off the hook."

"We gave him what he wanted."

"No, we didn't." Thalia reaches into the back seat and pulls out a bulging black leather purse. She drags it onto her lap and opens it, revealing the stacks of cash.

Harkness skids the Chevy to a stop in front of Jacob Wirth's, sidewalk tables clotted with tourists eating German food and drinking beer. "What the hell's that?"

"The money."

"What was in that other bag?"

"The box of photos," she says. "And some dummy stacks of cash that I put together last night after you fell asleep. Crisp hundreds on the top and bottom, paper in between. Painted the sides to look like cash. Got to say, they looked real."

"Are you crazy?"

"No, you are, Straight Ed. You were about to give twenty grand to a fucking felon you busted a couple of years back."

"We had a deal with Mach."

"Which means nothing. Mach never forgets. And he never forgives. So I figured, fuck him, we might as well get your gun back and keep the money."

"You knew all along that you were going to rip off Mach?"

She nods. "Pretty much. The guy's a shitbag."

"The guy's a sociopath," Harkness says. "Why didn't you tell me what you were up to?"

Thalia gives Harkness a hard stare. "So you could talk me out of it?"

"Yes."

"I couldn't give him the fucking money," she shouts. "I worked for him for years, Eddy. The guy wraps you around his finger and never lets you go. He'll just keep hitting you up for more. Besides, we need money more than he does. We can leave, Eddy. Go to New York and start over. No more parking meters. No more bars. No more bullshit."

"I can't, Thalia. My mother's got dementia. My sister needs me. My brother, too. You don't just flake on your family when you feel like starting over."

"You don't owe them anything."

"That's not the way I think about it."

"Then wise up, Eddy. You want to be emptying meters in Nagog the rest of your life? Or are you gonna make your move?"

Harkness watches the cars stream past. Much as he loves the city, Boston has jilted him over and over.

"C'mon, let's go," Thalia says. "There's a train to New York in half an hour."

Harkness shakes his head.

"Why not?"

Harkness gives Thalia a truth-inducing stare. "Were you really thinking about both of us when you came up with your big plan? Because I don't think you were."

She looks away. "Of course I was, Eddy. And I can't believe you're mad that I ripped off a guy who sells Thai girls for a living."

"I'm pissed because you keep lying to me."

Thalia's looking at the restaurant, the street — anywhere but at Harkness. "I'm your girlfriend. You got to trust me. I don't fuck just anyone."

"Neither do I."

"I didn't take your gun, Eddy. If that's what you're still worried about. Marnie did it on her lonesome. I had nothing to do with it."

175

Harkness reaches over and opens her door. "Just go, Thalia."

Thalia gets out and slams the door. She stands on the sidewalk, drops of rain in her auburn hair shimmering like mall diamonds.

The tourists turn to watch.

She glares at them. "What?"

"Catch your train. Go to New York," Harkness says. "Or wherever you want to go. This should get you there." He shoves the bulging purse through the open car window.

"Fine, I'm leaving, Eddy." Thalia starts to cry. "And yeah, I'm taking the money. I earned it. I hadn't set up this deal with Mach, you wouldn't even have your gun now. Your troubles are over. You'll be heading back to Boston. Don't need me anymore." She wipes the tears away with her fingertips.

"Quit fucking staring at us," she shouts at the tourists.

Harkness thinks about how easy it would be to tell his devious girlfriend to get back inside.

Thalia leans toward him, her eyes gleaming. "We're not over for good, you know," she says. "Just for now. Anyway, I'm not into the whole straight and narrow thing," she says. "The party hasn't stopped yet. At least for me."

"Never will," Harkness says.

She squints down the street. "My advice? Get out of Boston, Eddy. Or you'll die here. Right on the historic cobble-fucking-stones. Mach'll get you. Or some drug dealer you pissed off. Doesn't matter how it happens. Dead is dead."

Thalia backs up and waves to the tourists before turning back to Harkness. She smiles. "See you 'round, Eddy." Then she's skittering down the crooked streets in her tall boots and narrow jeans, her white leather jacket getting smaller and smaller like a puff of cloud that disappears in the summer sky.

27

R ED HARKNESS LIKED TO SAY that any fool could get rich but only a clever man could be interesting. Driving through the Back Bay, past plush townhouses and boutique hotels, Harkness remembers this bit of advice, which came long before he uncovered his father's clever but felonious version of investing.

Harkness has his gun back, nestled in its holster again and locked down by its leather strap. But Thalia's right, his troubles aren't over. To stay alive, Harkness has to be clever — and fast.

He pulls in front of Thalia's loft and runs up the stairs, slides the door aside, and steps inside.

"Thalia?" His shout echoes across the empty loft.

No answer.

Something heavy hits Harkness on the back of his head and he tumbles to the splintered floorboards.

So much for clever and fast.

Harkness wakes up handcuffed to the radiator. Thugs in suits are pushing over furniture, dumping out drawers, and breaking up the loft like a clumsy hand lurching through a dollhouse. The upside-down face of Mark Sarris hovers above him. "Tell us where they are!" he shouts.

"What?" Harkness says.

"The fucking photos."

"Gave them all to Mach."

"Sure you did."

Sarris kicks him in the head and the room goes black again.

· · ·

Sunlight floods the destroyed loft, quiet now. Sarris and the others are gone. Mr. Mach's face drifts above Harkness. He's holding up a prescription bottle.

"Feeling sick?"

Harkness shakes his head. His ears are ringing and his head throbs.

"Maybe you need this." Mach opens the bottle and pulls out a silver thumb drive.

Harkness presses his eyes closed.

Mach nods to his crew. Shinyman, white bandage over his missing earlobe, gives Harkness a hard stare as he unshackles him.

Mach sits on a windowsill, smoking a cigarette while rain clicks against the glass. Three thugs stand in front of the door, all mirrored shades and attitude.

"You cause a lot of trouble for me," Mach says. "But now it's over."

"If you came for your money, I don't have it." Harkness nods at the destroyed loft. "Guess you figured that out."

"I know who has my money," Mach says. "I'll get it back."

"Good luck with that." By now, Thalia's probably in New York.

"Love may make you blind, Edward. But it doesn't have to make you stupid. You've been played. Not the first time a man's been fooled by a piece of ass. And such a fine one. We'll have to compare notes sometime."

Harkness pulls his Glock from his waistband. The goons laugh.

"We gave you back your gun." Mach smiles. "But not the bullets. Do you think we are stupid?"

Harkness puts his gun back.

Mach stubs out his cigarette on the windowsill. "That tattoo of a red hummingbird just above her magnificent ass? Paid for it myself." A meaty rot wafts from Mach's yellow teeth.

"Good for you."

"I invest in people, Edward," Mach says. "That's my work."

"That's what you call it?" Harkness almost laughs.

Mach nods.

"So that's what you're doing out in Nagog? Investing in people? People who make drugs?"

"I invest in clever young people, in entrepreneurs. No matter where they are. That boy, Dex? He is smart, like a scientist. But wrong idea," Mach says. "People take drugs to forget, not to remember. Third Rail is interesting, but a niche product. And too expensive."

"So you're not selling it?"

Mach shakes his head. "Absolutely not. Waste of time."

Harkness stares at Mach until he looks away. Maybe he's more interested in Third Rail than he's letting on. "You found the thumb drive," he says. "What else do you want?"

"What everyone wants. Friends who are willing to help me."

Harkness says nothing.

"Consider your situation, Harkness. You lost girlfriend. You lost respect. You lost job. You need help from powerful people."

"You mean like Councilman John Fitzgerald?"

Mach shakes his head. "Not him."

"Thought you were friends."

"Connections. Thought he might be of use. But too angry and arrogant. He will never be mayor. I'm sure of it."

Harkness takes a moment to register this shift in alliances. "So what do you really want from me, Mach?"

"You helped erase history like it never happened, make a big problem a very small one." Mach holds up the thumb drive. "Now I need you to solve another problem — your friend Commissioner Lattimore."

"No way." Harkness shakes his head.

"The way I see it, you don't really have much of a choice." Mach nods at his three goons. "My ruthless young friends will slice your handsome face to shreds like they did to our mutual friend Jeet. By the way, he was screaming for you when he was getting cut to pieces — starting with that unfortunate blue Mohawk," Mach says. "Such a shame. Could happen to you."

Harkness feels sick.

"Or to your sister. Nora, right? And your crazy mother. Out in Nagog."

"Leave them out of this."

"You'll agree to help, then?"

"Help what?"

"When you're back in Boston, get Lattimore to back off. Let me know if they're investigating me. Or about to raid my club. That's all I'm asking."

Harkness closes his eyes.

"I know what you're thinking, Harkness. You're thinking about integrity. About how you don't want to make a deal with the devil. But I'm no devil. I'm just very good businessman. A businessman who just gave you your gun back."

Harkness doesn't point out that Mach stole it in the first place. Mach is about loyalty, not logic.

"One more thing you should know, Harkness," Mach says. "You like photos so much, you should see a couple of these."

One the goons flips open his cell phone and shoves it toward Harkness. A man with a bullet blast over one eye is folded in a fifty-gallon drum half filled with cement. In the foreground, someone holds a matte-black Glock so close to the camera that Harkness can see the scratch on the grip.

"While we had your gun, we put it to good use," Mach says. "This is Mr. Rick Ridell, who failed to pay me the five thousand dollars he borrowed for gambling. Here he is on his way to Georges Bank to do some deep-sea fishing. Very deep."

The goon swipes to the next photo, showing a beautiful young girl with caramel skin, her eyes wide-open, narrow chest a red wash of blood dotted with darker rips where the bullets entered. Again, a hand dangles his Glock in the foreground. Harkness shuts his eyes.

"This girl ran away after we welcomed her here from Thailand and gave her a job and a place to live. Ingrateful!"

"Why are you showing me these?"

"Wait, there are more!" Mach waves at the goon with the phone.

"That's enough."

"Okay. But know this — your gun means nothing," Mach says. "What you do with it is what's important. Like your heart and mind. When you are back in Boston you must be thankful, Harkness, in your deeds if not your words," Mach says. "Otherwise, we show them what your gun did when it was on vacation. And you'll have a lot to explain."

Harkness says nothing.

Mach crushes his cigarette on the windowsill and steps away, brushing dust from his blue pinstriped suit. "When we track down Thalia in New York, I'll tell her that you send your love. Because, really, what do we have, Harkness? It's not drugs and sex. And it's not guns or money or power. Those things are temporary. It's the love of our friends and family, Detective Harkness. That is what keeps us alive."

Mach strides through the debris, his men following. Their footsteps echo in the worn, dusty stairwell.

Harkness gets up from the floor and looks down at the street. A green Mercedes sedan idles at the curb, the car a respected businessman might drive — powerful but not flashy. As his driver pulls out, Mach looks up at the window and gives Harkness a crisp salute.

• • •

The afternoon fades over the South End. Harkness walks around the loft, stepping over splintered furniture and torn canvases, smashed bottles and piles of clothes. His ribs ache and his head throbs. He picks up a cardboard box and gathers up a couple of his shirts.

He wonders where Thalia is now, realizes that he has no idea. The lover you shouldn't love, the golden drug that can kill you, the money you shouldn't touch — there's no explanation for misplaced desire. And no antidote but time.

He finds a small canvas, untrampled by the goons. Thalia called the painting *Night Swimmer,* though there isn't any swimmer, just a red and brown river that reminds Harkness of the sickly canal behind the loft. The river is thick with clumps of green and black, some crossed out, others left alone. Thalia called them the *murk* — plans that never happen, songs you hate but can't forget, memories you can't leave behind, habits you can't shake, lost things that never get found.

He turns it over and sees *To Eddy* written along the bottom edge. He puts the painting in the cardboard box and moves on, knowing that their paths will cross again, like wires after a storm.

• • •

Harkness finds a hammer among the scattered debris. He counts seven floorboards from the wall, kneels on the loft floor, shoves the claw between two wide boards, and pulls up a floorboard with the metallic shriek of nails giving up.

In the narrow hollow below wait a dozen mailing envelopes, each stamped and addressed, old-style, to the *Boston Globe, Boston Herald*, the Massachusetts Attorney General, and others who might find the hidden past of mayoral front-runner John Fitzgerald newsworthy.

In each envelope waits a thumb drive identical to the one Mach's goons managed to find in the medicine cabinet, the most obvious hide ever. And on each thumb drive wait the high-res files of Jeet's photos, too incendiary to be explained away by press conferences and spin.

Mach may be a good businessman and a rich man, but he should know that no one buys just one thumb drive. They buy them by the dozen. Memory gets cheaper by the day.

Harkness scoops up the envelopes and puts them in his cardboard box. He was going to wait until closer to Election Day to drop these envelopes in the mail, but now seems like a better time.

He leaves the door open behind him. Thalia's loft is over, like a stage set when the show closes and the actors move on.

28

HARKNESS WALKS FROM meter to meter, rolling the coin transfer unit down the sidewalk past fairies carried by their mothers and ghosts in strollers. It's early afternoon but the youngest kids are already getting ready for Halloween night. After Salem, Nagog is known as the best place to be on Halloween — a creepy history, great costumes, and rich people who give away lots of candy.

His safe hometown seems fraught with new danger. When a green Mercedes pulls to the curb, Harkness is sure it holds Mr. Mach's crew. Instead, it lets off a gang of jabbering teenagers dressed like slutty witches. When he passes the Nagog Bakery, every scruffy young stranger who walks out is Dex, Mouse, or one of their friends. The weight of his gun in its holster does little to reassure Harkness.

His cell phone rings when he gets to the end of Main.

It's Nora. "George says you're a mess."

"That's his opinion."

"So you're okay?"

"Not really."

"What's the problem?"

"I'm still emptying meters."

"Maybe you just need to take a break from Nagog for a while."

"Sounds good. And unlikely." He looks at the redbrick storefronts of Main Street, explored with Nora and George until they knew every alley and trail, the secret cut-throughs and hideouts. He's across the street from where Colonial CDs used to be, during a time that seems impossibly long ago.

"You'll be back in Boston soon."

"Maybe." Harkness wonders if he'll ever escape Nagog.

"You got your gun back, right?"

"Yes, but . . ." He moves his right hand to touch his gun like a scrap of bone in a reliquary.

"But what?"

"Got some serious loose ends floating around."

"Then tie them up." His sister's matter-of-fact tone sounds like their mother before she drifted away.

"Easier said than done."

"Coming over tonight? There'll be plenty of trick-or-treaters if the storm holds off. And I'm making dinner."

"What're you cooking?"

"Gnocchi with marinara sauce. Thought it would look kind of bloody and scary."

"Save me a plate," Harkness says. "There's something I need to check out tonight."

"Crime scene?"

"Hope not."

. . .

Sergeant Dabilis, Debbie the dispatcher, and Harkness are on night duty at headquarters. The wind is picking up but not the rain, so the Halloween crowds are out in force. The usual calls come in — roving bands of teenagers causing predictable mayhem, smashed pumpkins, a couple of porch fires. When the nor'easter hits later tonight, there'll be power lines down, cars skidding on wet leaves, and worse. But that's for the next shift.

"Doing your homework, Harkness?"

"Finishing up some reports." Harkness doesn't look up. He's sitting as far as he can get from Sergeant Dabilis's office as he finalizes his meter tallies, the kind of paperwork that makes cops hate being cops.

"Well, make sure you're paying attention," Sergeant Dabilis says.

"We need to know exactly how many quarters you collected today. You should be able to get it right. Just check the math a couple of times."

Harkness says nothing.

Debbie shoots him an apologetic look.

Since the captain's death, Sergeant Dabilis has escalated from annoying to amoral. He's been lording his provisional power over every other cop, dispatcher, detective, and administrative aide in Nagog. Three cops have already quit after showdowns with the Sweathog. Tonight, Harkness is tempted to become the fourth.

Sergeant Dabilis walks into the captain's once-elegant office, which now looks like a Red Sox gear shop on Yawkey Way. Tonight he'll be typing doctored crime stats into an enormous spreadsheet and watching his favorite plays from the ESPN archives.

His shift over, Harkness is about to leave the station. He sets aside his reports and checks on Dex's big party. From what he can tell online, the party is happening now and it's awesome and outrageous but hardly life changing. It's good news that this loose end isn't unraveling.

A few minutes later, Harkness gets a text from Candace.

GET HR NOW DEXS FRKNG. HAS MAY.

Harkness pulls on his jacket and walks toward the door.

Debbie looks up. "Heading home?"

"Checking on a disturbance."

"Where?"

"Edge of town, Forest Road."

"Call in if you need anything," she says.

"Yeah, call in if you need help shutting up a barking dog or something," Sergeant Dabilis shouts from his office without even looking up.

• • •

The squad car hits ninety on the straight stretch of road to the Nagog Woods. Light rain flares in his headlights and the Buzzcocks blare from the speakers. Harkness drives ahead until the road clogs with parked cars — a clever way to keep the party inaccessible to anyone but insiders.

He backs out and drives to a narrow trail that shadows Forest Road, then speeds down it, squad car bouncing off rocks and ruts. When he sees something moving on the trail ahead, Harkness slows. Dozens of deer run toward him. They crowd past the squad car, hooves and antlers clicking against the metal. Eyes wild, frantic, they leap past his window and trample the underbrush as they flee.

Once the deer have passed, Harkness drives down the trail until it narrows and the squad car gets stuck on a low ridge of rock, hemmed in on all sides by trees. Harkness presses the gas but the wheels just spin. He leaves the lights on, grabs his flashlight from the back seat, and abandons the squad car, pushing the driver's side door open as far as he can and slipping out into the woods.

He runs down the trail, pressed into the forest floor by the bare feet of Micmacs and Wampanoags, marched by minutemen and redcoats, and now wandered by dog walkers, lovers, and weed smokers. He takes the path to the left toward what was once the Old Nagog Tavern, now the site of Headless at Freedom Farm, Dex's epic party, already under way.

A low orange glow filters through the bare trees and whoops and laughter echo from deep in the woods. The path finally opens up on the field behind Dex's house. Harkness walks out across the field, trying to be as invisible as a cop in uniform can be. Ahead, a bonfire sends flames and smoke high into the night sky. A band's playing on the stage and beyond it a white tent glows with strings of orange lights. From across the field, the voices sound like a buzzing human hive.

As he gets closer, Candace runs toward him, bracelets and leather jacket jangling.

"We have to find May." Candace's face is flushed, eyes bleary from crying. Her voice cracks and she bends over like someone punched her.

"What happened?"

She's shaking and pale, her black hair hanging in dark tendrils. "Dex is all fucked up and he won't tell me where he hid May."

"Hid her?"

"Didn't want to have a baby at his cool party," Candace says. "Might make him seem too normal. You have to help me find her, Eddy. You have to find her."

Harkness holds her by the shoulders and looks into her red-rimmed eyes. "Don't worry," he says, "I know right where she is."

29

H ARKNESS FEELS ALONG the wall for a light switch. Candace walks to the center of the dark barn and pulls a string to turn on a bare bulb high in the rafters. She looks around at the pile of lumber, the tools and trash. "Eddy, she's not here. What're we doing here? Where is she?"

Harkness unlocks the trash barrel and pushes it aside. When he opens the trapdoor, Candace peers down into the gloom.

"What the fuck is that?"

"You don't know?"

"I never come out here. Not since Dex and his stupid friends made it their man cave."

"It's more than that." Harkness leads her down the stairs and up into the lab. He turns on the light to reveal the wall of glass tubing gleaming with amber drops.

"What the hell?"

"Drug lab," Harkness says. "Third Rail."

"I know they take that shit. But I didn't know they made it."

Harkness walks past the lab table and toward the desk with the binders. He bends down to look under the desk. He pulls out May's empty car seat.

"Where is she!" Candace runs around the lab, kicking cartons and walls with her heavy boots.

Harkness walks to the other side of the lab, where cardboard boxes are stacked along the dusty floor. He holds up his hand. "Quiet for a minute."

Candace stops, and they stand still in the bright lab. They hear nothing. Harkness walks to where footsteps mark the dust and kneels down to push aside the boxes. Someone cut a rectangle out of the drywall, poked sloppy air holes in it with a knife, then taped the piece back with duct tape.

"May can't be in there," Candace says. "Dex wouldn't do that."

"I'll check it out." As Harkness peels away the duct tape he's back on Queensbury Street about to reveal Little Dorothy's dissolving body.

"She'd be crying," Candace shouts. "There's no crying!"

"It'll be okay." Harkness pulls away the last piece of duct tape and tries to pull out the piece of drywall with his fingernails. It's stuck.

"There's not any crying, Eddy. Don't look. Please. She's not in there. Can't be in there."

Harkness pries out the drywall with his knife, one corner giving way, then another. His flashlight reveals a dark space about as big as a microwave.

May sits shaking a few feet back on a dirty blanket, her face shining with tears. She's clutching an empty bottle and a filthy stuffed rabbit.

She screams when Harkness's flashlight shines in her eyes.

Candace reaches in. "Come 'ere, May," she says. "It's okay." The screaming gets louder. She puts her hands under May's arms and gently slides her out, then holds her tightly to her chest, feels her breathing in gasps.

In a few minutes, Candace pulls down the neck of her T-shirt and offers a breast to May, who takes her nipple with desperate eagerness.

"What kind of father . . . ," Candace just closes her eyes and shakes her head.

One who knows it may be the only safe place on the farm tonight. But Harkness doesn't say this. "She okay?"

"I think so."

Harkness reaches into the back of the space where May was hidden. There's stack after stack of hundreds carefully wrapped in plastic. He pulls a few out and shows them to Candace.

"What the fuck is that?"

"Pile of drug money?"

"Dex always told me we didn't have enough money to finish the house," she says. "That's why we're living like squatters." Candace moves May to her shoulder and pats her back. She looks around the drug lab. "I can't believe I was such an idiot."

"Love may make you blind," Harkness says, "but it doesn't have to make you stupid."

"Who told you that?"

"A Laotian drug lord."

"He's right." Candace lifts May and hands her to Harkness. "Take May for a second?"

"Sure." Harkness cradles May gently on his shoulder.

Candace kneels down to pull out the stacks of cash. She holds a bundle of cash toward Harkness.

"No," he says, "all yours."

Candace throws one stack of money after another toward the delicate wall of glass tubing, knocking pieces from it. Then she picks up a broom and smashes the rest of the tubing, which sprays down on the lab like an ice storm. She smashes a tall glass flask with the broom handle and Third Rail seeps over the table.

May rears back and starts to cry.

"Candace?"

"Cleaning house." She swings the broom at more of the lab, until nothing's left but glass shards, puddles of drugs, and hissing gas.

"So much for technology." She tosses the broom on the floor. "Let's get out of here."

Harkness considers finding the gas and shutting it off, but doesn't bother. He's late for a party.

"Walk down that path and you'll hit the main road." Harkness hands Candace his flashlight. "At the end of all the parked cars, you'll find my friend Officer Watt waiting in a squad car. He'll take you and May to the station or wherever you want to go."

Candace nods. "What about you?"

"Got to talk to Dex about a few things."

"Good luck with that." Candace walks toward the woods, then turns. "Be careful, Eddy. Be really careful. They're all superhigh."

The wind has picked up, whipping the long brown grass around Harkness in waves as he walks toward the bonfire. The rain is just beginning, the cool air so laden with water that his face is dripping, leather jacket, too. The band is gone now, stage empty, party retreated under the white tent. As Harkness gets closer, he sees someone walking from the party toward him, backlit by the fire.

The wind raises a wall of sparks as he walks closer. The figure throws a handful of shiny disks toward him and the air whistles.

A whirring noise passes above Harkness and leaves a small silver star with five sharp spikes sticking in the arm of his leather jacket, another on his shoulder. Harkness plucks them and tosses them aside.

"Dabilis said you were coming." Mouse wears a gray hoodie. "Welcome to Headless at Freedom Farm."

Throwing stars — retro, esoteric, and nasty. Weapon of choice for fake ninjas and anime fans. Of course Mouse would be into them.

"Harkness! Catch." Another batch of stars whizzes by, and Harkness reaches up instinctively with his fielding hand. Searing pain drops him to his knees on the muddy path. A pale finger lies in the mud in front of him. Blood drips from the red-tipped stump where his index finger used to be.

When Harkness closes his hand, the blood pumping from the crimson stump of his severed finger slows, but only a little. He presses his left hand deep in the pocket of his jacket. He clicks his radio on with his right hand, requests backup and EMTs, tells them he's injured. But no one responds.

Harkness's head lowers toward the ground. The field darkens. His blood-slick hand throbs. His chest burns. Warm blood drains out his sleeve like rainwater. He bends down to take a couple of deep breaths, then stands, swaying in the rain.

Mouse is gone, disappeared into the mist.

Harkness walks toward the party, gritting his teeth against the pain, eyes locked on the bonfire. On a low stage, high schoolers sing "We Are the Champions" and dive into the mud. They don't notice a policeman staggering past, leaving a thin line of blood behind him.

There aren't any ghosts at Headless at Freedom Farm, just idols. The white tent is crowded with Zuckerbergs in gray hoodies, unshaven Franzens in tortoiseshell glasses, and bandana-wrapped David Foster Wallaces carrying well-thumbed copies of *Infinite Jest*. At the back, Thoreau leans on his walking stick, talking to Louisa

May Alcott. On the other side of the tent, Harkness sees a couple of raven-haired Sontags, a star-spangled Wonder Woman, a Wurtzel dispensing candy Prozac from a bucket, and a mono-browed Frida Kahlo with a moon-faced Diego Rivera straining on a leash.

Harkness recognizes faces in the costumed crowd. Teachers, entrepreneurs, the intelligentsia of Cambridge, Boston, and further afield, they're all talking, their blurted words and frantic gestures giving away the real reason they're standing under a wedding tent in a rain-soaked field on Halloween night — free drugs.

An emo kid wearing silver boxer shorts and a hat with Mercury wings runs past carrying a trashcan of burning leaves, sparks trailing behind him like a human comet. He throws the can in the dark river and stares at the sizzling, steaming water as if he's accomplished something brave and important.

Dex steps out from beneath the tent. "Hey! Look who's here! Who invited you?" he crows into a bullhorn.

"Party's over."

Dex laughs. "No way, just getting started."

"Now, Dex. I'm shutting it down."

Dex shakes his head, wet strands of yellow hair plastered to his face. He takes a few steps forward. "Get out of here, fake cop," he says, bullhorn distorting his voice. "Been planning this for months."

"Small-town drug dealer," Harkness says. "That how you want your daughter to think of you?"

"Shut up about my daughter," he says.

"She's not going to be your daughter much longer."

"What're you talking about?"

"The state doesn't like to see kids stuck in a dark hole in the wall."

Dex takes this news in.

Three men step out from the tent and stand behind him. They're wearing suits, not costumes. For a moment, Harkness thinks pain is making him hallucinate, but Mach's goons are real. Of course they're here, protecting their boss's interests.

The less addled superheroes drift away from the tent to their cars. The high schoolers jump off the stage and head toward the woods. But the hardcore fans circle around to see what Dex is up to now. They're entrepreneurs, digerati, grad students, winners of prizes and grants. They're airplanes flying far above the mundane world of waitress jobs and parking meters. But on Third Rail, they're just drug hungry and looking for a new thrill.

Dex throws the bullhorn to the side and holds out his right hand. One of Mach's thugs reaches beneath his jacket and slaps a gun into his palm. Lit by the flickering light of the glowing bonfire, Dex's friends cheer and circle around to watch his latest audacious distraction.

For a moment Harkness thinks he's back on the Brookline Avenue Bridge, surrounded by jeering Sox fans.

"Put that down, Dex," he says. "Now." Harkness turns to the side and radios for backup. No one answers.

Harkness wipes his eyes with the back of his blood-washed wrist and stares through the rain at Dex walking toward him, white shirt plastered to his skin, rain-tangled yellow hair dangling in his face, gun in hand. He's smiling off in the distance, Third Rail already rewriting this scene to transform him into a superhero.

Harkness clenches his ruined left hand and shoves it deep in the pocket of his leather jacket. He's lightheaded and his legs shake like he's been running for hours.

"Put the gun down now," Harkness says, "and this is all over."

Dex walks closer. He's armed and dangerous. And he's not obeying clear instructions shouted by an officer. Deadly force is allowable.

Harkness draws his Glock and feels its familiar weight in his hand. "Stop," he shouts.

"What are you going to do, shoot me with your plastic gun, fake cop?"

"Last warning." Harkness raises his Glock, clicks off the safety, and aims.

"Fuck you." Dex lifts his gun.

Harkness fires, and the explosion echoes across the yard. A red rip opens in the thigh of Dex's jeans and he drops to the ground. He kneels and stares at the wound as if he can think it away.

Called in by Watt, State Police helicopters spin on the horizon.

"Stay. Right. There." Harkness wants the incident to end now with the State Police hauling Dex in. But Dex struggles to rise from the mud, turned tenacious by Third Rail.

Dex walks toward him, teeth clenched, leg dragging.

Harkness's Glock is steady in his right hand while his left drains a steady stream of blood.

"Get out of here, now. All of you," Harkness shouts at the last clumps of bystanders. They run out from under the tent and into the heavy rain, slipping in the mud as they race to their cars.

Dex walks closer, waving his gun.

Just stop, Harkness thinks.

Harkness aims, inhales, and holds his breath. He pulls the trigger. The shot hits high on the shoulder and knocks Dex on his back in the mud.

Dex stares up at the roiling gray sky, rain beating on his face. His eyes widen with surprise and confusion, blood soaking his white shirt. He rises and staggers toward Harkness, Third Rail telling him to keep going.

As he trudges toward Harkness, Dex raises his gun and fires a shot that burns past Harkness and into the woods.

Enough. Harkness fires and hits Dex above the right eye. A thick wind of scalp, blood, bone, and clots of brain sprays behind him. Dex gives a contorted smile, his face an abandoned storefront. Then he falls back on the muddy ground.

Some people are too smart for their own damn good.

• • •

Except for the ticking of freezing rain on the field, all is silent as Dex lies motionless in the mud and Harkness stands, gun in hand. He clicks his useless radio. "Man down, Forest Road. Request ambulance."

The last partygoers rush to their cars, their rain-soaked costumes flapping in the wind.

Dex stares, his wide-open eyes unmoving, at the black sky and the lights beaming down from the helicopters. Mach's thugs approach beneath three black umbrellas, as if Dex's funeral is already under way and they've come to pay their respects. One reaches down to pluck his gun from Dex's hand. Then they hurry across the dark field toward the barn, passing Harkness as if he's just as dead.

Harkness's stomach lurches and he drops on his knees into the mud.

Thalia warned him that Mach was working an angle. Ever the

businessman, Mach saw a new opportunity in Third Rail, so different from other drugs. And much more lucrative.

Mach's thugs cross the field like a trio of clever crows flying toward a shiny silver nest.

Mach gave Harkness back his gun so he would clear away a business obstacle — Dex. As Harkness lowers his head, the Glock's barrel presses on his forehead like the warm finger of a perverse priest. With one pull of the trigger, he could join his fathers, one clever, the other tempted.

When he finally looks up, Harkness watches Mach's thugs joking and pushing each other, on the way to a new payoff. They'll bring Third Rail to the city, finding new markets and users. Mach has the vision, organization, and charisma to turn Third Rail from an invisible menace to a name brand among the smart and daring. And soon he'll have hundreds of full vials, and binders of Dex's hard-won chemical secrets will tell him how to make more.

Harkness stands and wavers, almost falling back in the mud. He turns toward the barn and waits until the thugs clump onto the threshold.

One of the thugs pulls his leg back to kick the door in. Harkness raises his Glock and fires in the air to get their attention. When they turn, he takes his ruined left hand from his jacket pocket and raises a bloodied middle finger. Even from across the field, it's clear that they're confused, wondering why a half-dead cop would dare to piss them off. In unison, they reach inside their jackets for their guns.

Harkness levels his gun and swings it toward the back of the barn. He sends one shot across the field, then another. Nothing happens. The thugs are pointing their guns now. He pulls the trigger and the third shot hits metal. The barn explodes in a fireball that lights up the field and sends planks and bodies flying like cardboard.

When he left the gas whistling from the ruined burners, Harkness figured the world would be better off without the secrets of Third Rail.

Even better without Mach's thugs.

• • •

A State Police officer scoops up Harkness's severed finger and puts it in a Dunkin' Donuts cup. An EMT wraps his bleeding hand with white bandages, tightens a tourniquet around his wrist. Watt runs toward Harkness and says something he can't hear over the helicopters and the ringing in his ears. He puts his arm around Harkness and helps him toward the helicopter.

"You're gonna be fine," Watt shouts.

Harkness nods, exhausted. His shoulder aches and he pushes aside his jacket to reveal his blood-slick shirt. A throwing star juts below his collarbone like a silver latch. Harkness stops and tries to pull it out, but it's stuck. The warm metal turns slippery with blood pulsing from the deep rip in his chest.

One of the EMTs runs toward him. His face whitens when he sees Harkness's jacket open, his good hand struggling to pull out the star. He shakes his head in an urgent *no*.

Harkness tastes salty blood, then nothing.

30

FINNED AND FIRM with muscle, Harkness swims through the murk like a primordial night creature forever on the move.

On the riverbank Thalia Havoc waits with her box of brushes and bag of dope, carnival-haired Marnie sprawled in the mud next to her like a Technicolor catfish. The Sweathog and Ted Williams play catch on the banks.

He passes through Nagog, where clever Red Harkness sits at a desk stuffed with money spilling out of every drawer. Robert Hammond perches at the top of the town monument. Harkness's mother and sister trudge up a mountain, topped by a wooden podium where Henry David Thoreau speaks to the crowd, wielding his walking stick like a mighty sword.

Harkness swims past a cornfield where Little Dorothy tap-dances, smoking wreckage strewn around her. Nine redcoats carry their severed heads, yellow teeth chattering. Glock 17s fall like hard rain. But Harkness can't stop to catch them. He has to keep swimming.

. . .

Harkness opens his eyes for a moment. Patrick's slumped in an orange plastic chair, a vase of red flowers on the table next to him. He's encircled by a personal galaxy of newspapers, coffee cups, and food wrappers.

Patrick rouses and rushes toward him. *"He's awake, he's awake!"* Harkness closes his eyes again and dives back into the murk.

• • •

Chest wound. Perforated heart casing. Punctured lung. Trauma. Massive blood loss. Partial digit reattachment. Nosocomial infection.

• • •

Harkness wakes in a blazingly white room.

Candace sits in the orange chair where Patrick was sitting just a minute ago. There are new flowers in a vase on the table next to her.

"I'm sorry," he says.

"What, Eddy?" She rises slowly, as if she might scare him away.

"I'm so sorry."

"You're awake." She stands and walks toward him, the chains on her engineer boots rattling. "Sorry for what?"

"For shooting Dex," he says, then wonders whether Dex's party was just part of his nightmare. "I shot him, didn't I?"

Candace nods slowly. "Yeah, you did, Eddy."

"Is he dead?"

She nods, presses her eyes closed.

"I'm sorry, Candace."

She cries, tears streaming down her face. "It's his own stupid fault," she says. "Got in way too deep." She touches his hand, the one that isn't encased in bandages. "You didn't shoot Dex. You saved May."

"That's one way to think about it."

"That's the only way I think about it."

Harkness stares at the city lights outside the window.

"Can't carry around guilt, Eddy," Candace says. "Dad taught me that."

"Where am I?"

"Mass General. Been here for about a week. In and out of it. Mostly out."

Before Candace can say more, the room dims and he's swimming again.

• • •

198

When Harkness opens his eyes, Commissioner Lattimore paces around the room, past new flowers and Mylar balloons. He's wearing a black suit and white shirt, carrying a newspaper folded under his arm. His frenetic energy multiplies in the small hospital room. Harkness just stares and wonders if he'll ever be able to move that fast again.

"Harkness! You're awake!" Commissioner Lattimore leans down. "Did you know that good news has a positive effect on recovery outcomes?"

"No, sir," Harkness says, his unused voice cracking.

"It's true. There's good data on it. Been reading about it online. So I was going to wait to tell you after you get out of here. But seems better to tell you now." Commissioner Lattimore leans closer. "We want you back, Harkness. To lead Narco-Intel again. Are you in?"

"Of course," Harkness says. "I'd be proud to."

The commissioner waves the newspaper in front of him. "I've been trying to get you back for months," he says. "But this pissed-off chump was making noises about becoming mayor and throwing us all out. Got the whole BPD distracted, playing defense, trying to save our jobs. Not a problem now. Check out this morning's *Herald*. Definitely game over."

Harkness stares at the cover, trying to decipher the photos. The first shows the ashen face of City Councilor John Fitzgerald, backlit like a deer by the flash, one hand trying to shield his face as he walks out the front door of his campaign headquarters. Below is one of Jeet's photos, showing Mach and Fitzgerald with Whitey Bulger and their other hard-guy friends.

The headline — FITZEY ENDS MAYOR RUN AFTER MOB TIES REVEALED.

"Nice photo, huh?"

"Yes," Harkness says, thinking of Jeet. "It's a great photo. A classic."

• • •

He writes a book in his head, *Twice,* imagining every line and even envisioning the indigo cover with two clouds printed on it, one white, one black. The book is about birth and death, love and hate, rise and fall, freeze and melt, war and peace. During his long swim Harkness has plenty of time to plot it all out.

He lost his gun and found it. He loved Thalia and let her go. His two fathers died. Two Doyle brothers held Pauley Fitz over the Pike. Mouse and his brother served Dex. A missing hand, a severed finger.

Harkness opens his eyes. "Twice," he says.

Candace looks up from her magazine and tosses it aside. She picks up her cell phone. "Told your sister I'd call if you woke up."

Harkness waves her toward him and she puts the phone down.

"It all happens twice," he says.

"Really?"

"Yeah. Been thinking about it. Got to remember."

"See that big bag?" Candace points to a puffy clear plastic bag hovering above Harkness.

"Uh-huh."

"That's saline solution. Keeps you hydrated until you can go out for a beer with me."

"Okay."

"But that one next to it, the smaller one?"

"Yeah?"

"That's called meta-morphadroxadrine," Candace says, tongue wrapping around every syllable. "The nurses told me about it. It's like super-duper synthetic morphine from Merck! So just know this, Straight Ed. You're ridiculously high right now. Ironical, yes?"

Harkness laughs and feels a burst of pain in his chest.

Candace shakes her head. "*Do not* laugh. Sorry. Laughing comes next week, if you're better. And if you are, I'll let you hold my hand."

"The real one or the plastic one?"

"My real one."

Harkness looks into her eyes. "What's going on?"

"That throwing-star thing grazed your heart lining. They had to restart you. By the way, they tried really hard to reattach your finger but it didn't work."

"Nine fingers," he says. "Nine headless redcoats."

"Enough with the coincidences and numbers," Candace says. "After listening to Dex go on and on, I can tell you this — things only seem connected because we connect them. Or because we're high."

"Oh."

"So don't quit your day job to become an Internet cult leader."

"I like my day job."

"Yeah, I hear you're back in Boston," she says. "Your friend Watt's been around here a lot. Flirting with me shamelessly, though I completely iced him, by the way. But he told me a lot of stories about you. Didn't know you were such a rock star."

"Me neither."

She walks back to her chair. "Here's the proof." She holds up the *Globe*. "It's from last week. Watt saved it for you." The grainy cover photo, taken from a State Police helicopter, shows the dilapidated white house by the river, the bonfire's blackened circle, and the sagging white party tent. Fire hoses stretch across the rain-gutted field to the shell of the burnt-out barn.

She reads, *"The leader of an Internet drug cult died last night in a muddy field outside the quiet town of Nagog when a Halloween party ended in chaos."*

Candace pauses.

"You don't have to read that."

"It's okay," she says. "It happened. Can't pretend it didn't." Candace raises the paper again. *"In a violent shoot-out, Officer Edward Harkness of the Nagog Police shot and killed the group's leader, Declan Nevis, 26. Three reputed Chinatown drug dealers died in a related explosion in a drug lab. Nevis's young daughter, May, was treated and released from Nagog Regional Hospital."*

She lifts May's car seat from the floor. She's sleeping. "See, good as new," she says. "Not a scratch on her."

"Beautiful."

Candace stares at him for a moment, her eyes starting to glisten. "You've probably been wondering what I knew about the whole drug thing, Eddy. Since you met me, even."

He nods.

"I guess I knew they were up to something, but I didn't know it was such a big deal. Or that they were selling so much of that Third Rail stuff. Dealing seemed like too much work for those lazy assberger fucktards. The investigators interviewed me for three hours. Sworn deposition. I told them I didn't know what was going on at the party, except that everyone was going to get high and weird, of course. That was always Dex's specialty. But I didn't know he was going to freak. Or that those assholes from Chinatown were going to be there. I never would have asked you to come if I did."

"I'm glad you did." Harkness watches May's pale face and calm eyes.

Candace keeps reading. *"Investigators still searching the crime scene are focusing on a powerful synthetic drug, Third Rail, which makes users act irrationally and violently. State Police and the DEA are now investigating. Officer Harkness—involved in the infamous fatal shooting on the Brookline Avenue Bridge after a Red Sox division win last year—is currently in the intensive care unit of Mass General Hospital with life-threatening injuries."*

"Life-threatening?"

Candace looks at Harkness, then kisses him on the forehead. "Not anymore, Eddy. That was last week. Go back to sleep. The doctors say you need to rest."

Harkness closes his eyes and drops back into the murk.

• • •

When Harkness surfaces again, he's in a new room, bigger and even brighter.

Patrick struggles to stand, then rushes forward, bobbling a coffee cup, which hits the floor. He's looking around for something. "I'm supposed to press that thing that tells the nurses you're awake," he says.

Harkness shakes his head. "Patrick?"

"Yeah?"

"Am I dead?" Harkness whispers.

"What makes you think that?"

"Feel weird. Bad dreams. Life-threatening injuries."

Patrick laughs. "No, Eddy. If you were dead, I wouldn't be talking to you. I'd be crying. Besides, you're out of the ICU now. Nice room in the normal part of the hospital. Check out the view." He pulls open the shades on a window and Harkness sees the winding streets of Beacon Hill, the dome of the statehouse. "You don't die and go to Boston. That's really not how it works."

"Guess not."

"You're in Mass General. Been here for a couple of weeks."

"Seems like a lot longer."

"Time kind of grinds when you're in a coma."

"Or emptying meters," he says.

Patrick leans closer. "You'll never empty another meter in your life," he says. "I guàrantee you that. You're the golden boy again, Eddy."

"I don't feel golden, Patrick."

"You will." Patrick sits next to the bed. "Commissioner's been by the office twice already to rally the troops. Fitzgerald's going down in flames. Narco-Intel's gearing up to full speed, waiting for you to get back. Been wanting to ask you — you wouldn't have any idea where those photos came from, would you, smart guy?"

"Can neither confirm nor deny."

"Well, they did the trick. Mach's disappeared — they're searching for him down in New York. Fitzgerald's got a good shot at ending up in Walpole."

"I can die happy," Harkness says.

"But don't, please." Patrick stares out the window at the city. "Got lots of drugs to find. Perps to pop. And lots of fans cheering for you."

"Like the Sox."

"Just like the Sox," Patrick says.

"History repeats itself."

"Sure does," Patrick says. "Like it's got Alzheimer's."

31

FROM THE STREET, Harkness can see through the uncurtained windows of the tidy house with a thick crust of snow on the roof. Dabilis is eating a bachelor-style dinner, half standing, half perching on the arm of an Ikea couch, plate in one hand, fork in the other, beer bottle on the table in front of him. He stares at the flat-screen intently, searching for some vital secret. Harkness guesses it's the Patriots game.

Harkness takes out the digital wiretap, repaired after its dive in the Nagog River. He sets it on the dashboard of his car and inches forward through the slush.

Dabilis is still captain of the Nagog Police, one of the most powerful men in town, as he's glad to tell anyone. He only got a hand slap for not sending backup to Dex's party, claiming it was a radio malfunction due to the nor'easter.

If he turned on the digital wiretap, Harkness knows he wouldn't hear anything incriminating for as long as he could stand to listen. The two other men involved in the bribes — Dex and Captain Munro — are dead. Dex's friends, who could ID him as the corrupt cop who picked up the payoffs, couldn't be found. No one has real proof that Dabilis did anything wrong besides being a bad cop, which isn't news.

No one except Harkness.

He flips the digital wiretap over and turns the silver arrow from RECEIVE to BROADCAST, a trick he and his men pull when they get bored during long stakeouts. He points it at the wires running to Dabilis's house and presses START.

Dabilis stands up, confused. He sets down his plate and beer and walks toward the flat-screen, pressing buttons on the remote. But every channel broadcasts the last inning of the final game of the '04 Series against St. Louis, the one when Lowe clinched it. Dabilis throws down the remote and sits on the couch, staring at his favorite game as if it were beamed by God through a celestial cable box.

Harkness turns up the power.

Now the game's coming out of Dabilis's computer and radio. Wherever he turns, he hears the announcer's voice and the roaring fans, an onslaught that sends him rushing around the house, trying to turn everything off. To drug dealers staggering around in a haze, Kanye West coming from their beepers is equally mystifying.

Dabilis scurries through the house, turning knobs and clicking remotes, but he can't turn off the game. Harkness cranks up the power even more. Now the game is beaming from everywhere at once. He switches to new content:

> *Through careful detective work that seemed beyond his abilities, Sergeant Dabilis discovered that I had fathered a son out of wedlock—and used it, over the years, to extort me by threatening to tell Katherine of my transgression. He forced me to fire several officers simply because he didn't like them. He received payoffs from local businesses. And in a final moment of weakness, I looked the other way as he received payoffs from the operation at the Nagog Tavern, which I now recognize is home to a dangerous drug lab, one that I intend to shut down.*

Dabilis walks into kitchen, confused.

While the first tape was a revelation, this confession, captured on the second tape the captain left behind, was about revenge. Any listener would suspect that Dabilis killed Captain Munro to quiet him forever.

Harkness drives his car forward for a better angle, takes out his binoculars, and watches as Dabilis races into the kitchen, looking for relief from the accusations and sonic overload. He opens the fridge to find a beer waiting right in the center of the first shelf, Sam Adams Light, his favorite. Dabilis is vain about his growing belly.

Dabilis twists off the top and raises it to his lips, taking a thirsty swallow intended to chase away the relentless voice of the dead captain. He doesn't notice the Third Rail — it's tasteless, odorless. Like water, like nothing.

When he broke into Dabilis's house this afternoon, Harkness considered dosing the beer with more than a couple of drops. Enough Third Rail, and Dabilis would curl into the fetal position and thrash around for a few moments, legs rabbit kicking and spastic arms flailing. Then his brain would short-circuit and his body would go into seizure — white foam spraying between clenched teeth — until his heart stopped.

The punishment would fit the crime. Harkness remembers Mrs. Munro's instructions to him about her husband's killer. *Hunt him down and make him pay. Without an ounce of mercy.* Vengeance would be his. But it would be like a movie where the devious villain gets blown away at the end with a fast shot to the head. Crowd pleasing, but too easy.

Instead, Harkness gets out of the car and walks to the back of the house. The door is unlocked. Cops are notoriously slack about safety at home. Like nurses who smoke, doctors who drive too fast, and motorcyclists who don't wear helmets, they like to tempt fate.

Dabilis stands in the living room, his eyes wide-open as the information keeps pouring into his brain — his past rewritten and replayed at 1,000× speed, memory cracked open. His awestruck smile droops when he sees Harkness.

The captain's voice echoes through Dabilis's house, repeating over and over like a mantra of guilt.

Dabilis tries to run but Harkness grabs the back of his shirt and throws him against the television, knocking it off its stand with a short-ciruit flash.

"You'll get a citation for this," Dabilis says from the floor.

Harkness feels his boot rising to stomp Dabilis's head but he stops short. "I don't work for you anymore," he says. "I'm in Boston now. No citations. No backtalk. I came back here to make you an offer."

"Fuck you." Dabilis crab walks away from him, sliding along the floor until he hits a wall.

Harkness follows, points up at the ceiling, where the captain's voice echoes from in-wall speakers. "You killed him, didn't you?"

"You mean *your daddy?*" Dabilis sneers. "I always knew you were a real bastard, but still . . ."

Before Dabilis can flinch, Harkness reaches out to grip the back of his ear with three fingers, then uses that leverage to press his thumb into Dabilis's right eye, backing him against the wall in a practiced move that bouncers call *eye for an eye.*

He presses harder, until Dabilis squirms, then screams.

"You know, you're not very popular in Nagog," Harkness says, releasing him. "You've fucked with every officer. You made the captain's wife a widow, and lied to her. You took bribes from drug dealers. And you drowned your superior officer."

"He jumped off the Carson Avenue Bridge," Dabilis says, face dripping with sweat. "Had leukemia. And a pile of debt."

"That's the story you made up," Harkness says. "And the Third Rail I put in your beer is making you think it's the truth. But when you wake up in the morning, you'll know it's not. You'll remember how you held him underwater on the banks of the Nagog until he wasn't moving. Right?"

"Maybe. But I'll still be in charge," Dabilis sputters, twisting his damp face.

"Not for long. You're resigning and leaving Nagog. Florida's nice this time of year. Spring training starts in a couple of months."

"What if I don't?"

Harkness takes the tape from his jacket pocket and holds it up. "I'll take this to the town manager and you'll be under investigation in no time. If that doesn't work, I'll be glad to come back and revisit my decision to let you depart gracefully."

Dabilis juts his face forward maniacally, inspired by Third Rail. "Why don't you just shoot me now, Detective Harkness of the fucking BPD? Too scared, bastard boy?"

Harkness shakes his head. "Because then I'd be just like you, Sweathog," he says. "And I'm not. If you don't follow the rules, they're not rules anymore."

Dabilis smirks. "I know you don't believe that."

"There're all kinds of rules," Harkness says. "Some bend. Others don't." He reaches toward Dabilis's other eye with his thumb, ready for a second round of *eye for an eye.*

Dabilis's screams, the captain's confession, and Harkness's low threats form a brutal trio, echoing deep into the night.

As he drives away from Dabilis's house, scene of a successful home invasion and interrogation, Harkness knows that his purgatory in Nagog is over. Dex is dead, his followers and customers dispersed to grad school and tech start-ups. Freedom Farm is slated to become a community garden. The town of Nagog, no longer awash in smart kids and amber vials, awaits a new temptation. Someone else is emptying the parking meters.

Inspired by Harkness's visit, Dabilis will resign soon enough. If he doesn't, Harkness will be glad to provide new motivation. He comes back to Nagog a couple times a week to visit his sister and mother. Dabilis's house isn't that far away, just a few streets west, near the elementary school where Harkness went so many years ago, where his mother was principal.

It's a small town.

By the Harbor

CANDACE LIVES IN the seaport now, in a new neighborhood still figuring itself out, with parking lots and construction sites, an old seafarers' church lit blue by cerulean waves captured in stained glass, and whiskey bars that throb with techno deep into the night. Developers call it the Innovation District, hoping to dream up a new Silicon Valley from gritty warehouses gentrified by scrappy artists who were edged out by people with more money.

Now this urban work in progress is thick with cranes and crews in hardhats. They're building office towers, research labs, and highrise apartment buildings. But they're not building a casino. That idea withered along with the reputation of its promoter, former mayoral candidate John Fitzgerald, now facing a federal investigation into his ties to organized crime.

Her condo, paid for with what was left of her father's money, is on a high floor in a gleaming tower completed just a couple of months ago, keeping it free from history, memories, and misery. None of the ghosts of Nagog have followed Candace and May.

From the nineteenth floor, Harkness looks out the living room window at the East Boston drydocks, jets taking off from Logan, and cranes putting up new buildings where old piers once jutted out into the harbor. It's six in the morning but the city is already awake. It's the morning that matters in Boston, the early shift where all the honest work gets done.

The spring light beams off the water in patterns that mesmerize Harkness for a moment. He checks his watch, checks that his badge is in his pocket. He moves his hand slightly to the right to the Glock 22 in the waistband of his jeans. The commissioner gave him the gun when he came back on the force. It has a custom grip, a textured frame, and a larger magazine catch, making it excellent for street work. Harkness misses his old Glock 17, with its scraped grip and mixed history, turned in when he left Nagog. Like lovers, their time together was brief and tumultuous.

Candace walks in from the bedroom wearing Harkness's faded Black Flag T-shirt, shorts, and slippers. "Hey." She leans up and her long, slow kiss almost derails Harkness from his shift.

Candace reads his mind. "Not enough time."

Harkness reaches out to touch Candace's black hair with his left hand, most of the index finger missing. He's almost used to it now — adaptation.

"No uniform?" she says.

"On a raid. See that wharf over there?" Harkness points.

"Yeah?"

"Furniture importer's been bringing in bootleg Vicodin behind the back panels of bookcases."

"How'd you find that out?"

"Got suspicious about someone importing thousands of bookcases from Indonesia. Not exactly a lot of demand. Gone the way of the CD rack."

"Don't get killed today, okay?"

Candace's bluntness doesn't surprise Harkness anymore. "I won't."

"Or any other day. May's getting kind of used to you, you know, stopping by." Candace wanders into the kitchen and the coffeemaker starts burbling.

Harkness moves to the side window, facing east toward the city. He can almost see Chinatown from here. Sometimes when he's walking down Beach Street he'll sense someone watching him — one of Mach's goons, Thalia, someone. But there's never anyone there, at least no one he can see.

No matter what Marnie thought, Boston isn't rotten underneath. The latest rot waits in trashed-out Somerville triple-deckers and plush Marlborough Street townhouses, venerable North End social clubs and shimmering office towers on Route 128. Harkness knows he'll never find all the outliers with their drugs and big plans. But it's his job to keep looking.

Candace comes back in with two coffees and hands one to Harkness.

They stand at the window for a moment, listening to rustling sounds coming from the bedroom.

"Our little friend up?"

"Up with the sun," she says.

May wanders in dragging a gray blanket behind her and takes a meandering path across the living room. She makes it all the way to Harkness, stumbles, and wraps her arms around his leg.

"Dada."

"No, honey." A darkness shades Candace's face.

Harkness picks May up and she nestles her head on his chest. The truth — that he isn't May's father, that he's the man who killed her father — can wait until she's older, when she can make sense of it all, if that's even possible. For now Harkness and Candace let the secret hover above them, safely out of May's reach.

It's joined by the memories of Dex lying in the muddy field and Captain Munro floating in the millrace. Because unlike memory, which circles like leaves caught in an undercurrent, life runs in one relentless direction.

You crawl from the murk and walk on down the street.

You find what's lost and put it back in the right place.

Harkness hands May to Candace and zips up his blue hoodie, ready to drive his unmarked gray Chevy to today's bust.

"Even without the uniform, you still look like a cop, Eddy," Candace says. "Anyone ever tell you that?"

"Never."

"Aren't you that Harvard Cop?" She smiles. "The one who shot that guy and messed up the Red Sox?"

"Not anymore." Harkness gives Candace the look that says *Don't mention the curse*. It's early in the season, but the Sox are on a winning streak. There's already talk of winning the Series. Sportswriters are already calling this year's team the *Fenway Phoenix*.

He pulls Candace and May toward him for a moment to feel their warmth, to breathe their comforting scent.

In the burgeoning spring, the city's reward after a hard winter, bullets will cut down street-corner thugs in Mattapan and Mission Hill, pierce the chest of an unfaithful Cambridge husband, put a quick end to a convenience store robbery in Southie, and leave a player slumped behind the wheel of a black Escalade in front of a Boylston Street nightclub. But they won't find Harkness, made invincible by love — and the best Glock on the market.

He's safe, for now.

Acknowledgments

Special thanks to Andrea Schulz, Dan Conaway, and Megan Abbott for getting *Third Rail* out to the world beyond Nagog, Massachusetts—and to John Schoenfelder and Allan Guthrie for inspiring it in the first place during a couple of long nights in New York City and Edinburgh.

Thanks to Katrina Kruse, Emily Andrukaitis, Stephanie Kim, Naomi Gibbs, and the rest of the Houghton Mifflin Harcourt team—as well as Tanya Farrell, Emily LaBaume, and Wunderkind PR.

Cheers to Russell Banks, Gregory Maguire, Castle Freeman Jr., Doug Johnstone, Wesley Brown, Ron Slate, Craig Moodie, Scott Phillips, Glenn Gray, Madison Smartt Bell, Hamilton Fish, Christopher O'Riley, Bill Cicciarello, Chris DeFrancesco, Lynn Landry, Esther Piszczek, Stephen Fredette, Verena Wieloch, Samantha Kane, Sandy Poirier, Julie Sorkin, William Mansfield, and all my friends and family.